YOU'LL NEVER SEE STARLIGHT AGAIN

A _LIQUID COOL_ CYBERPUNK DETECTIVE NOVEL
Book Ten

AUSTIN DRAGON

Published by Well-Tailored Books, California

You'll Never See Starlight Again

(Liquid Cool, Book 10)

978-1-946590-19-0 (paperback)

978-1-946590-13-8 (ebook)

http://www.austindragon.com

Book cover design by Leslie K.

Printed in the United States of America

Table of Contents

Introduction

Cupid still reigned as one of capitalism's leading rainmakers.

In my household, Valentine's Day was every bit as much of a major holiday as all the Puerto Rican, American, and Chinese ones we observed and celebrated. Who knew love could be so profitable? For the megacorp retail and restaurant industries, it was a huge deal ranking second behind the Christmas super-holiday. For me, it was my favorite—no parents, no parents-in-law, no kids, just the wife and me. The season was also my time to remember how I met Dot to begin with.

Also, I was enjoying being back on my own patch of the ultimate supercity on the planet—Metropolis. No more out-of-country or off-world excursions for me after my recent UFO Case or my Jules Verne's Island or Luna Colony cases. I was staying put in my domain where my street team was on hand. Being without my team was like being naked in the middle of a freeway with no arms or legs, with a pack of hungry dinosaurs stampeding through a time portal from a parallel universe looking for some sweet meat. (Don't laugh. It was the plot of Cruz Jr.'s cartoon show we watched the other day.)

However, this Valentine season would have more planned for me than fine romantic dining. I'd even changed my look, which I felt was long overdue. I didn't want to be known as The Man in the Tan Fedora forever.

Then along came another big case.

As the cases pile up in a street detective's career, they, or their clients or criminals, bleed into one another. That's why I didn't like loose ends when it came to cases. Though my posthumous mentor, Wilford G., who worked the streets of Metropolis as a private detective for seventy-plus years, said simply:

"Don't expect closure in every case. It doesn't always happen in life, so why should it be any different in a detective's life?"

I remembered a favorite saying of mine: "Men are canine and women are feline. But so are cases." Canine cases required so much vigilance, because they were so damn dangerous. The danger was physical, extreme, right in front of you, in your face—but you didn't only see it. You heard it and felt it—hopefully, not in the form of a laser blast between the eyes.

Feline cases were just as dangerous—but deceptively so, even at their most calm and cerebral. Quiet one moment, and then the violence came at you in a flash. Then all was quiet again, like a wily cat sitting on a ledge, always watching you with one eye. Cuddly and soft, but razor-sharp claws right beneath that fluffy fur.

This case had a lot of "cats and dogs." And I'm not a pet person at all.

I could have easily called it the Crazy Pre-Valentine's Day Caper. The cases that took me out of my role as street detective and turned me into some kind of assassin or urban commando had highly annoyed me. In this case, I was more like a secret agent.

The case could have also been called NeuroDancer 2.0. I knew the dead villainess had groupies and followers. I knew they'd come looking for me one day.

But I was a Metropolis detective in my Metropolis. I was not armless, legless, team-less, gun-less or naked. Far from it.

Officially, the case was called Starlight.

PROLOGUE
When Cruz Met China Doll

It was like I was a kid and being sent to the principal's office. I didn't like the feeling when I was a kid and I liked it even less as an adult. I didn't even do anything. My taxpayer dollars hard at work. Yes, my OCD "issues" were getting out of control, but that didn't give the Metropolis Court System the right to mandate that I attend group therapy sessions for six months.

I arrived in the district of Neon Blues—overcast, gloomy, and rainy. As I descended out of the sky traffic, the tower's silhouette gave the impression it used to be a church. Church and government? There's a combination in hell for ya. Well, at least there was decent parking across the street, so I set my Pony away from all the other hovercars in the lot and hopped out. Living in Metropolis with a classic red hovervehicle meant I was more than used to walking to keep my prized possession away from any potential riff-raff. As I wrapped myself snuggly in my tan slicker and pulled my tan fedora down a bit, I glanced around. I saw the security guard station in the corner at the other end. I saw a couple of human guards watching me and cameras on the street lights above, following my path out the lot. Good. Actual security.

I had enrolled myself in the Phobias Anonymous Support Group. The Metro Court said I had to enroll in a group but not which one. There was no way I was sitting in a support group twice a month for six months with real OCD people. One person turning off a light six times before he could enter a room. Another person walking around a chair four times before she could sit. My OCD issues stemmed from legitimate germophobia, which I had mitigated. I don't know what caused my recent relapse, but I didn't need the courts sticking their noses in my business. But when do governments stay out of your business?

When I came up the stairs, I was glad to be out of the rain, but as soon as I entered the well-lit interior I said, "This was a church." It definitely had that look and feel. More like the community room of a church, library, or the like. Nearest the entrance were chairs arranged theater-style facing away toward the front of the room. At the other end, a group of chairs was arranged in a circle. Good grief, I thought. Already there were several people quietly seated and watching me like robot hawks. I smirked and approached. From the number of chairs, there would be thirty-five of us plus the facilitator in tonight's group session.

Which one was the facilitator?

I'd reached the group. They were still watching me. I stood there and gave them a quick once-over. A couple smiled—it was a man and woman, both looked in their forties. There was a heavyset guy, probably around my age. There was a guy who looked like a kid, though he probably was older than both the heavyset man or me from his wrinkled hands and neck. Then there was another guy. Clear glasses, his hair tied up in a bun right at the top of his head—a style for men I loathed. I looked at him and he looked at me. We smiled at the same time.

"Yes, it's me," he said.

"Are you testing us, Facilitator?" I asked. "Sitting amongst us crazies to glean some secret insight?"

"Actually, it's part of the ritual. Anyone new arrives, we say nothing and see what they do. Everyone acts differently. Most people ignore everyone else and sit down. Once in a while, a visitor gets so unnerved they walk back out until I intervene. You're a high-functioning introvert, so you don't greet everyone, but you're not shy about speaking up. You're anti-authoritarian, so you need to seek out the person in charge, size them up, see if they're worthy or not. How am I doing?"

"Facilitator, I don't care what you say, how you say it, when you say it. Just record my attendance at each session so I can ditch this group therapy session at the earliest possible opportunity. Good behavior means I get out of the sessions three months early. Mr. Facilitator, I will be your best student. What are you drinking? What can I get you?"

I got smiles from him and some others; the couple laughed.

"Now, for the rest of you, I'm not getting you anything. You get your own coffee or beverage or snack. The facilitator is special, so he gets special treatment," I said.

The class was for thirty-five, but there were only six of us, including the Facilitator, and we were twenty minutes into our ninety-minute session. But it didn't matter. Our facilitator, Mr. Oken, already had us make our introductions and asked if anyone was willing to share why they were in the session. Under no circumstances would I ever "share" anything, but there was always one rat in the group gullible enough to run into the mental mouse trap. The heavyset man had to raise his hand. He didn't want to get something off his chest. He wanted to get it out of his chest, his back, and backside. I thought I had problems being scared of germs and isopods. This man had a phobia of mirrors and anything with a reflective surface. I didn't need any degree from Freud College USA to know the man's problem was he didn't want to see his "big-boned" self in the mirror. The man just needed a good shake and to be told to go about his life. Maybe force him to hang out with some Mexican Sumo wrestlers. One week with them and they'd rename him Slim.

Then she walked in.

Metropolis may have been the largest supercity on Earth, but it did not differ from any other big city. It had its share of beautiful women. The woman who quickly strolled in was one of those women. She never needed to wear a lick of makeup to be mistaken for a movie star. She was Asian; I guessed probably Chinese ancestry, dark hair, perfect skin, lean and toned build. She was also one of the best dressers I'd ever seen. Fashionable electric blue slicker, sheer scarf around her neck, a heavy scarf over her head for the rain, tight leather jeans, trendy black-heeled boots. Her eyes looked out from behind a pair of expensive dark shades with a tinge of blue.

"Sorry, sorry, I'm late. The sky traffic was dreadful."

She literally came around to each of us and shook our hands. She was a high-functioning extrovert, but not the annoying type. When she got to me, I could smell a hint of perfume as we shook hands. I also notified the exquisite finger nail paint she had. Yep, we were among "royalty" here.

"Here," I said. "You can sit next to me. What are you drinking? What can I get you? We have some decent beverages, even the coffee."

"Oh, thank you. I'd like some tea, but that would be too much trouble."

"No trouble at all," I said as I stood from my chair.

"What about me?" the facilitator asked me as I made my way to the food table.

"Silence!" I scolded. "Don't mess with my world. She's special, so she gets the special treatment. You can get your own beverage."

He chuckled.

I made her the best cup of tea I could manage at the food table with the tabletop beverage machines at hand. All the while, she was the center of the group conversation. No, she was leading the conversation.

That's how I met China Doll—real name Dot. And the future Mrs. Cruz.

As the months went on, our Phobias Anonymous Support Group class would finally get up to its thirty-five court-appointed attendees, but we'd learn none of us had anywhere near the phobia of China Doll. We were a group of people afraid of water bugs, mirrors, and silly things. We should have been ashamed of ourselves. Dot, however, had been a professional amateur hover-go-cart racer as a little girl with a competitive streak to match any seasoned race driver three times her age. One fateful day of racing, she pulled ahead of her two rivals before going under a bridge, but she was going too fast. She didn't react as she should have; she didn't dive. Her vehicle and body went under the bridge... but her head didn't. A taut illegal neon wire that shouldn't have been there saved her head from smashing against the bridge. The stars were aligned in her favor, too, because medics were standing right there. Dot became a cyborg that day—neck, top of shoulders, and spinal column all bionic. However, the nightmares of such a horrific freak accident haunted her into adulthood. She had been conscious during the entire incident. Wouldn't you fear bridges too, if that happened to you?

After meeting China Doll, I decided to put an end to my phobia demons. The entire class did. Our phobias could never compete with hers—not even close.

PART ONE

Nothing Like a New Black Suit and Hat

Chapter One
Harry the Hatter

How magnificent is the man in a brand new suit!

That's what I said to myself when first I admired my new look in the full-length mirror at home. I'd had my old look for so long, the new one was a pleasant change. Too bad the family didn't get to see it yet, so the surprise for them was still to come.

There were a million fine men's attire shops in Metropolis to find a good suit in, but I chose a store recommended to me by, of all people, Phishy, my slider-associate friend. If I picked a store recommended by my best friend, Run-Time, then I wouldn't be able to afford it, or at least it would cost more money than I wanted to pay. A Phishy recommendation meant if he could afford it, then I could too. Even a high-end suit, which was what I bought, in a Phishy-recommended suit shop, wouldn't do too much damage to my wallet. Of course, one might say I was on the road to madness if I was taking dress suit tips from the likes of crazy Phishy.

I was very picky with my clothes and it took me well over two hours to find the suit I wanted. Stylish. Well-fitted, but not too much so, since I carried concealed weapons. Nice fabric, but strong enough to withstand running, jumping, and diving for cover from a shootout. Finally, I wanted black. I'd worn everything but black my whole life, including at my wedding. But it was time to put my contrarian streak to the side and wear basic black to blend in with the masses of the well-dressed persuasion.

To fit my style, there was one more piece to add to the "uniform."

No matter how many centuries we homo sapiens advanced in time—hovercraft and spaceship transportation, bionic and biotic tech, laser and gun-tech weaponry, orbiting space station and off-world colonies—the suit remained the standard formal attire for the professional and corporate world. Matching coat and trousers, some traditionalists added a vest, others the pocket hankie. Purists wore the clip-on ties. I added a fedora. "Out" with the sandy color tan and "in" with sophisticated basic black.

I stared at myself in the wall mirror, touching the tip of my newly purchased black fedora. I had completed my new look. New black suit, new black aqua-shoes, and now a new black hat.

"Simplicity is the ultimate sophistication," I said.

"Leonardo da Vinci," Harry responded.

I glanced at him. "I'm impressed, Mr. Harry."

"No need to be. People in my business make it our business to know every famous quote throughout time about the science and art of dress."

"A science and an art?"

"Always both."

I was in Harry's Haberdashery in Woodstock Falls. I bought my own fedoras at the place, mostly to give as gifts. However, my new black one was custom made with the precise craftsmanship his establishment was known for. Woodstock Falls was a working-class, multi-ethnic neighborhood like my own Rabbit City. But its clientele came from all the upper-class, booshy districts too and I knew he even had Up-Top customers from as far as Mars.

When I stepped into the store, Harry was making his rounds, brushing each hat on display by hand. Yes, he could have employed high-end hover-robots to do the work for him, but this was Metropolis and this was Harry's Haberdashery. People in Metropolis didn't like robots, and people like Harry achieved their reputation by an unwavering mark of quality, distinction, and refinement through the human hand, not by any robotic contraption.

His store was more a museum than a retail store. Harry was a dark suit purist, and he always wore a lighter-colored vest under his jacket, complete with a sharp tie and nice pocket handkerchief. Hats galore adorned the wall in every shape, style, and color imaginable, for men and women. To spend any length of time in Harry's place was to get a visual history lesson of humanity through the perspective of hats. Modern times never really bothered to create its own styles. How could any compete with the classics? With classic hats, older would always be better.

"We often use the phrase, but he was one of the original Renaissance men—painter, sculptor, architect, thinker, theorist, scientist, and inventor. Interesting that you'd quote him for, of all things, a new hat," Harry said to me.

"Mr. Harry, I like my new hat. Great work as always."

"Thank you, Mr. Cruz. A happy client is a lifelong client."

"I like my new look." I tugged the tip of my hat again as I admired myself in the large full-length wall mirror in the middle of the store.

"You do, however, look more like a government worker than a private detective."

"Government worker? Not in Metropolis."

"I was thinking more along the lines of a secret agent."

I grinned. "A secret agent is a government worker to you."

"You work for who pays your salary and expenses."

"That's true."

"May I ask what made you change from your standard attire?"

My work "uniform" had been my trademark tan fedora and tan slicker. My clothes underneath changed, often a vest over a dress shirt; casual, fitted, stretch pants; and non-slip gripping shoes. However, people only remembered my tan fedora and slicker. In Metropolis, most people didn't wear hats—hoodies were the preferred choice, and people stuck with dark-colored slickers. The masses never wanted to stand out in the crowd, but I was a contrarian, despite never wanting to stand out.

"Time for change," I said.

"If you say so, sir."

I finally pried myself from the mirror. "I'll wear it."

Harry nodded. He took the hat for me. I stepped over to the main counter as he grabbed a hat box and wrapping from one of the wall cabinets. At the counter, he stacked them nicely in a big shopping bag and handed it to me.

"Mr. Harry, I have a feeling you don't agree with my change."

"The customer is always right, Mr. Cruz, but you're known as the Metropolis street detective in the smart tan fedora and slicker. When the masses get accustomed to seeing you a certain way, they don't take to change too kindly. That has been my experience, at least."

"I think they'll like the change. Besides, I'll be able to blend in better with the masses. They wear dark clothing. Now, I do too."

"Is there a reason you want to 'blend' in, sir?"

"I just want to stay out of trouble."

Harry laughed a bit. "Sorry, Mr. Cruz. Too late."

"That's my mission at least. Stay low-key in this high-tech, low-life world."

"If I could give you some advice, sir."

"Please do."

"Never run from who you are, especially when it's exactly what makes you so good at what you do. If I ever need a detective, I'll be calling you and not any of the more famous, high-end detective firms that even frequent this shop."

"Thanks for that, Mr. Harry. I really appreciate it. But I've been wearing my trademark attire since I was a kid in high school. Just trying something new for a bit. See where it goes."

"Then change it, sir. I'll walk you out. And don't forget to say 'hi' to your family for me."

#

As I stepped into the rain outside the store with my big shopping bag, I buttoned up my new black slicker. I definitely had a new look for what I mentally was calling the "new me." I was so glad to be back on my home turf of Metropolis. My last major case (The UFO Case) was still making news around the world. I was learning the hard way that fame was a double-edged, laser-tipped samurai sword. More clients seeking your services, but also more crazies.

But I wasn't trapped on a luxury hoverjet 40,000 feet up in the sky flying 700 miles per hour above other countries. I was in my supercity—the largest in the world. The rain, flashy neon signs, crowds of people in their dark slickers and glowing-colored glasses, the chatter of a million conversations on the street, in many languages I didn't speak, and the noise of busy hovercar traffic above us, and the megaskyscrapers towered above even that. I loved it all. This was my domain. The streets of Metropolis were where I could control my own destiny.

I stepped out into the street for the parking structures with my aqua-shoe covered feet and yelled out. A nasty garbage hovertruck illegally flew above and dumped buckets of muddy water on top of me.

"Damn!" I yelled.

My new look was drenched. I looked around and just my luck, I was the only one who seemed have gotten the wrath of the supercity's Trash Services.

There was no way I was going home to change back into my old trademark clothes. Wait. The garbage hovertruck did only dump muddy water on me, right?

Chapter Two
Good Kosher Man

I didn't need to go back home to change. All I had to do was step back into Harry's and he squared me away. He had a simple hand gadget that steam-cleaned my suit to its pristine former self, then he did the same for my new hat. I even got a full shoe-shine service. Classic establishments like Harry's had their loyal clientele for a reason—always the best service for the customer, no matter what.

When I walked back out of the store, I had a clear plastic slicker over me to protect my new look from the elements or any wayward hovergarbage trucks. But I wasn't taking any chances as I double-timed through the crowds toward the parking structures.

My next stop was Woodstock Falls. Back in the day, before I was born, it was one of the elite Metropolis bohemian districts filled with hipsters. Nowadays, Woodstock Falls was a safe, working-class, multi-ethnic, mostly Jewish, neighborhood. Like similar working-class neighborhoods, residents and business owners fiercely kept the trash—human and otherwise—away. Residents didn't just work here; they lived here. The bottom half of the monolith skyscrapers were the businesses and all above to the top was residential.

I coasted down Graffiti Alley, where despite its name, there wasn't, and never was, a speck of graffiti anywhere, ever. The street may have had no graffiti, but it should have. Secluded and dark, though it was a major street, it had the feel of an out-of-the-way back alley where bad things were supposed to happen. There was never a lot of traffic—that you could see. Actually, there was plenty of traffic, and all to one place: The Good Kosher Market.

After all these years, I couldn't tell you the name of any other business in the district. Good Kosher took up the entire length of the street, and that's saying a lot, since streets were ginormous in Metropolis. Food came in three categories—processed (practically everything sold on the market), organic (supposedly the "healthier" alternative), and natural—or, as I would say, "straight from the dirt." I never shopped anywhere else. I didn't eat processed and felt the whole "organic" thing was nothing but a scam by the unholy coupling of government and megacorps to overcharge people for basic food. Only natural foods for me, and Mr. Watts and his five sons had been serving nothing else, continuing the tradition for more than a century. Good Kosher was not into anything gimmicky or faddish. Mr. Watts would say, "Nothing gets on my shelves that hasn't been in the general market and people have been eating for at least a thousand years." Funny, but true. I'd been a devoted customer since I was a teenager.

When you were a fixture of a neighborhood for so long, owned such a popular business for so long, employed the same workers and catered to the same clientele, it didn't take long for everyone to feel you truly were family. Every family had a sage—the wise, ol' uncle or wise, ol' grandmother. Mr. Watts was our sage. You did your shopping first, one of his five sons rung up the order at the cash register, and then you spent however long chatting it up with the Good Kosher Man himself.

In direct contrast to the streets outside, inside Good Kosher was always packed. I always felt people teleported into the store from space because my words when entering were always, "Where did all these people come from?" Customers came from all across Metropolis to shop—every age, ethnicity, nationality, class you could think of was here.

The interior looked like an underground football stadium with neon rows of product. People zipped around on hovercarts of all sizes. In traditional markets, the products came to you. Here, you got your own stuff. Other than the hovercarts, there really wasn't any machination of any kind, which was rare for any modern store. But it was a "natural" market, so robots wouldn't work with the store's image. The sons, however, wore mech-gloves with store inventory displays on the wrist area, and the hand section was telescopic to pull down things from the top shelves without ever having to get a ladder. The gloves probably had a million other uses, like a Swiss-army knife.

But this time, I wouldn't be grabbing a small hovercart near the entrance for grocery shopping. I was there for only one thing. Straight down one of the main aisles I went as soon as I saw him.

I didn't know how old Mr. Watts was. He had to be in his late fifties at least, but there was nothing old about him. He had a full beard and mustache with the hair graying at the temple and the edges of his beard. Like his sons, the uniform was a khaki jumpsuit with a fully equipped utility belt, beaded strings around the neck, and a pointed Chinese bamboo hat to protect from the constant exposure of the artificial daylight ceiling lamps, on which all its indoor natural plant life depended. The skin techs at Eye Candy, where my wife worked, would be proud of his discipline. He probably had the rare hats shipped directly from the Southeast Asia territories, back when they were affordable.

When he saw me, he did a double-take, then stared at me. As I approached him, his squinting eyes studying me, his blank expression changed to a smirk.

"Mr. Cruz, I almost didn't recognize you," he said.

"Mr. Watts, how do you like my new suit?"

"I don't."

"You don't?" I asked, surprised. "Why?"

"For the same reason you'll never walk into Good Kosher Market and ever see me or my sons wearing pink top hats. It would confuse the customer. Customers don't want confusion. They want consistency."

"Change is good, though, isn't?"

"Change is good when your status quo isn't working. When it is, change is stupid. Cruz, please don't follow the advice of people quick with quotes but have never run a business."

"I'm just trying it out. I think a nice new black suit looks good on me."

"You look like an undertaker."

"What? No, I don't."

"What did Mrs. Cruz say?"

"I'm surprising her."

The Good Kosher Man made some kind of disapproving grunt. "What I thought."

"Actually, I came here for her. I need some nice roses."

"Okay, you haven't lost all your senses yet."

"What do you have for me?"

Good Kosher had its own interior gardens in the back and off-limits to customers, growing a wide variety of roses, tulips, and other flowers. Watts led me back into the massive room, which had its own climate-control system with a steady rain mist falling. Good Kosher was a secret flower shop too, and no one had better—if you wanted real ones and not the synthetic "garbage" everyone else sold that could survive a nuclear blast.

He didn't ask me. He walked to the roses section and handpicked a bouquet of large crimson red roses for me. They looked so perfect that I could barely believe they were natural.

"How do you grow such perfect roses?"

"A Good Kosher secret," Watts said to me.

Suddenly, he was in front of me and pinning a single rose to my suit lapel. "Better," he said. "At least, you don't look like an undertaker anymore."

"I do not look like an undertaker. I look cool."

"You looked cool before. Now you look like everyone else in a suit. Not cool."

"What's that saying that the customers are always right?"

"Are these roses for V-Day?" he asked.

"Yes," I replied.

"Why are you getting them today then? You said it was a surprise for your wife."

"I can keep them hidden until then."

"Mr. Cruz, take your lapel rose and go. Come back on the appropriate day and not before. Go to work."

"But I don't want to go."

Chapter Three
Dog Man

My third stop, since I hadn't eaten yet, would have to be Dog Man. I was already on the Circuit and wasn't in the mood to drive anywhere else before my client calls in the office.

I found myself, once again, on the bustling streets. Unlike Woodstock Falls, which hardly had any pedestrians, I was in my business district of Buzz Town—another embodiment of the city's neon urban jungle. Looking up from the ground, when visibility was clear, the buildings seemed to have their own halos, courtesy of the rooftop lights. On rainy days, that same illumination gave the sky a faint glow. Either way, the city's lighted buildings pulsated with flashing neon signs of commercial ads and government PSAs (public service announcements). Both always trying to be as outrageous and provocative as they could get away with, but people ignored the visual "noise."

I moved through the crowds in their gray-toned or black slickers, some with umbrellas with glowing-colored handles, others wearing hoods, most with headphones, everyone wearing colored glowing glasses. Fifty million-plus living in the supercity of Metropolis, and the many, many other metropolises exactly like it, though smaller, on Earth. But Buzz Town was my business corner of the universe.

Only hover-garbage trucks were more ubiquitous than hover-food trucks in this city. In Metropolis, you never had to venture into the rain on a food run if you didn't want to; the food would come to you. But most hover-food trucks staked out their turf either in the air or on the ground.

Dog Man had the perfect corner, with six lanes of pedestrian traffic on the ground, and the same above him in the air. His hovertruck never flew anywhere anymore; it was a permanent fixture on the corner, open twenty-fours a day. His food truck "owned" this street, which meant he paid a wad of cash to City Hall for exclusivity for his main truck here and, these days, ten more at the other end of six other streets. I bet he easily made more money than I did as a street detective. But not because he had so many food trucks. He made damn good hot dogs. Already as I approached his truck, I saw the line of customers. But you never had to wait long.

He saw me from inside the truck, then did a double-take and stared.

"Cruz, is that you?" he yelled.

"Dog, who else would it be?"

He laughed. "Didn't recognize you at all. The usual?"

"Yeah."

Most of the customers in line didn't know who I was. Though a few did—one of them was wearing a tan fedora and smiling. I paid no attention as I walked to the counter to pay the man.

Dog Man was big time now. He collected the money as his crack team of culinary artists—all three of them in the truck—created his hot dog masterpieces. The aroma was narcotic. He got you your beverages to wash it all down.

"What's the deal?"

"What deal?"

"The new clothes. What happened to the real ones?"

"A slight change in wardrobe," I said.

"Personally, I like the old clothes better."

"I gathered that."

"No one will know who you are."

"No one knows who I am, regardless."

"Come on, Cruz. That's not true. You're famous."

"You're famous. My wife is famous..."

"And you, too. I heard about your airplane case. Scary stuff."

"That's an understatement."

"A shootout thousands of feet in the sky on a hoverjet. You sure know how to pick 'em, Cruz."

"I was on vacation."

"Weren't you on vacation on that Jules Verne's Island murder case too?"

"Following my cases, Dog Man?"

"Of course, Cruz." He set my beverage on the counter. "Your dogs will be up in a minute," he said.

"Thanks," I said as I picked up my cup from the counter.

"Might want to ease up on those vacations of yours."

"My wife already beat you to the advice."

"Oh I get it," Dog Man said. "These black clothes are for a special occasion."

"No. This is going to be my new look."

"Temporary though."

"No. My new look. To replace the old look."

"But temporary."

I had been trying to drink my drink, but was getting flustered. My new suit and hat looked damn good on me, but all I was getting was negativity.

"Dogs up! Let me get you your sauces. Can't have dogs without the sauces."

Finally, I was going to eat something. Someone was tapping my shoulder, and I turned around.

It was the customer wearing the tan fedora. "Hey, Mr. Cruz. I agree with Dog Man. We like the old look better."

"Do you now."

"Yeah. It's the Liquid Cool look that you made famous. I have my hat like yours."

I did the whole fake smile thing, grabbed my dogs and beverage, and strolled away from all the uncalled for, vicious, negativity toward my cool new suit and hat.

"Come again soon, Cruz!" Dog Man yelled at me from the truck. "But make sure you're dressed properly next time."

He laughed.

"No more tips for you!" I yelled back.

"I always add it into the price!"

#

A light drizzle came down as I sat in my vehicle eating my late lunch. The alleyway where I parked wasn't far from the office, and I'd used it often. It was a real alleyway, meaning it was barely wide enough for two hovercars to pass each other, driving in opposite directions, and right off the pedestrian street. I was in the exact center in a neon blind-spot, so my red Pony was in the dark.

A woman stepped into the alleyway at the other end in front of me, about ten feet away. I could she was female by her build and walk. Dressed in neon everything—hair and clothes, then it was as she turned off a switch as she changed into an average gray person—gray slicker with hood. Neat trick, couldn't have done better myself. I was known by my trademark fedora and slicker but was good at disappearing too when the situation called for it.

She waited and another taller and larger female joined her. I watched them talk as I continued to eat my food; that larger female was one of those people who talked with a lot of hand movements. Suddenly they were looking in my direction. I couldn't tell if they were staring at me in my vehicle, or just in my direction down the alley. We had a staring contest, only I didn't know if I was playing by myself. The larger female extended a middle finger in the air, and both of them disappeared out of the alley.

Interesting, I thought. My cue to get lost. I didn't want anyone sneaking up on me and damaging my classic Ford Pony.

Chapter Four
Punch Judy

Buzz Town was a busy business district. Not a wealthy one like Paisley Parish or Peacock Hills, but it was a solid working-class district. My opinion of the area had risen over the years since becoming a fellow business owner. My Liquid Cool office was in one of the many mega-towers along Circuit Circle—called the Circuit by some; the Circle by others. I'd gotten offers to move to a more upscale district, but I wasn't moving, and it wasn't just because it was a legacy—owned outright for life. Buzz Town was Liquid Cool's permanent home.

I came out of the elevator on the 100th floor. Always quiet, or most of the time. As I approached, I stopped in front of the door of the empty adjacent office. It had belonged to the tenant I called Mr. Grumpy, who had led the "pitch-fork brigade" to get my office legacy taken away because of all the "violence and mayhem"—his words—I attracted to the floor. Nonsense. Well, one day, he just up and sold it to me. Now, I had more office space than I knew what to do with. I had only one employee, and that was plenty.

From outside the door, I admired the name placard with flashing neon letters: LIQUID COOL DETECTIVE AGENCY. Already, I could hear PJ's French music from inside the office. Today it was jazz, other days it was ska, electro, or dance.

But that wasn't the reason I stopped outside my office. I was getting far more sophisticated in my tradecraft. In my right ear was a mini-rear-viewing camera. The feed went to my mobile in my hand.

I saw the gray-slickered figure peek out from the end of the hallway and disappear. It had to have been the neon lady in the alleyway who met the larger female. So I was being followed, and they knew which floor I was on. But it didn't necessarily mean anything nefarious. Unfortunately, the price for being famous, or least known by a lot of people, was that sometimes the odd fan thought it amusing to "play detective" and follow you. However, I always assumed the worse. A trait my posthumous mentor, Wilford G, said made for a long life in the detective business.

Inside my office I went, passing under our hidden scanning arch over the main door for detecting weapons (my omega gun excluded) and cyborgs (PJ and my wife excluded). At her desk, staring at me, was my one ex-felon cyborg employee PJ, with her short crimson hair. No one called her by her street name Punch Judy anymore. Her gang days were long gone, like my own hovercar restoration and illegal amateur racing days. I was a street detective, and she was my right hand.

"Who are you?" she said with her French accent.

"What do you mean, who am I?"

"Do you have an appointment, sir?"

"Stop that. You know who I am."

"No, I don't."

I started walking to my private office, and she immediately stood from her chair. "Sir, you're not allowed to go into my boss's office."

Her face had a simulated dot of a mole, and she'd given up the pinkish lipsticks for more conservative darker reds. She wore sleeve-less women's business suits these days, but she'd never give up her heeled boots.

"PJ, what is wrong with you? I'm your boss."

"My boss wears a tan fedora and slicker. My boss doesn't wear a black fedora and a cheap black suit with some flower on the lapel."

"This isn't a flower. It's a rose."

"Are you a highwayman?"

"What?"

"In Neo-Paris, we call them highway men. They wear cheap suits with flowers on them and they rob people."

"PJ, I have no idea what you're rambling about."

"Where's your clothes? Did a highway man rob you of your clothes?"

"PJ, I'm going to my office."

I marched past her and opened the door to my private office.

PJ ruled the main reception and waiting area. It would be like an ex-posh gang member to have an haute couture interior design decorating sense. With her punk rock playing in the background on an infinite loop, she had turned the space into some hipster, scenester receptionist-waiting room of the stars. Psychedelic posters on the wall, her fancy "modern" glass desk with see-through glass drawers, and a boombox on top along with her own mobile computer. All of her workstation was behind a metal barrier, but it didn't look like a barrier with the decorations.

The waiting area had these geometric, purple couches around a glass table on a shimmering, neon powder blue rug. The reception table had French fashion magazines, which I thought was stupid because how could people read them, but then I realized—fashion magazines—so that meant lots and lots of pictures with few words, so it didn't matter, and numerical prices were universal. I added the sports and hovercar racing magazines.

PJ had turned the reception-waiting area into a shrine... to me. Framed pictures hung on the wall of me with clients, celebrities, CEOs, and other VIPs. There was even one of me shaking hands with the mayor of the damn city, no less. Potential clients would see them and decide I had to be a legit detective. But getting new clients ceased to be a problem years ago.

Outside on the wall to my inner office was a LIQUID COOL DETECTIVE AGENCY sign in neon letters. It was the first thing people usually noticed when they entered. I, as boss, at least got to rule my private office which had been redecorated by my wife. I had my main desk with my droplet-covered bay windows behind me. In the corner, I had my own arrangement of plush chairs around a glass table, the whole setup on another neon dark blue rug. My wife had added the snazzy, eight-foot-tall, four-panel Chinese screen with midnight black faux-wood borders to the side of my sitting area.

"Where's your normal clothes?" PJ said with her hands on her hips at the entrance to my inner office.

"I'm changing my look."

"Non, you can't do that."

"Why not?"

"What is wrong with you? You're a businessman now. Successful businesses understand branding. Your tan fedora and slicker are not a tan fedora and slicker. They are your brand. You cannot change them."

"What are you talking about, PJ? I'm not wearing a tan hat and slicker forever."

"That is your brand, so yes you are. People identify with your brand. No brand, no brand loyalty, no successful business."

"Solving cases is what makes Liquid Cool successful, not my clothes."

"The clothes make the brand."

"I thought the clothes make the man."

She disappeared from my door and I heard her bionic fingers typing on her desk keyboard.

"What are you doing, PJ?" I hated to even ask.

"We need to send you to business school."

I popped out of my office to look at her at her desk. "Business school? Why would I need to go to business school when I have a business and staff?"

"You're starting to go business-senile. Forgetting the basics, so we need to send you to school."

"Changing the style of my clothes doesn't necessitate having me go back to school."

"Why black? You hate black. You've said a million times you don't want to look like everyone else. Now you look like everyone else. You're ruining the Liquid Cool brand."

"I never said I hated black."

"Yes, you did. Many times."

"That's not true. I never said that." I went back into my office and sat at my desk.

The call came in when I at my desk re-prioritizing my messages. I had the "hot" pile, the "hold" pile, the "hell no" pile, and a few other miscellaneous ones.

My eye noticed that one of the outside lines was lit on my main phone. I could faintly hear PJ whispering from outside. I knew she was up to something.

"PJ, who are you talking to?"

"I'm calling Run-Time!"

"Don't do that. He doesn't need to be bothered with your nonsense."

"He said you always said you hated black, even as far back as middle school!"

"That's different. Leave him alone, PJ!"

"Tan fedora, tan slicker, red Pony. No black."

The light went out, but then immediately lit up again. Who was she calling now?

The light went off and PJ appeared at the entrance to my office. "Your wife asked what's the special occasion."

"PJ! Why did you call my wife?"

"You're wearing strange clothes. You're forgetting things you've always said. Are you suffering from PTSD?"

"Why would I be suffering from PTSD?"

"Your last case, the UFO one."

"Why would a bunch of crazy maniacs aboard a hoverjet cause me to have PTSD?"

"You were up in the sky in a plane with shooting and explosions. You could have been blown up. The plane and all the passengers could have been blown up. Flying men, giant mantises. That would give me PTSD."

"No, it wouldn't. You'd just punch the flying men to pieces and punch the giant mantis off the plane."

"True, I'd punch them all."

"Is there any point to this conversation at all, PJ?"

"No. So when are going to talk about our new office space next door and being my own boss too?"

"I'm not talking about Mr. Grumpy's office."

"Our office!"

"TBD."

"What's that?"

"To be determined."

"Well, hurry up and determine it. I want two, maybe three assistants to boss around. This is why I'm upset with you potentially damaging the Liquid Cool brand. We can't expand and hire my staff if you damage the brand. Brand awareness, integrity, and nurturing is key."

"Whatever you say, PJ. Who needs business school when all I have to do is listen to you?"

"Exactly, Professor PJ it is. When do I get a raise?"

#

From my pop-open mini-kitchen, I made myself a cup of silk coffee.

"Do you know the difference between B2B, B2C, B2D, and B2A?"

"PJ, I'm not playing your games. B2D and B2A? You're making stuff up."

"Business to Business! Business to Client! Business to Data! Business to Algorithms, or AI! You must know your basic business vocabulary if you ever want to make Liquid Cool into a private investigation empire."

"Empire? Heaven help us."

With my cup of coffee, I sat back down at my desk and stared at my messages. I had thirty minutes to my first walk-in client. I got up again and walked to the section of the wall in my private lounge area.

From a corner, I pulled out my hidden wall mirror. I stared at myself in my new black suit and fedora. I liked my new look but so far I'd been called an undertaker, a Neo-French highwayman, and more than one person had to do a double-take to recognize me.

"Are you supposed to be a secret agent?" PJ said, now standing in my office.

"I'm supposed to be a street detective with a new look."

"Well, you can't be a secret agent. They don't wear black suits."

"Yes, they do. What do they wear then?"

"They wear all kinds of clothes to blend in, so the enemy doesn't know they're a secret agent."

"The enemy, huh?"

"What really happened up there in the Falcon Express?" PJ asked.

"More than enough for me to know that Mrs. Cruz and I will take our vacations right here in Metropolis from now on."

#

I was sitting at my desk, planning out my week, with the intercom on and PJ was at her desk, typing. What she was typing, I had no idea.

"You remember that ancient show about early space travel? You know, the warp drive nonsense. When sci-fi thought such nonsense was plausible even in sci-fi," PJ said.

"Oh yeah," I said.

"Well, one of the main stars—the pointed ears one."

"Oh yeah, the elf."

"He wasn't an elf."

"Yeah, an elf."

"The show was not mythical fantasy. He was an alien from another planet and their race all had pointed ears."

"Yeah, the elf."

"Okay, ignoring you now. He grew to resent all the fame he got as an actor from his character and wrote a book that wasn't that character name."

"Elf."

"Ignoring and continuing my story. Well, he got older and wiser and said wait: why would I resent the very character that brought me all this fame and changed people's lives? I created the character. The character is me. So he wrote a new book. I am the character. Cruz, you are the tan fedora and slicker. Why would you want to change it? It's your calling card. People expect it because you made them want to expect it. Then you're upset because they expect it. Make up your mind. It's branding. Megacorps pay billions for that kind of branding. Embrace your branding, man."

"Wow, PJ. That was actually very profound persuasion on your part."

"And?"

"I am considering the return to my tan fedora and slicker."

"That's more like it. Sounds like a raise is in my future."

"Distant future."

"Near future."

"Ancient future."

"Tomorrow future."

Chapter Five
Spiders

Detective firms in Metropolis fell into two main categories: the high-end, one-hundred-man firms that looked and smelled like high-end legal practices, and the bottom-end, small firms that always seemed to share space with some bail bonds outfit. What made my agency unique in its own small way was that I was carving out a middle lane. A sole practitioner firm that did the small Average Joe and Jane cases, the routine government cases, mostly for the municipal courts, like skip tracing and civil witness statements, and the high-end megacorporation cases, most often corporate espionage cases. I prided myself on being a generalist detective rather than the specialist. Variety is what I wanted, and fortunately for me, it paid the bills.

The afternoon, however, was filled with only the smaller cases. My first client was a domestic surveillance case, which likely would turn into an infidelity case. I hated them, but there were so many of them, so it was a choice between leaving lots of money on the table or holding your breath and doing them. He was a very shifty character, but nothing came up on his background check. As a matter of practice, I did background checks on all my clients without their knowledge. A practice that kept me out of far more trouble and danger than I could count.

The second client was a property damage case. A pair of business owners wanted me to find out who was vandalizing their commercial retail property after hours. The Metro police had real violent crimes to contend with, so such matters were always at the bottom of their pile. That left plenty of work for the supercity's private detectives. It took me no time at all to find the culprits. With the information, my clients could have the criminals arrested and be able to sue for damages. It thrilled the business owners as they left.

My next client case was interesting. A real estate firm had hired me as a security consultant to look over all their security proposals. I'd done the same for my own Liquid Cool offices, so I guess I was an expert of sorts. As PJ would say, quick case to resolve, quick case to get paid for.

Another client was a no-show, but they left a message to reschedule. I had to give PJ her credit. Requiring clients to leave a deposit for appointments, only refundable upon showing up and me determining I couldn't help them, cut out no-shows by ninety percent. Huge!

I had two clients in a row that I couldn't help. One wanted me to do some traveling, which after my UFO Case was not going to happen, but I referred them to someone else. The other client wanted me to partner with a bigger firm for a corporate investigation case. I saved the silver-haired executive some money by telling him that the corporate competitor he was so concerned about would not be a competitor for too much longer. The man thanked me with a big smile, shook my hand, and left. I came across lots of information from my street, corporate, and police contacts. If I could save a client some money, why not? In the future, they'd return the favor.

#

"There he is! The man in the killer black suit!"

My next client strolled through the main door of my offices. He was a lanky guy in a dark hooded poncho draped over him down to the thighs of his jeans. Blue glasses covered his eyes, but their glow was mild compared to his beaming smile.

"Spiders!" I came out of my private office and we gave each other a bear hug.

Spiders was one of those friendly blasts from the past. I met him at the same Phobias Anonymous Support Group back in the day where I met my wife. Funny, he met his wife at the group too. We had lost touch with each other, but with friends like him, it doesn't matter how much time passes, when you see each other again, you simply pick up from where you left off.

"How have you been?" I asked.

"Couldn't be better. So look at you. Looking good, Cruz. Looking good in basic black. Is this how detectives dress?"

"Thanks, Spiders."

"Hello, excuse me, client," PJ said from her desk, shooting a dirty look at my friend.

"Well, hello," Spiders said as he strolled to the desk. "Who are you?"

"I am PJ, VP of Client Services for the Liquid Cool Detective Agency."

"Listen to all that, Cruz. You always knew how to pick the right females."

"This female is about to punch you," she said.

"Punch me? Why? I'm a friendly guy. I'm friendly to everyone."

"Be careful, Spiders. PJ has bionic arms, and she has been known to punch a hovercar or two through walls."

Spiders smiled. "Like I said, Cruz. You know how to pick the right people. But Ms. PJ, you didn't tell me why you wanted to punch me. What did I do?"

"You, Mr. Spiders, have undone my efforts to salvage the Liquid Cool brand from the self-sabotage of its founder and chief executive."

"Cruz, she's smart too, because I have no idea what she said."

"Welcome to my world," I said.

#

Spiders was a glass half-full kinda guy. He always had something nice to say about someone. Never a negative vibe about him. His compliment about my new look was nice, but, frankly, if I was naked except for a garbage bag, he'd say I looked "amazing." I chuckled thinking about the many conversations we had in our Phobias Support Group. People could have almost died and suffered excruciating humiliation and depression, but he'd always find the bright side of the situation. Then he'd have you believing it. It was an uncanny ability.

Yes, his phobia had been spiders. But most of us never really believed him because he was always so positive about it all. Yet, he insisted he was terrified of the eight-legged freaks and needed group therapy. All he did was counsel the rest of us. He was quite good at it.

"I got it," he said, seated in front of my desk.

"Got what?"

"I'm a licensed therapist and counselor."

"That's great, Spiders. Didn't we all say you were a natural and should make it legal?"

"You all did. Took me forever, but one career ends and another begins."

"That's great. I can now say I know a counselor I'd actually recommend to people in need."

"Legitimate need," he corrected.

"That's why you'll be good. You don't want lifetime clients. You want them to cease being a client as quickly as possible. Spiders, you will go far."

"Thank you, Cruz. Had to become as successful as you and China Doll."

"No, we both had to become as successful as the wife. She was successful when we met her."

"Two, right?"

"Cruz Jr. and Kat."

"One. Thor."

I grinned. "At least you didn't name him Tarantula or Arachnoid. So Spiders, what's the case?"

I'd seen plenty of wet-wear in my day, especially when I was on the illegal hovercar racing scene. Worn by cyberpunks or tech-heads, "wet-wear" was the colloquial term for wearable computers. Spiders lifted his black poncho to reveal all the wires, components, and screens literally wrapped around his arms and torso. He was wearing his computer, or many of them, on his body.

"You gotta tell me about your last case," he said as he sat down again. "Give me all the details about this Falcon Express and these flying men."

I realized he had no interest in any such thing. He just wanted me to talk out loud while he did whatever he was doing. Already he was typing on a virtual keyboard, which from my vantage point, looked like his fingers were fluttering around in the air.

"Sure, I'll start from the beginning when I boarded at Metro International," I said as I sat.

I knew my office wasn't bugged. I was very cautious about that, but that didn't mean that outside forces couldn't use devices to listen in to conversations. Many hackers told me that any window was nothing more than a beautiful broadcasting device to the world. I had measures against that too, but I knew they weren't fool-proof.

I swiveled my chair around and at that very moment some giant hoverdirigible passed right by my bay window.

"That was close," I said.

"I'm surprised there aren't hovercraft crashing into the building every hour," Spiders said.

"If people stay in their virtual lanes, and avoid stunts like that, there would be no crashes, or near-misses like that."

"Go on and continue with your case story," Spiders said.

"Oh, yeah. Where was I?"

Spiders wasn't typing on the air anymore. He was writing on a small notepad with yellowed pages showing its age, resting on his thigh.

I continued my story as he wrote. Every so often, he'd say something as if he were really listening, but he wasn't.

Finally, he finished and looked up. "I don't know how you do it, Cruz. All that fun and excitement and money too."

"That's one way of looking at it."

He stood and handed me the notebook.

"As my first act as a licensed counselor-therapist, I'm giving my first session ever to... you."

"Me? Do I need to lie down on my couch?"

"Do you have an uncontrollable urge to lie down on the couch? A simple nap will cure that condition."

His response made me chuckle.

"Cruz, lose the black suit and hat," he said.

"I thought you liked it."

"I lied."

"But it looks good on me."

"It's not about a black hat or tan hat, Cruz. It's about you. Confidence. With one you have it; in the other you don't. I don't know what happened to you in your last case that made you doubt yourself and the very essence of yourself. I can guess."

"I don't agree with your analysis but for the sake of conversation, what's your guess?"

Spiders shook his head slowly. "Figure it out. I can't tell you."

"What if I don't know?"

"You do know. Even now, you know." He lifted his palm computer to his face. "However, I will send you an email with the answer, password-protected, but you have to promise me one thing."

"What's that?"

"You will only open it when you know the answer."

I smiled. "You said I know now."

"Your subconscious knows, but your conscious self is too stubborn and refuses to listen. Wear your new look for a while longer until your conscious self becomes less stubborn."

He pointed to the rose on my lapel.

"Does it come with a bouquet?"

"For Dot," I said.

"Early start to Valentine's Day. Thanks for the reminder."

He stood from his chair. "It was good seeing you, Cruz."

I got up too. "Are you leaving?"

"Opened up the new practice in the new city last week. They're waiting on me. Remember, I'm a country boy. You're the city boy."

"Returning to your roots."

"Yes."

"Thanks for the work."

"I needed a librarian I could trust." I was speaking in code, of course.

Spiders may have graduated to being a licensed therapist and counselor but he was also a sought-after scraper, one of the best. In the past I'd used a kid named Tag, but I wanted to use someone no one knew about, but connected to me and who I could trust. Scrapers were the people other people paid to sift through all the endless data (or garbage) on the Net. I'd secretly hired him years ago to monitor the Net for clues matching specific criteria. He came in because he'd found them.

In Metropolis, there were only three libraries left in the City. Sure, from the comfort of your own home, you could download any content you wanted to your digital book reader, but frankly, who had time for that. There were a gazillion books out there in cyberspace. Being a librarian was actually a serious profession with value; they had advanced degrees in data mining, sifting, and record compiling. Libraries sifted through all the clutter of data garbage to give you the best of the best of what you wanted, or needed. Spiders had been a full-time contractor for one of them forever.

He was perfect for the job I hired him for. He was good, thorough, and exceedingly paranoid.

"Say hello to China Doll for me then."

"Of course. Maybe we can see your new county digs one day. I don't think I've been to the county before. Oh, I have. A cow tried to stampede into my vehicle."

Spiders burst out laughing. "Only you, Cruz. A one-cow stampede."

"Yeah, he could have scratched my paint job."

He gave me a hug before he left. Once again I felt all the gadgets and components under his poncho. I heard a slight buzz as he stepped back—I instinctively knew it was some kind of anti-audio surveillance barrier.

"Be careful on this one, Cruz. I wasn't the only one in the Net cell looking for these clues. If I was aware of them, they were aware of me."

Chapter Six
Suit Soldiers

My former floor neighbor, Mr. Grumpy, wasn't wrong about Liquid Cool attracting unsavory elements to our once-sleepy Buzz Town office tower. There was a shootout that spilled into my office the day after I acquired it. We'd also had sword attacks and explosions. But it wasn't my fault.

Anyway, we'd turned the offices into a virtual fortress and I invested in all kinds of surveillance that covered the elevators, lobby, parking lot, and roof. I was not worried by the woman who followed me to the office because we had her on surveillance tape, so we'd know who she was soon enough.

I walked Spiders out and noticed that PJ was glued to her computer screen at her desk rather than being her cheerful self, saying her goodbyes in English and French to a client.

When the door closed, I asked, "What's wrong?"

"We have company."

I joined her at her desk. She had all the surveillance feeds on her display screen. The hoverdirigible that buzzed my window had illegally set down on the roof of the tower. Streaming out were dozens of corporate soldiers in shiny suits and wearing colored glowing glasses. I couldn't tell if they wore black gloves or if they had bionic hands of black metal.

"How much you wanna bet they're coming here?" she said.

"Well, they almost crashed into my office window, so they're coming here all right."

"I hope you didn't leave you weapon in your real clothes at home."

"I have my gun right here."

She reached under her desk and out came her laser shotgun. "Good. We'll tell them we don't tolerate violence in our place of work. Who's that?"

I saw the woman come off the airship too. She was a Caucasian woman in a kimono-style slicker flanked by a male and female samurai soldier, swords strapped to their back and laser machine-guns in hand.

"That, PJ, is the president of the Council of Corporations," I said.

PART TWO
The Cabal of Corporations

Chapter Seven
Madame President

I'd met Madame President before in my Electric Sheep Massacre case. I had nothing to do with politics. Whenever I needed advice in that area, I called my best friend Run-Time. However, the one thing I knew was that Metropolis was a city of powerful forces, none becoming more powerful than the other. A détente existed between the government represented by the Metropolis Police Dept., five hundred thousand strong, and the megacorporations represented by the Council of Corporations. But that uneasy equal relationship was always being tested by either side. Metropolitans were more than content because combined, both kept the criminal class to a manageable size.

Already, I'd seen a sight that no other Metropolitan had seen—the supercity's entire five-hundred-thousand jet-packed police force in one place during my first major case, when the former criminal organization, known as the Animal Farm Syndicate, thought they could take over the city. They fatally thought wrong. The Animal Farm Syndicate no longer existed in Metropolis or anywhere else on Earth.

But, one day, that sight was topped on the beach at a place called the Valves. On one side was the chief of police in military battle armor, flanked by platoons of other fully armored police troopers and the sky black with police hovercruisers. On the other side was Madame President, flanked by the same male and female corporate soldiers, and dozens of helmeted samurai soldiers with swords strapped to their backs and laser machine-guns in hand. The sky was black with their own air-armada of hovercraft. It was a scary thing. Two deadly forces of nature were about to come to blows. Fortunately, a world war on a beach didn't happen.

However, we didn't have the full Metro PD backing us up. The only thing facing off the Council of Corporation delegation would be PJ and me. We were good, but not that good.

"We need more guns," PJ said.

"I think we need more of something. Let's try the cool approach instead," I said.

"Does that actually work in real life? I'm seeing lots of guns and swords on my screen. If you'd hire me some assistants for me to boss, I'd have all of them heavily armed right now, a laser-rifle in each hand, and ready for some fighting."

"You're back with that gun in each hand nonsense again. I told you that only works if you have two heads and four eyes. Two hands. One gun."

"Two people and two guns? I see many people and more guns. The cool approach looks like the wrong approach for me."

"I'll handle it."

"We're about to find out. Here they come."

#

The first two suit soldiers pushed open the door. Both looked up as if they had X-ray eyes behind their shades and could see our hidden scanning archway. They handed their machine guns to other suit soldiers in the hallway. They stepped into the office and stood across from PJ and me. Their over-boss seemed to glide in after them. She moved as if she was powered by some kind of hover-tech, but the arch alarms didn't go off.

"Madame President," I greeted. "Welcome back to the Liquid Cool offices."

"Mr. Cruz," she said. "The last time we met, there was a corpse on the ground before me. I believe you were responsible."

"Simply doing my civic duty ridding the Earth of a multiple murdering crazy maniac. Police sanctioned," I added with a smile.

"Yes, it was."

"But you've been here in my offices before. My Alien Hunter case. You were waiting for me right there in the waiting area with a bunch of people in suits."

"Yes, I vaguely remember. My mind doesn't hold too tightly to anything of the mundane."

"Nothing mundane about your visit then, or your visit now."

"Our first encounter, however, is etched in my mind like yesterday. Corpses and cops. All on a dirty beach."

"Not a particularly fruitful day for you, as I remember. You weren't able to acquire a piece of tech you wanted."

"The incident, and the day, are of no significance to the Council. We do not dwell on the past, especially when the status quo remains unchanged."

"Is the status quo at risk of being changed today, Madame President?"

"I wish to consult with you, Mr. Cruz. Possibly hire you."

"As flattered as I am, Madame President, why would you need to hire a street detective who probably makes in a year what you make in an hour?"

"More like a minute," she interjected.

"Your Council includes every major detective firm in Metropolis. Why would you want to hire me?"

"You know why."

"No, I don't."

"More games. I'll make it easy. Two words. Neuro. Dancer."

PJ looked at me. "Her? She's dead."

"Yes, she is. Your boss killed her. Though I am not saddened by that. She was a very dangerous person. More than you'll ever know. Mr. Cruz, you know why I wish to hire you rather than the many thousand-person private investigation firms in the Council. Simply put, I can trust none of them with the case. Shall we sit and talk, Mr. Cruz?"

"Why not?" I said.

"Splendid."

#

Her two bodyguards remained outside as I led the Council President into my private office. PJ remained where she was. I knew she'd keep an eye on both of the suit soldiers, and watch the army of the others in the hallway.

"I almost didn't recognize you, Mr. Cruz," she said as she took a seat in one of the two chairs in front of my desk.

"Please, not you too," I said as I sat behind my desk.

"I always thought of your trademark look as a disheveled mess, but now that I see you trying to dress up, I realize I was wrong and you were right."

"You don't like the new look either."

"The suit doesn't suit you."

"Yes, funny," I said. "Why not?"

"Is this your attempt to blend in with the masses? The Shakespearean king visiting his soldiers' camp in disguise. To converse with them, share their experiences and deepest fears."

"I'm a detective, not a king."

"You've met quite a few, despite your station in life. The king of the Saud Empire considers you a friend. Not even I've had the pleasure of meeting him in person. You were his honored guest at his palace."

"I was. He gave me the grand tour. May I ask why you tried to crash your ship into my window?"

"I wanted to encourage your client, or should I say contractor, to move on."

I watched her with squinted eyes.

"Mr. Cruz, do you believe you're the only intelligent person in Metropolis? I will commend you for immediately recognizing the danger of the tech used by the late NeuroDancer and taking steps. From our last encounter, I also know you have a simplistic, although acceptable, code of conduct, concerning which I've convinced others within the Council that you'd rather destroy the tech rather than handing it over to the Council or your friends at the Metro PD."

"Chief Hub would do the same thing."

"Would the mayor? The City Council? The captains under Chief Hub's command?"

"I don't care about them. They don't run the largest police force on the planet."

"We know all about your friend, Mr. Spiders."

"Do you?"

"Yes."

"The Council doesn't have data scrapers?"

"We have the best in the world. We pay them to listen to the whispers of the corporate world in the physical world, Net world and in the Dark. A network of intelligence you couldn't even imagine."

"Spies, you mean. I could imagine it, actually. I always suspected I was being monitored."

"Not only us. Your friends at the Metro PD have their own spy agency too, even though they deny it."

"I always suspected both my enemies and friends would monitor me. So busy watching me they weren't looking out for criminals like Venn Diagram, and who knows how many others."

"Another person we have to thank you for eliminating for us."

I grinned. "So, did you find it or not?"

"I was about to ask you that."

"If you know about Spiders, you know the answer. I don't even know why you're here."

"I learned that you've completed courses on being a federal profiler. You're a very interesting person. A street detective who becomes a profiler too. But then you were a hovercar racer and restorer before becoming a detective. You're a real life polymath, a person whose knowledge spans across many subjects, assimilating all that complex and divergent knowledge to solve specific problems. If you had any true ambition and the ego to match, you could even rise to run a megacorporation yourself."

"I'm content with my detective agency."

"Yes, a tiny shop in Buzz Town." She looked around my office in an annoyingly condescending way. I wondered if she was being her contemptuous self because she couldn't help it, or was subliminally pushing my buttons for her true aim. Her next words confirmed it for me.

"We did our own extensive psychological and behavioral profile on you. It said you hate incomplete tasks and unresolved situations. It said you would never stop."

"I don't like loose ends."

"No, you don't. A criminal used a mind-control device and almost made you dive off a rooftop. Yes, Mr. Cruz, we know about that too. She used the same method on a few people."

"But the Council never eliminated her."

"No, we didn't. We couldn't."

"In case others in her crew had the tech."

"We had to take the view that such a thing was a possibility. Sometimes when you eliminate one king, you create a hundred more. We now know that our fear was not a possibility. One device. But she couldn't take it with her to the afterlife. Do you have an idea how many factions have been searching for it? I'm sure you can imagine. In the shadows of the corporate R&D world, the search is like the quest for the Holy Grail, the Fountain of Youth, faster-than-light warp propulsion, or cold fusion."

"Don't forget time travel," I said.

"Or sentient toilets," she said with a smirk.

The Council of Corporations truly had been keeping tabs on me.

"Of course. Carnegie Cosmo is a member of the Council. Though with the dip in his financial net worth, you all will kick him out any day. But we Buzz Town business owners have our own council and will gladly welcome him in."

"I'm not trying to unnerve you, Mr. Cruz. Only to impress upon you, we take this matter as seriously as you do. There are few hands on this planet or off-world that this tech can be allowed to fall into."

"I'd say the true number is zero. No one should have it."

"There are many who disagree with you strongly... and violently."

"Madame President, I'll be brief. You don't have to tell me about the search because I'm one of the searchers. You all want it to mind-control people. I want it to destroy it. We all know that already. Why are you here?"

"To hire you."

"Hire me to do what, Madame President?"

"Please, call me Ms. Gem, especially with another new M.P. in the nation's capital."

"Another in a long line of useless politicians to mirror a long line of useless male ones. What did I learn in civics in school? The feline cat and masculine dog think themselves so different when they're both smelly animals."

Gem laughed out loud. "Spoken like a true Metropolis resident. Supremacy of the supercity. All beyond its borders be damned."

"Why bother with anything outside the city? I want to hop in my hovercar and be able to drive to my representatives to curse them out. If I have to fly to one end of the nation or another to get to see them, then I'm not interested. I've had my fill of Metropolis International."

"Yes, you've had quite a few bad experiences for a simple private detective."

"Experiences? Near-death experiences, you mean."

"But we all have our civic duties to fulfill. Strange to me that Metropolitans vote for their mayors but not for the country's presidents."

"Vote local," I said. "Or is it: voting is loco. I forget."

"You're not a pet person either, Mr. Cruz."

"Don't you know how many crawly critters can hide in their fur?"

"We've digressed quite a bit, haven't we?"

"Hire me to do what, Ms. Gem?"

"The device may have been found."

My poker face was good, but my heavy sigh blew that. She had my attention, and she knew it.

"The last time we met, Ms. Gem, you were trying to get your hands on another evil device. You were going to have your corporate samurai soldiers shoot me for it."

"Technology isn't evil, Mr. Cruz."

"Lots of dead people over the ages would strongly differ with you. VR-killing device. Then a space artifact. A supposed mind control device, now. Makes me wonder what other devices the Council has collected."

"More amazing and terrifying than you'll never know."

"I bet. But my Venn AI case told me that the Metro government is doing the same thing."

"Of course, as does the criminal underworld, to a far lesser and unimpressive degree. The VR-killing device, as you call it, belonged to us."

"You mean you had Council of Corporation lawyers claim ownership for you?"

"We bought it. But all a moot point, Mr. Cruz, since you blew it up."

"I'm sure you've been working day and night to re-engineer the tech, but I don't play VR games and the global VR community can be more ruthless than any crime boss in protecting their virtual universe and its code."

"That we know, Mr. Cruz. That day, your police partners were so surprised you would not be their puppet."

"Neither of you were going to have it."

"You're the original Boy Scout, or is it a priest?"

"Amen! Hallelujah!"

Her expression was one of amusement, but I knew it was all an act. She was leading me down a story lane. What was true and what was false would take me some time to figure out, but not a lot.

"What about the NeuroDancer device?"

"Oh, so that's what we're calling it."

"Yes."

"Just tell me what you need from me before one or both of us says something crass to the other."

"Very well. Let's begin after the Second World War."

"That many world wars ago. How long is this story? Are Cruz Jr. and Kat going to be in college when you're done?"

"It might not be as exciting as one of your private detective criminal cases, but espionage can sometimes be even more so."

"I'm a detective, not a secret agent."

"But you are dressed for the latter," the CC president said with a smirk.

"Now you don't like my black suit, either."

\#

"Governments have been working on mind-control for a very long time. The CIA had a Project MK Ultra."

"I saw the movie as a kid."

"No movie, Mr. Cruz. It lasted some two decades. Thousands of military veterans experimented on people using psychotropic and hallucinatory drugs, electroshocks, hypnosis, sensory deprivation, isolation, verbal and sexual abuse, brainwashing, psychological and physical torture."

"But in our times, do all the above with the touch of a button."

"MK Ultra was illegally conducted at military bases, colleges and universities, prisons, and local hospitals. It wasn't the only government program in the world over the ages, and America was far from the only nation with similar programs in its history.

"We have been able to achieve some level of brainwashing and brain-tech in the early days of cyborgism, but all hardware. None had ever achieved true mind control… until the late NeuroDancer. But how did the pop singer-actress do it?"

"She was a biology major in college," I said.

"Biology? She was surely a living, breathing billboard for the reverse harem lifestyle."

"Biology, and I don't mean sex ed."

Gem watched me seriously for the first time. "What then?" she asked.

"You know."

"You shouldn't know."

"Why? Was it the Council that erased her past records? Neuro-psychology, hypnotherapy, neuro-linguistic programming, and every other psycho-manipulation technique out there, clinical and theoretical, meaning quackery. Why would a leggy dancing singing actress need all that?"

"It wasn't us. She had the records erased a long time ago."

"But she couldn't erase the students who took the classes with her. A center-of-attention, social butterfly like her. Boyfriends everywhere. Not hard to piece together."

"If one was looking."

"I was looking. The woman almost made me do a swan dive off this building."

"My apologies then. You aren't playing at the detective thing, after all."

"No, I'm not, and I plan to live longer than my posthumous mentor. One hundred fifteen sounds nice, so I can play with the great, great grandchildren. What do you want to hire me for?"

"Find it. Your friend Spiders gave you what you needed."

"You've had me under surveillance all this time, but you don't seem to know much. I had Spiders monitoring the Net for clues that it had been found, anything similar found, talked about, or used."

"And he did."

"No, Ms. Gem. He didn't."

"What do you mean?"

"I pulled him in to see who'd come visit me. And here you are."

Her face became cold.

"Again, you underestimate me because I don't live in the right district, belong to any of your country clubs, don't have the right booshy contacts. My suit doesn't cost what most Metropolis residents make in an entire year."

"But you married upward."

I smiled this time. But I could never forget that a person like her only became head of the Council of Corporations by killing her way to the top, figuratively speaking, or literally, when the situation called for it. Who knew what non-metal weapons she had under her sleek, stylish kimono dress? "I married well," I said.

"Then you are lucky, indeed. Most, including myself, cannot say the same. Regarding my underestimation of you, like any human, I make mistakes too. But never more than once." She looked past me through the window. "We're not alone."

I would not fall for any tricks. "PJ!" I yelled.

PJ stepped into the doorway of my office.

"Is there anything behind me?" I asked, but I already knew there was by her expression.

I turned to see a Metro PD battle cruiser hovering outside my building.

"You should be very careful about being right about things, Mr. Cruz." Then she yelled something in another language. It wasn't Japanese, but it was some kind of Asiatic dialect.

One of her suit soldiers came in and handed me a gold plastic card.

"I'm hiring your services officially."

"For what? You still haven't told me what this is about."

"Your friends will be here soon, so all I will say is that the Council of Corporations needs you to find the person or persons involved in the theft of Council property."

"What property?"

"Do you use legal counsel?"

"When I need to?"

"Then once you sign the non-disclosure documents, you'll be given a full briefing and can begin. The Council will pay ten times your normal hourly rate."

Of course, PJ was smiling, but it made me want to take the case, whatever it was, even less than when she glided into my office.

"We'll speak again soon, Mr. Cruz. Very soon," she said, did a slight Japanese bow, and turned to leave my offices back the way she arrived.

Chapter Eight
Monitor P.I.

In my Electric Sheep Massacre, these two forces had faced down each other with me in the middle. Now both of them were in my Liquid Cool offices. One of them by themselves had enough firepower to reduce my offices and our entire business mega-tower to dust. I wanted them far, far away from me.

Madame President glided back out of the offices with her two main suit soldiers, who immediately claimed their machine guns from the others in the hallway. To me, it looked like there were a lot more of the corporate samurai soldiers waiting than before. Regardless, they marched back to the elevator capsules for the roof.

"They move fast for corporate soldiers," PJ said to me as we watched them on the display screens on her desk.

"As long as they get away from here."

"But the cops are here now. What's going on here? Are they going to hire you too?"

"Maybe they're going to hire me not to be hired by the Council."

PJ nodded. "Yes, that sounds like the cops. Didn't the Council give you a retainer?"

I handed her the gold card.

"That's what I'm talking about. Get a card from the cops too. We need more money for the remodeling."

"What remodeling?"

"For the office expansion. You're hiring me some assistants to expand the Liquid Cool empire."

Madame President and the suit soldiers were soon back on their hoverdirigible. The silver vehicle blasted off from the roof at the very second a Metro PD battle cruiser landed in its place.

"What's wrong with these people?" I said. "They almost crashed into each other."

"They're frenemies. Frenemies do things like that. We should know."

"Well, these frenemies won't be becoming friends, just worse enemies. Dangerous for you, me, and everyone in Metropolis."

"Don't be negative. They're just playing tough with each other. Showing off. We have nothing to worry about. Cops are your friends. They like your tan hat."

PJ quickly made a face, realizing that it was my new black fedora sitting on my head.

That's when all the lights in the office and hallway went out. We stood there in complete darkness.

#

I was so annoyed. I'd left my mobile at home by mistake (okay, yes, I left it in my tan slicker) so I was without a flashlight device. PJ was useless, unable to find or remember where she stored her spare flashlights.

"Find it," I yelled.

"Patience! I'm looking for it." All I heard was chaotic noise from her clutching at everything in her drawers and cabinets in the dark.

Then there was light!

PJ and I stood there with our mouths open. My Liquid Cool offices were filled with slim, helmet-headed, black robots—androids. I hated androids. I'd tangled with them far too many times in my relatively short detective career. Bastards killed my posthumous mentor, which meant I hated them even more.

I quickly counted twenty of them in a semicircle around us, watching us with their single visor eyes. At least they didn't have guns in their hands, but that meant nothing. They were androids. Possibly their arms, heads, or chests could have been any manner of lethal weapon.

Then a man in a black uniform walked through the open front door.

"Detective Do-Little returns," I said.

I hadn't seen him in years. When I first met him, he was Detective Monitor in the Metropolis PD. Not too long after, he was Captain Monitor. He came from a wealthy Old North Euro family; the latter being irrelevant, the former being very relevant, because he was on the career fast-track to the top. Metro beat cops hated him, hence their nickname for him back then: Detective Do-Little.

But the last laugh was his. The black uniform reminded me of Interpol—Up-Top's intelligence services, but the robots had Metro PD insignia—very distinct MPD letters on the chest above the heart area. Most people didn't know that every police uniform, casual or dress, and every silver-and-black body-armor had the insignia. I knew. Monitor and the black robots were Metro PD. Or were they?

"I haven't been called that in a long time, Cruz."

"I came by one day at Police Central and you were gone."

"Bigger and better things," he said.

"Does the police union know you're employing androids for non-extreme hazardous duty? People don't like robots, and especially androids. Why you be taking jobs from humans, Monitor?"

"Let's cut out the crap-talk, Cruz."

"Are you the elusive division known as Police Intelligence?" I asked.

He flashed a badge I'd never seen before.

"P.I." I said, staring at. "Sorry, but PI is already taken. It stands for 'private investigator.'"

"PJ is taken too," she said from her desk. "Find something else."

"I have you to thank," Monitor said, now standing right across from me. "My division's budget was doubled after the Venn business."

"Androids killed Wilford G. What do you think Wilford G. Jr., the head of the police union, will do when he sees you with an army of them at his side?"

"Cruz, I'm not here for conversation, and Wilford G. Jr. will never see me. No one will. We are a super clandestine division. Very few people will ever see us in their lives."

"So we're lucky, are we?" I asked.

"The president of the Council of Corporations was in your office. Why?"

"She said there were a lot of suspicious looking black androids hanging around her offices and she wanted to hire me to find out who was sending them."

Monitor knew I could play games all day. He sighed and just stood there, thinking about what to do next.

"You are so far out of your depth on this one," he said.

"I've been told that before."

"What's with the new black suit?"

"New look."

"Wrong look. For a second, I thought I walked into the wrong offices."

"Thank you for joining the chorus of people dumping on my new look. What's your rank anyway, since you claim P.I. is yours?"

"Commander Monitor. And it is my division."

"So you're above Chief Hub?"

"Metropolis PD is in its own unique place in the world. No one is really above it, or him. But at least I don't have to babysit half a million cops."

"So you're calling the Metro Police babies? Well, they don't like you either." I stepped forward and tapped the metal arms of one android. "But who needs friends when you can have a factory make you some?"

"Obviously, you're not listening to me."

"I'm listening to every word coming out of your mouth, Commander. What do you want me to do?"

"Are you here to hire him, too?" PJ asked.

"Can I hire him not to take the Council's case?" he asked her.

"Monitor, what do you know about the Council's case? Were you actually listening through the keyhole, as they say? Isn't that illegal?"

"Not if you have a warrant."

"I bet Police Intelligence is the same as Intelligence. You do the crime and get the back-dated warrant later. Leave me alone, Monitor. Whatever depth I'm in or about to be in is my business. You've done your job and warned me off. Heard and rejected."

"They call it psi-tech," Monitor said, knowing he'd get to see my brain race at light-speed.

"They can call it whatever they like. Some tech is meant to never be possessed by humans."

"Do you know NeuroDancer's body is still in a lab being studied to this day? Every test, scan, everything that could be done to find out how she did what she did was employed. Was it biological somehow? Was it a drug that dissipated in the body after a certain period? Was it a device operated by others, out of sight?"

"A lot of questions there, Commander."

"I knew you wouldn't talk to me. But here." He reached into a pocket on his uniform and handed me a thick silver business card. "Call my boss when you're ready to talk."

"Your boss? I thought you were the boss."

"Everybody has a boss, Cruz. It's his private, secure line."

He turned and headed for the door.

"Don't turn off the lights again!" PJ yelled. "I don't want to be fumbling around for flashlights."

The lights and power all went out again.

"What is wrong with him?" I said in the dark.

"He's thinks he's mysterious and powerful. I say he's stupid. In fact, I'm calling him stupid man from now on."

"Let's just stand here and wait... Still waiting... Still no lights or power... Still waiting."

The lights finally came back on. Monitor and the androids were gone.

We got back to her desk as the feeds came back on. Their Metro PD battle cruiser was already departing from the roof.

"There's no way they got to the roof so fast," I said.

"It's a trick. They're spooks. Spooks play mind games."

"Is that what this is?"

She looked at the business card he gave me.

"Chief Hub is the head of P.I.?" PJ asked. "He's the head of PD and PI at the same time? That's too much work."

"It's too much something."

"It's a spooky mind game. Maybe this is all a big show."

"That's a real Metro PD cruiser leaving our roof."

"Is it?"

PJ had me thinking. "You're getting as paranoid as me," I said. "Good, very good. Your priority for today is to identify everything about this P.I. Who, what, where."

"But they're secret."

"That's what detective agencies do, PJ. They uncover secret things."

I looked again at the card that Monitor gave me. I held it up to PJ. "Maybe the real name that should be on this is Ms. Gem, President of the Council of Corporations."

PJ grinned. "I bet you that's it. She's the spooky mind-gamer. You think you're calling him when you're calling her. Woman pretending to be man, robots pretending to be people. We just need man pretending to be woman and we have the full trifecta."

"What are you even saying now, PJ?" Actually, I was ignoring her at this point. My inner paranoia was growing as I looked all around the office.

"Why didn't the alarms go off when the power came back on with the robots lined up in the office?" I asked aloud. "What's the real reason behind him cutting the power?"

We both looked around the office suspiciously. PJ reached for the phone. "I'm calling him now!"

"Tout suite," I said.

"Tout de suite," she said. (Right away.)

Chapter Nine
Bugs

We were so right. But not even we were prepared for what they found.

We called him Bugs. He reminded me a lot of my posthumous mentor, Wilford G. Bugs may have been old, but he was always on the go and worked harder than kids sixty years younger. His trademark uniform was his overalls over his purple suit and holding some contraption in his hand. Bugs's business was listening device detection, motion detection security, intrusion defense security, video surveillance, door and wall defense security, door and lock augmentation, trap doors and panic rooms. He did everything that had to do with office security and he had turned Liquid Cool into a proverbial fortress of tech to keep PJ, any visiting clients, and me safe inside.

He strolled into the Liquid Cool office with a dozen guys in purple overalls, each with different devices. He greeted us with a nod of the chin as he entered and saw me seated in the lobby waiting area, but it was clear he didn't recognize me.

"Hello, Ms. PJ," he said to my smiling cyborg secretary.

"Mr. Bugs. Do we have a job for you?"

"Where's your boss?"

She started laughing. At first he didn't know why she was laughing, then he slowly turned to where I was sitting. His forehead crinkled up as he squinted.

"Cruz?"

"In the flesh," I replied as I stood and walked over to him to shake his hand.

"I didn't even recognize you. Are your clothes at the cleaners?"

"Well, I'm not naked. Don't you like my new look?"

He studied my suit and hat. He had the look of a cat that swallowed a bird but didn't want anyone to know.

"Well?" I asked.

"Probably not a good thing when your friends can't recognize you on sight. You need your clients and potential clients to recognize you. Not walk right past you. How long is this new look experiment going to last?"

I shook my head. Experiment? I was making a major life change, and he implied it was a passing fad. "Still thinking about it," I said, just to end the conversation as quickly as possible.

He had PJ and me wait in the hallway, and they swept the entire office.

"Mr. Cruz, come back inside," he said to me. But his tone was a happy one.

PJ and I walked back to where he stood at PJ's reception desk, with his six men waiting.

"What's the news, Bugs?" I asked.

"Who was in here?"

"Police Intelligence, or so he claimed."

"Police Intelligence?"

"Is there a Police Intelligence Division?" I asked.

"There is but they wouldn't come here. They never leave their offices."

"Their guy was an ex-police captain named Monitor."

"Yes, I knew him when he was on the force. A real schmuck. Who else?"

"He arrived with a bunch of black metal androids."

"Anyone else, before or after?"

"Madame President, herself, of the Council of Corporations."

Bugs nodded.

"Would Monitor be with this Police Intelligence?"

"I don't know. Maybe, but even they have standards. This is not intelligence modus operandi."

"Intelligence would plant listening devices."

Bugs smiled. "Real Intelligence shops don't have to. They can listen and watch you from the sky, or space."

"That's nice to know."

"More likely you were being played by the Madame."

"He works for the Council. PJ, you guessed right."

"Cruz, I don't know how to tell you this, but I'm going to need to fumigate your offices."

"Fumigate? That's for rats, roaches, and isopods. This is a clean establishment."

Bugs shook his head. "This establishment is so far from being clean. Every piece of furniture, every item in your office, has been fitted with a listening device. They're the newest generation. Not even made on Earth. Straight from Up-Top. I believe the Martians make the best of them. Most sweepers can't detect them. The quickest way to get rid of them is fumigate."

"I suspect the term 'fumigate' is different from what I'm thinking."

"You'll be buying new furniture and computers."

I stood there shaking my head.

"But I just got my new mobile computer," PJ said. "I had to wait forever to get the right color I wanted."

"You'll be okay," he said to her.

"They turned off all the power and lights, so we couldn't see," I told him. "But not that long."

"Androids could definitely move fast enough to do this work."

"Madame President had my offices bugged," I said, annoyed.

"We'll ban her for life. No more entry for her," PJ said. "No matter how fat the retainer. Second time is the last time."

I noticed that Bugs wasn't finished.

"What's wrong?" I asked. "There's more?"

"Yes. Listening and visual surveillance devices."

"Eavesdropping and peeping tom bastards!" I said.

"Uh, Mr. Cruz, they're active right now," Bugs said.

PJ and I looked at each other with our mouths open.

"No obscene hand gestures, please," Bugs said to us. "My grandson is not allowed to see that kind of stuff."

"Oh, stop it, Gramps," one worker said to him, grinning.

Chapter Ten
Wize Gal

Bugs had plenty to tell me when we were far enough away from the office and he was sure we weren't being monitored. The good news was that his team could easily remove all the bugs in my office. The bad news was it would take days. Bugs told me that some devices were microscopic robots that burrowed deep into wood, wall, or wherever. They weren't just next-gen surveillance tech; they were so new that most of Earth, including law enforcement, hadn't got their hands on them yet to come up with countermeasures. However, the worse news was it was all going to cost me a lot of money. I was furious. PJ even more so, because there went our fat retainer from the Madame herself, and then some.

"She did this on purpose," PJ told me. "If we didn't find her bugs, she could spy on us forever. If we found them, we'd have no money left from her retainer."

"If we found them, I'd be forced to take her case to get my money back."

"She's doing the spooky mind game manipulation on you. Forcing you to do what she wants."

"I'll get even, PJ. I always do."

We were effectively kicked out of our own offices, but Liquid Cool still had to be open for business. PJ already had a plan of action. She sent me away to the parking structures as she set up a pop-up reception desk in the ground floor lobby of our building. I didn't think such a thing was allowed. But it was in the hands of my VP of Client Services and I was glad not to have anything to do with it.

While I'd changed my attire, an owner never changed their classic vehicle. My Ford Pony was every bit as Miami Vice bright red and a classic as when I first built it from scratch back in high school. My high-performance, super-charged, advanced nitro-acceleration hydrogen engine made a low purr as I flew out of my parking structure into the hovercar traffic. The power hadn't gone off in the parking tower, so it was under constant guard by security personnel, and my vehicle had advance security shields, so I was fairly confident it wasn't infested with any trackers or bugs.

I nestled right into the slow lanes out of the Circle, and soon, out of Buzz Town. Hovercars and hovercyclists whipped past us all in the fast lane, but I was in a pensive mood so slow suited me fine for the moment. Visibility was perfect, no rain or drizzle. I had a big, grayish hovercar in front of me, a sleek black one behind me, both at a safe distance. Nothing out of the ordinary in any of the lanes, around, above, or below me. Though a hovertruck below us was driving much faster than it was supposed to.

What I was thinking about wasn't that Madame President hired me and then had her fake Police Intelligence bug my office. I was thinking about all the damn people who didn't like my new suit and hat. I'd pass by my place in Rabbit City on the way, but I wasn't stopping. I didn't care what any of them said or about stupid branding. A man can change his look once in a while if he wants to. What's wrong with that? I wasn't changing anything. I'd be the Man in the Black with Fedora for at least this year. No matter what anyone said.

#

I had to thank the man himself, Wilford G., for introducing me to her. He loved his gambling. Cascade City was in Old Metro, the ancient part when Metropolis was just a city, not a supercity yet. That's where I drove and every mile of sky-traffic I passed reminded me more and more of The Man, Wilford G.

Wize Gal owned a casino-restaurant-club, appropriately named Wize. It was a high-end gambling place and a fine restaurant where even the waitresses wore business suits. Her father, Wize Guy, was the previous owner, but he'd retired to warmer, sunnier climates and he didn't care he had to learn a brand-new language at his age to live there. His daughter ran all his businesses now.

The establishment was huge and upscale, but catered to all—from the booshy elite to the Average Joe and Jane, as long as you dressed with class. Male and female valets were all seasoned professionals, but I still parked in a secure parking structure way down the street.

She was a certified paralegal—but as good as any full attorney—smart, relentless, cutthroat. But she had no desire to be a real one. Wize Gal was my legal counsel for whenever I needed it. I needed it now.

When I got inside, it was as bustling and noisy as always. People gambling, drinking, dancing, and watching large monitors on the walls and ceilings everywhere of every sport, fight, or race worth betting on. One didn't have to wonder why her legal work was a hobby rather than her main career. She was rolling in money fit for royalty by the hour, whether or not she came into the office.

A waitress escorted me to her grand office in the center of the establishment. Casinos had more surveillance than Fort Knox, so she was waiting for me. She was a petite brunette dressed in a sharp purple business suit. When I stepped in, her head jerked back as she stared at me with a wrinkled brow and pursed lips.

"Who are you?"

"Don't you start too."

"I take that to mean everyone isn't liking the new black suit look."

"I like it. That's all that matters."

"So Mrs. Cruz hasn't seen you yet."

I sat down in the plush chair in front of her large silver desk. "Did you receive it?"

She didn't miss a beat as she swiveled to the side and grabbed a heavy tablet. She laid it on the desk in front of her. "Received the file thirty minutes ago. The Council of Corporations. You're working for them now?"

"Maybe," I said.

"It's going to take me longer than thirty minutes to review a non-disclosure agreement of this size. My legal advice is not to sign it."

"Wize, just make sure I won't be selling my soul, giving over my kids, wife, or any family member or my business or any genetic material, and I'm good."

"Will you be good? From what I gleaned, you'll be privy to the most secret of Council proprietary information. Why would you be good about that?"

"Because in this rare case, I agree with them. It should remain the most secret of secrets."

"What's the play, Cruz? You don't trust the Council of Corporations any more than I do, or any sane person."

I said her name. "NeuroDancer."

Wize Gal's charm and playful smirk disappeared. "The mystery mind control stripper-singer-actress diva. Didn't you kill her years ago? But still on the case. Another fatal flaw you have in common with the former G-Man. You won't let it go."

"How can you let go of something like that?"

"G-Man said the same about the Venn case."

"And he was right."

"He was, and it cost him his life. Are you willing to make the same trade?"

"I won't have to."

"Listen to me, Cruz. I'll give you your due. You're slightly more intelligent than the average biped, but this is the Council of Corporations. You think they don't know you're only doing this to find out what they have, so you can destroy it?"

"I know."

"What do you think they'll do? Just because you're friends with the chief of police and head of the police union, and are friendly with the local beat cops, doesn't mean they can make you disappear. Are you hearing me, Cruz? You're a one-man show, and your cyborg sidekick doesn't count."

"Don't let PJ hear you calling her that."

"I'm serious Cruz. The last time I warned you not to do something, who were you sitting next to?"

Wize Gal knew how to hit below the belt.

"Wilford G. is dead, and you're walking a path to join him."

"Then let me ask you the reverse," I said. "Why are they doing this, then?"

"They're using you. They think you know something, and will manipulate you to get that information."

"Wize, I need to know what they know. I'm not stupid. If I need to bring the entire Metro PD into this, I won't hesitate a second."

"You think they'll ever let you dial even the first digit of 9-11? Also, as your legal counsel, I'm obligated to tell you that knowingly planning to breach a corporate non-disclosure agreement is a felony. You can be prosecuted and will. They'll send you to jail, seize your business, seize your legacy properties. Since we're in a casino, let's go with that analogy. They hold all the cards. You have none in this game."

"I hear you, Wize. I do."

"I don't think you do. Are you signing this document?"

"Yes."

"Then you don't hear me. Is your will in order?"

"Oh, please stop."

"You're wearing the right color suit."

"I'll be fine."

"Give me until tomorrow to fully review it."

"Thanks."

"Okay, Cruz. You know, my father was a real-life gangster in his youth."

"I heard some rumors."

"You know why he's sitting on his fat butt on a lounge chair on a sunny beach resort? Because he listened to someone. They told him to walk away from the gang life. He did. So he didn't end up dead. If he hadn't, I'd be dead. He was the one who saved me from self-destructive, suicidal teenage years. I'm a successful businesswoman because of my father. He gets to sit on his fat butt, retired and smiling with endless drinks all day, and playing poker all night. I run his business empire and do my legal stuff on the side to keep myself amused."

"Wize, the one thing I'm not is stupid."

"Cruz, do you think you're untouchable? A guardian angel, or two of them, sitting on your shoulders. Luck runs out eventually. I know. This isn't the only casino I own."

"Maybe it's not luck."

"You have skill and street smarts. No doubt about it. But luck runs out for all of us."

"If we're not careful," I said.

"Will you be careful?"

"I will."

"I'll have the document couriered over to your office tomorrow morning."

"Send it to my residence instead. I'll be working from home."

"What happened to your offices?"

"We had a visit from the Council."

"And?"

"And a guy claiming to be with Metro's Police Intelligence Division."

"Still not hearing the reason you're not working out of your place of business. I don't work from home. I work at my business. Why aren't you?"

"It's only for a few days while the place is swept for listening devices."

"I see. Gifts from the Council."

"Probably."

"The people you wish to partner with."

"They're hiring me."

"They're distracting them."

"I'm fooling them."

"Interesting word choice. Fool. Okay, Cruz, I have to get to some actual work. I'll have the agreement to you tomorrow morning for you signature. Then I'll deliver it to Council headquarters for you."

"Thanks. Wize, I know you're not happy with my decision, but if we're the good guys, then let's be the good guys and not simply say the words. Despite all jokes, I'm doing this for Metropolis and beyond, just like G-Man would have done and did for over seventy years."

"Remember, Cruz. G-Man is dead. You're the Man now. But the caveat is that you must be around for a while for it to stick."

"I already promised G-Man that I would. I don't break my promises."

She nodded. "Then I'll see you when I see you C-Man."

I smiled. She told me she'd come up with a nickname for me, just as she did for my posthumous mentor, Wilford G.

Chapter Eleven
Run-Time

My hands gripped the steering wheel as I shot into the hovertraffic express lanes. Wize's words were not lost on me. All I wanted to be was a successful street detective with basic cases. Time after time, I found myself in larger-than-life cases that would kill any average private investigator in this supercity. I had to get some questions answered if I was going to be playing footsy with the Council of Corporations again. One case they were an enemy, another case an ally. Despite them wanting to hire me, they could still be either on this case. At the very least, they saw me as a means to an end to acquire tech that, besides them, every government, nation, and crime boss would kill lots of people to get their hands on.

But I was back on my home turf of Metropolis, with my entire network of friends and associates. That was my ace in the hole. Wish I had thought to say that to Wize Gal when I had the chance. Above all of them was one, and I'd brought him into my secret case years ago. Now I was only minutes away.

Peacock Hills was one of the premiere "new money" business districts in Metropolis. From the hovertraffic lanes, the monolith towers looked like gargantuan fingers extending into the sky to the clouds. The buildings were illuminated along the edges in neon white, light yellow, and blue. The roof lighting of each structure also gave the appearance of them having angelic halos.

Like most executives and owners in Peacock Hills, not one of them was over the age of forty-five, including my best friend Run-Time. Middle-school drop-out at eleven years old. Body shop go-fer at twelve. Hover-car mechanic at thirteen. Valet attendant at fourteen. Hover-taxi driver at seventeen. Hovertaxicab owner at nineteen and bought three more at twenty-one. Millionaire at twenty-two. Founder, President, CEO, and COO of Let It Ride Enterprises at twenty-five. Mega-multi-millionaire by thirty. He owned all the top car washes, hovercar body shops, hovercar rental shops, hovercycle rental shops, hovertaxicab, and hoverlimousine services in the city. Anything that had to do with private transportation, Run-Time had his hands in it. The hover-car remained the top luxury item in the city, despite ubiquitous public transportation and commercial hover-taxicab services.

Run-Time may have been a "Who's Who" among the wealthy elite, but there was nothing "elite" about him. He came from the working class and kept that sensibility, despite his wealth. For me, he was my source of any information having to do with politics or the corporate world. I had lots of questions and he'd be able to give me straight answers.

Let It Ride Enterprises took up all its monolith tower on Electric Boulevard. I was glad to be visiting as I coasted into its parking bay off the freeway exit. Let It Ride was one of the few places I'd allow valet service to get anywhere near my Pony. Here, I always knew my vehicle was in great, secure hands. If I wanted, they'd even wash and detail it for me.

I came out of the elevator on the penthouse level, two hundred and fifty floors up. All I did was smile as I saw them. Three women sat at the vaulted reception area, evenly spaced apart from each other. "Good morning, Mr. Cruz," the receptionists responded in unison.

I realized, like Wize Gal's place, they could see me on their monitors from the parking lot to the elevator.

"Good afternoon, ladies," I greeted.

The Caucasian woman with the British accent was dressed in purple, the Asian woman with the Southern accent dressed in green, and the Black woman with the West Indian accent was in blue.

"What happened to your clothes, Mr. Cruz?" Mrs. Bliss asked in her British accent.

"We didn't recognize you, Mr. Cruz. What's the occasion?" Mrs. Utopia asked in her Southern accent.

"Is this supposed to be a disguise, Mr. Cruz?" Mrs. Eden asked in her West Indian accent.

In Metropolis, not only were you exposed to countless languages, but countless dialects and accents.

"No one stole my clothes, and the occasion is to keep everyone on their toes. I have to surprise my friends too every now and again. The criminals get to see that from me. I need to share the fun."

"Mr. Run-Time was expecting you today," Ms. Utopia said.

"And here I am."

"Mr. Cruz, thanks for coming so fast." I turned to see one of Run-Time's three VPs walking toward me. It was the tall Lebanese woman, Mrs. Phoenicia, in a shiny ivory suit.

As I stood in place, she waved a hand scanning device over me, from head to toe. PJ had one too for our Liquid Cool offices.

"Clean," she said.

"Is this a new practice for visitors?" I asked.

"Mr. Run-Time will explain."

#

Up the steps to his private second floor of the penthouse level, we went. Ceilings of purple stone, white marble walls, and plush purple carpet. Run-Time's office was at the very end of a long hallway.

The door was already open to his spacious office. Its decor theme was ivory whites and smooth black metals. My best friend came into view with a smile. Run-Time had his own trademark look—flat cap over a close haircut, slim-fit business suit with slim ties.

He greeted me with a hug. "Mr. Run-Time, at last."

"Mr. Cruz."

"How's Crystalline and the kids?" I asked.

"Fine as wine. Dot and the kids?"

"Same."

"He made good time, sir," Mrs. Phoenicia said.

"I never made the call," he told her.

"We read minds," I said to her.

"Want anything to drink?" he asked.

"No, thanks. I'm going to head home after this. I just wanted to stop by."

"I'm glad you did."

"What were you going to call me about?"

"Warn you."

Run-Time walked to sit behind his huge ivory desk, and I took a seat in one chair in front of it.

"Thanks, Mrs. Phoenicia." His VP closed the door as she left.

"Cruz, what's the new case?" he asked.

"It'll be for the Council of Corporations," I answered.

"They want to hire you?"

"They do."

"Is that wise?"

"My last stop said the same thing."

"You should listen."

"This is a case I need to stick with."

"You did something today, didn't you?" Run-Time asked. "Something out of the norm."

"Other than my new suit and fedora? And thanks for not dumping on my new look like everyone has been doing all day."

"That's what friends are for."

"Why do you ask?"

"Part of Mr. Mick's division is to monitor the Net and all its deep dark circles."

Mr. Mick was Run-Time's VP of Covert Operations. I was glad that I'd never be big enough of a company to need such an employee, or department. At least, that's what I kept telling myself.

"A few hours ago the chatter exploded," Run-Time continued. "Some of that chatter mentioned you."

"Why would I be mentioned?"

"Most of it mentioned a former client of yours."

"NeuroDancer," I said without hesitation.

"So you did do something."

I shook my head. The surveillance on me and my friend Spiders was obviously more extensive than I'd suspected. "I hired a scraper to monitor the Net for me, ever since Ms. NeuroDancer was sent to the afterlife. We knew this day might come, eventually."

"We did. I'm sure it comes to no surprise to you that a lot of megacorps in Metropolis have been secretly preoccupied with that former client-villain of yours, including me. You had the foresight and the initiative before everyone else."

"We still don't know how she did what she did."

"So you took it upon yourself to find out?"

"I'm the one she almost made do a header off my own business tower."

"What did your scraper find?"

"Clues."

"What clues?"

"Someone may know how she did it."

Run-Time sat quietly for a moment. We both knew the implications, and they went far beyond the Council of Corporations.

"What do you plan to do?"

"You know exactly what I plan to do."

"How does the Council come into this?"

"Officially, they want to hire me to find stolen corporate property information. That's my guess. Hinting that it has something to do with Ms. NeuroDancer's mind-control powers. Unofficially, they're trying to find out what I know."

"I would try to get you to drop this, but I know I'd be wasting my words."

"What I came here for is to know about a division of Metro PD. The Police Intelligence Division."

"What about them? Their services are shared by Metro PD, all the major supercities in the country, the Feds, and Up-Top too."

"The Council?"

"No."

"Do they use androids for soldiers?"

Run-Time almost laughed. "No. Who are you talking about, Cruz, because it wasn't Police Intelligence?"

"Remember, Captain Monitor at Metro PD."

Run-Time pushed a button on his desk. "Mrs. Phoenicia, can you do a search? Commander Monitor, formerly of Metro PD, still with Police Intelligence?"

There was a moment of silence. "Commander Monitor is with Police Intelligence."

"Thanks."

"You're welcome, sir." Run-Time touched the button again to disconnect.

"You sure they don't do work for the Council, too? Who runs it?" I asked.

"Anything's possible with the right amount of money. Chief Hub runs it. But if that's the case, then it's illegal."

"The chief?"

"Illegal or..."

"Or what?" I asked.

"They're working together on a specific case."

That made much more sense to me. The Council of Corporations and Metro PD in a temporary alliance. "That's a possibility."

"Monitor told me the truth, then. The Chief runs it."

"The chief may have nothing to do with day-to-day operations, but they all report to him. The division is under him. He approves all operations, and he has ultimate oversight."

"Intelligence Services involvement?"

Run-Time chuckled. "Where did that come from?"

"A story Madame President told me about a CIA operation in the far past."

"CIA? No such organization anymore. That was before Metropolis, Space Station colonies, Lunar Colonies, Martians, cyborgs, VR, hovercars."

"I know. But our Intelligence Services."

"What story?"

"MK Ultra."

"Sounds like she was telling tales like your Falcon Express story of sentient toilets. Equally irrelevant to your current situation."

"Let's not mention them again. Leave that in my UFO Case file, never to be opened again. You said this chatter started today. The same day I was being followed, but I am followed all the time. Then the Council visits me to hire me. Then Police Intelligence with an army of black-metal androids shutting off the power and lights to the tower so they can infest my office with listening devices. Or maybe she did it."

"The same day a group of clients tried to bug my offices. Very unique listening devices," Run-Time revealed. "As if they knew you'd be visiting me."

"That explains the hand scanner before."

"Cruz, what have you gotten yourself into now? That chatter included megacorporations, foreign governments, criminal syndicates. This is big."

"Everyone that matters," I said, reciting the name I once thought of giving to one of my past cases.

"Big, and extremely dangerous."

"I'll likely be at the Council's headquarters tomorrow, with Madame President herself, so I'll be safe."

"What about before you get there and when you leave?"

"I'll take precautions."

"Do you know how NeuroDancer did what she did?" Run-Time asked me directly.

"No, but I will find out. Or, I'll make so that no one else does."

"You really have been on this since you killed her."

"The very next day. No one can get it, whatever it is. Machine, drug, whatever. No one can get it."

"You did this," Run-Time said with a smirk. "You set all this in motion, on purpose. The explosion of chatter in cyberspace."

I didn't say a thing.

"Cruz, I admire your resolve."

"I don't like loose ends."

"That I know."

"Not on this one."

"Heavens knows I agree with you completely. But you're not the only one out there. These people will do anything to get it for their own purposes."

"That's not what scares me, and has scared me every day since I blasted that crazy maniac client villainess of mine. What scares me is what any other crazy maniac would do with that power if they got it. Everyone should be scared."

"Believe me, Cruz, everyone in the know is scared. That's what scares me. Scared people do dangerous things, and these type people are already dangerous and scary enough when they're calm."

"I guess I should go home and get ready for my Council headquarters visit tomorrow."

"Ever been to their headquarters before?"

"No. Liquid Cool is too far down on the corporate totem pole to ever be allowed anywhere near there. Not even on their totem pole, I should think."

"They're in Aurora Borealis."

"Never heard of it." But then I remembered. "No, once we passed by it when I was on the illegal hovercar racing circuit. It's near Silicon Dunes and Opus Fields. That's where they'd be."

"The Council of Corporations' property takes up the entire district."

"The whole town?"

Run-Time grinned. "And everything in it. One of the few districts with their own police force."

"That's allowed in Metropolis."

"It's the Council, Cruz. But Movie Town does too. Silver City is the other. Think of yourself as the ant and the Council of Corporations' headquarters and its property as Mount Everest."

"I will be on my best behavior."

"Maybe you shouldn't."

"Why?"

"Cruz, don't let their pristine and faux palm trees fool you. There are drive-by shootings in Aurora."

Chapter Twelve
Board of Evil

I lived in Rabbit City, a working-class residential neighborhood, nestled amongst many others. Not the dumps like Free City or booshy-upscale like the districts I'd soon be visiting. I didn't have to wait long at my residential tower called the Concrete Mama. It was legacy housing willed to me by my maternal grandparents. I loved its ugliness. A giant chunk of granite set down on Earth from space was a monolith residential tower that could withstand a nuclear blast or an asteroid crash. Not just my home anymore, but the entire Cruz family's.

Wize Gal sent the reviewed non-disclosure documents early in the morning. If she was happy with it, with her legal eagle-eyes, then I was too. I didn't even take it back up to the apartment to read it. I sat down in the lobby, used the electric pen, and signed the document to hand back to the courier. As I watched the young super-slim courier guy wearing a soft backpack walk out of the building, I knew that my path was set. There was no going back, there was no escaping. I'd get hired for the case, but everyone involved knew this was far, far more than a simple case for a street detective. Could we get to the end without anyone getting killed? Doubtful.

#

In all the years I'd lived in Metropolis, I'd never actually been inside the Aurora Borealis district. It was like the sun. You saw it in all its splendor high above, but you'd never go there. It was among the top five wealthiest districts in the entire nation, probably the top twenty on Earth.

The late Wilford G. had that one ultimate case that he never let go of for fifty years—the Venn Diagram/A.I./I.T. Case. He even came back from the dead to solve it with me at his side. He defeated Venn, with my assist, and saved Metropolis, but at the cost of his own life. I would not let the late NeuroDancer be my swan song case. I had every intention of ending up like Wize Gal's father—sitting on my fat butt on a Caribbean beach in retirement. But it was much more than that.

A narcissistic sociopath like NeuroDancer having mind-control tech was scary enough. The woman was sufficiently insane to think she actually could take over the supercity of Metropolis like a real dictator. The problem was that governments, megacorps, and crime gangs would always be more ruthless and powerful than any one individual, no matter how clever he or she thought they were. Even I knew I needed a solid team to assist me in solving my cases and beating out all the crazy maniacs I came across. If she hadn't gotten herself killed—by me, someone else would have done the job.

The first traffic signs for Opus Fields came into view as my hovercar changed from a fast virtual lane to a middle one. The last time I was in the wealthy district was also for my NeuroDancer case. Opus Fields was Movie-Town, with its open fields, massive filming studios and offices. But the scandal I uncovered from that case put a lot of its talent in prison or out of work—those that didn't commit suicide, that is. The business still hated me, even after all these years. Wear a Liquid Cool T-shirt in that district and you'd get shot or rundown by some hovercar for sure.

Beyond Opus Fields was Silicon Dunes, another uber-wealthy district but more like a real city with its monolith towers. Once past there I'd finally see the mythical Aurora Borealis district—the headquarters of the Council of Corporations, the most power megacorp chamber of commerce in the world. My detective agency would never get to be a member, as their starting annual membership fee was in the millions. However, Run-Time's Let It Ride Enterprises had been a member for years. He'd told me he'd never wanted to be a member, but there came a time when not being one was far more dangerous for his business. Membership meant protection. He came to the realization around the same time he determined he needed a VP of Covert Operations and also had to hire a small army of in-house corporate soldiers to protect the company he founded and ran to this day.

Very few Metropolis residents had any of idea of the endless corporate wars that went on between Earth megacorps. The Council of Corporations was the entity that kept the peace. Even I had to admit they were a necessary evil. My Blade Gunner case taught me the hard way that there were sinister megacorps in the shadows out there that had to be forced to play by some standard of rules. A war among the megacorps could destroy the planet, and that was only half of the equation. The police were the other force who provided a constant reminder to the Council that if they didn't keep the peace, the police would. Self-regulation and self-governance were what the megacorps wanted, besides making lots of money.

I could see the district now. From my vantage point in the sky-traffic, it was like I beheld a city of pure light. For any city to look so angelic was the first telltale sign that it was filled with devils. Yep, Aurora Borealis was dead-ahead.

The city was also quite large. A combination of residential and commercial properties that truly appeared to be made of muted yellow light. But one's eye was transfixed by the three-hundred-plus-story megatower in the center—the official headquarters of the Council of Corporations. I was told it was virtually a gated city within the supercity of Metropolis. Those who lived in Aurora Borealis never ventured outside the district, except for business or vacations. They had everything they needed, including their own police force and even their own standing army.

The exit came up fast, but I was ready and shot down the virtual lane from the expressway directly into the district. Directions were simple here: drive toward the big, bright light until you have to stop. I wasn't in my classic Ford Pony. I'd rented a silver sports hovercar, and it was super-expensive to do because people hardly rent hovercars anymore. You either took a hovertaxi or drove your own hovercar. But I learned another quirk of the district of Aurora Borealis. Hovertaxis weren't allowed. I'd never heard of something so ridiculous, but that was the law, so I had to scramble to get a rental because there was no way I was driving my classic Ford Pony to the headquarters of the Council of Corporations. They'd already infested my offices with tech junk; they would not infest my classic vehicle with trackers.

Due to constant rain and drizzle, Metropolis was a supercity not known for its sunny disposition. But sunlight seemed to beam down from the heavens through the overcast of the rest of the city to the Aurora district alone.

No, they couldn't have, I thought.

They did. Aurora Borealis was so filthy rich that I realized they had giant hoverlights high in the sky, probably between the troposphere and stratosphere, to keep the district in perpetual daylight. Lights in the sky and buildings made of light. This one district likely consumed more power than the entire supercity.

As I flew toward the Council HQ, I noticed two other things. First, I was the only person on the lane. Second, the flock of seagulls above my vehicle were not birds; they were drones and were following as fast as I was driving, all around me. I bet every scan that was possible was being done on me and my vehicle. They were probably also doing a full instant criminal and intel background check on me, which would be complete as soon as I stepped out of the hovercar.

"Now, what's this coming at me?" I said.

Two flying silver androids were flying toward me. Did they not hear about my UFO Case? I didn't want any "flying men" around me ever again.

#

As I followed my two shiny silver android escorts to a parking bay on one side of the mega-tower, I noticed I was in control of the acceleration, but not the steering. Being on the illegal hovercar racing circuit, every mechanic made external remote control of one's vehicle impossible, as I'd done, but this was not my vehicle. But would it have mattered? Here, the Council was doing it. I let my foot off the accelerator and still the hovercar moved on its own. My vehicle was completely under their computer control. More than a few people, including Run-Time, told me the Council of Corporations had technology found no place else in Metropolis.

My vehicle set down in a wide empty parking space on a sparsely filled level. The two flying androids stood at attention, waiting at the side of the stall. The six-foot models looked very humanoid, except their faces had no facial features of any kind.

When I stepped out of my car, without warning, one android reached into my slicker and took my gun from my concealed shoulder holster.

"Your weapon will remain in your vehicle," it said.

I was not stupid enough to bring my omega-gun, but I had to at least try to see if I could sneak in some kind of weapon. Now, I might as well be naked.

I stared across the parking level as I noticed a shimmering effect in the air. My stomach jumped up as if I was on a roller coaster that had dropped, though as far as I could tell, my feet were firmly planted on the ground. Suddenly, a young woman with tan skin in a black kimono appeared in front of me with a very tall, scary-looking corporate soldier on either side of her. Their suits were shimmering gray with black ties. They wore black shades, one had no facial hair, the other had a mustache and goatee.

"Mr. Cruz," the woman said as she gave me a customary Japanese bow and nod. "Follow me." Her golden-brown hair was tied back tight in a ponytail and when she turned, I could see it went to her waist. I followed, and the suit soldiers followed me.

I held by breath. Everything was changing around me. The androids and parking lot disappeared to be replaced by a giant open glass-domed lobby. It was as if I was in some kind of VR (virtual reality) simulation game, only I wasn't wearing any VR glasses, a helmet, or any device to be plugged into. The lobby was bustling with people around me. Far ahead of us in the giant cavernous lobby of glass were elevator capsules. Behind us were the auto-opening doors of the parking bays. People appeared to be walking on air, but were really on some kind of invisible moving walkway. Others rode mini-hovertrolleys above us.

Then everything around me changed again, and we were outside of another glass lobby but truly outside with the sun (or their hoverlights in the sky) beaming down on us as if we were in the tropics. The structure was ultra-modern, but planted to the side of a giant revolving door entrance was an old stone-marble plaque. PECUNIA EST RADIX OMNIUM BONORUM, it read.

"Money is the root of all good," my escort said to me.

I had the incredible, and useless, superpower of knowing what the language was but unable to speak a word of it. "Latin, huh? Why such an old language?"

"To forge forward into the future, one must always hold on to the past, Mr. Cruz. A reminder to humanity," she said.

"Or a warning," I said.

The Council's architect and interior designers seemed to only know two colors: white and silver, except for the material of the tower exterior that made them look like they were made of light. We all went through the revolving doors in one pass. Everything changed again, and we were already at the elevator capsules, which only a moment ago were about twenty feet ahead of us. There was a bank of five elevator capsules on either side of the corridor. One arrived, and she led us in. We had the entire capsule to ourselves. I could fit ten of my Ford Pony's in the compartment. It was that large.

One had to always remember that elevator capsules were actually rockets. How else would one be able to get up and down three-hundred-story megatowers in less than a minute? Of course, the modern Earther was used to the G-force from the time of infancy.

I didn't know what floor we were on, because there were no visible displays on the panel or walls, nor any audible announcements. The door opened, and she led the way.

"You may sit there," she said, gesturing me to what could only be called a waiting room for royalty. "Ms. Gem will have you in shortly."

The three of them walked through a wall and disappeared. I laughed to myself. I sat in one of the single chairs and slowly sunk into the plush fabric until my body finally stopped.

The receptionist area was like Run-Time's penthouse megatower one, but theirs was empty. I was completely alone in the area, or so they wanted me to think. Didn't even ask me if I wanted some water or a beverage? How rude.

"May I offer you some water or a beverage?" I heard a voice say.

My head jerked to my left and there was the same young woman with a tray in her hand with an assortment of tiny bottles, some clear, some colored.

That was creepy.

"I'll take a water."

"You might prefer a silk coffee," she suggested.

"Sure. Why not?" So the Council knew I liked my silk coffee in the morning. How very CIA of them.

She handed me a ceramic-like bottle that was warm to the touch.

"Thank you," I said.

She nodded and stepped backwards. Again, she disappeared.

I imagined the building was a complex construction of holo-floors and walls, nano walls, holographic projectors, sonic pulses, and an assortment of tech so you never really were sure where you were, what was there, who was around you, and what was real.

A smile came over my face. On the center reception table were hovercar racing magazines from around the world. The mags were there for me, not any of the booshy ultra-wealthy class that might sit in this room. I wiggled out of my chair and got to my feet. The chairs were arranged in a rectangle around the reception table. At the end was one normal single chair made of faux white wood. I took out my analog pocket watch from inside my jacket.

"Madame President, let's stop with the games and get started. I'm on time," I said aloud once I sat down again.

Then everything in the room around me changed again.

#

Logically, I could figure out how it all was done, but the tech was like true magic. One second I was in a spacious white reception area, the next I was in a dimly lit room with Madame President of the Council of Corporations standing a few feet away, facing me in a crimson kimono-style dress and a fat pearl necklace around her neck. She had a new 'do—her pitch-black hair cut very short with a bang on the right landing just above her eye.

"Mr. Cruz, welcome to the executive boardroom of the Council," she greeted.

I stood from my chair and looked around. "A fitting megacorps boardroom. Lots of shadows and darkness."

"Did it ever occur to you, Mr. Cruz, that we may actually be playing to your stereotypes, and the masses, of the wealthy elite for our gain?"

"I once visited Free City and one of their fine residents said the same thing to me," I said with a smile.

"Free City." Madame President laughed to herself. "I don't believe I've ever even flown over that place."

"The poor do exist, Madame President, even in Metropolis."

"I'll take your word for it."

From the shadows behind her, the same young golden-brown haired woman in a black kimono stepped forward. "You've already met my chief aide, Ms. Akarui."

"Hello, Ms. Akarui. What's it like to work for one of the most powerful people in the world?" I asked.

"Is she?" asked one of the male board members.

Overhead lights turned on. The executive board room was far from empty. The man who'd spoken was wearing a white suit with his chest hairs billowing up from his open black shirt. What I was staring at was the man's oversized incisors.

"Hello. Does the Council allow vampires on their board?" I said, stepping to him with an arm extended to shake his hand.

The man smiled and shook my hand with an iron grip. "Call me Mr. Atila."

"Of course you are," I said, smiling.

"I'm the Senior Executive Chief Vice President of the Council of Corporations, so I must be one of the most powerful people in the world, too."

"Who's everyone else?" I asked, looking at the crowd of impeccably dressed men and woman gathered around.

I met the first VPs, second VPs, third VPs, VP of Security, VP of Business Development, VP of Member Satisfaction. It went on and on. I realized that every one of them was some kind of vice president. My smile never left my face as I met everyone. Some smiled too—very fake smiles, but most simply glared at me, as if I were some lowly intruder or peasant, and not wanting to shake my hand at all.

One reason I was so successful as a detective was my street smarts. Like any real Metropolis resident—born and raised—we could sense danger like we had an internal radar. It wasn't something you could learn. You either had it or you didn't. My spidey-sense had kept me out of trouble all my life. I could size up people quickly. My senses were screaming at me, like they did whenever I came across the criminal, violent, or psycho. The Council of Corporations board of directors was more than businessmen and women. They were extremely dangerous people. I could feel it in the air. They were capable of any manner of violence or evil. But what did I expect? To be more powerful than the real criminal underworld, the business over-world had to be worse.

"Who are we missing?" I asked.

They all looked at me suspiciously.

"Why do you think we're missing anyone, Mr. Cruz?" Madame President Gem asked me.

"Don't all boards have to have a Finance VP? It's in your bylaws. After all, 'money is the root of all good.'"

I got them to laugh. Good. The tension in the room dissipated.

Ms. Akarui showed me to my chair as the other board members moved to their seats around a huge dark faux-wood table which stood out in the room of white and silver by design.

"You weren't surprised by the 'shifting,'" Mr. Atila said.

"You mean your magical megatower here," I said, "where nothing you see is real and can change in an instant. I've seen it in VR games, of course. But the Council has expanded it to the real world."

"Real is a matter of perspective and acceptance," Atila said.

The door opened, and another man came in. He was in a silver suit, balding, wearing orange tinted glasses and carrying a shell-laptop in his hands. Ms. Gem was already sitting at the head of the table. Atila was seated to her right, and I was seated to her left. I never expected them to allow me to sit around their corporate board table. The new man sat at the opposite end of the table and placed his laptop in front of him.

"Numbers, you were missed by our guest here," Atila called out to him.

"Is Madame President going to finally explain why a non-board member is in the boardroom?" he asked.

"Our Treasurer," Atila told me.

"Because the Council of Corporations has hired him," Gem replied.

"Why would we hire some solo detective off the streets? We have all the most prestigious detective firms in the world in our membership."

"Because I wanted someone I could trust."

"You can't trust the membership and you can't trust the board. Madame President, you seem to have trust issues," Numbers said.

"I do. That's why I sit here and you sit where you do."

For a moment, the two stared at each other across the long table with such deadly contempt that I was scared one of them was going to shoot the other.

"This happens all the time," Atila said to me from across the table. "They absolutely hate each other."

Ms. Gem snapped out of her death stare. "We all hate each other, Mr. Atila. That's why we're such effective Council Board Members for the good of the membership."

"Our Treasurer asked a question that hasn't been answered," one of the male board members called out. He was a small man who reminded me of Mr. Viper from my Blade Gunner case.

"I've hired Mr. Cruz to acquire the object for the Council."

Instantly, everyone's expressions went from unemotional coldness to genuine fear.

"We said we wouldn't search for it," a female board member yelled.

"Why? So they can get it?!" Ms. Gem yelled.

"We have agreements!" Atila yelled at her.

"The Council will have that object, because it's on the market!"

The news shocked everyone around the board table. I had to admit that I had no idea what she meant or what was going on.

"How do you know?" another board member asked.

"Feelers have already been broadcast," Gem said to him. "We can either get in the game, or be destroyed by the others."

"Madame President, this is unacceptable," Numbers said as he stood from his chair. "We may be strong, but we can't fend off the others if they unify. This will do that."

"No, it won't. We have only three choices here: let them get it, let another party get it, or we seize it."

"How do you plan to seize it, then? You haven't done so in all these years. What has changed?"

"What has changed is Mr. Cruz," Gem said.

I felt my stomach drop into my butt. What did I have to do with this? What did Madame President really hire me for? What game was she playing with me as the clueless pawn, risking my life without my consent?

"How so, Madame President? What does that one have to do with our business?"

"He's been looking for the object longer that us. And he found it. He just doesn't know it yet."

My eyes had locked on her, as surprised by her last sentence as everyone else. Fortunately, my peripheral vision was working. I threw myself back, tipping my chair over just as the shooting began.

#

Going to a gunfight with a knife was stupid. Going to a gunfight with no weapon at all was stupid, suicidal, and deranged. As I hit the ground hard, I remembered what Run-Time had told me about drive-by shootings in Aurora Borealis. But I'd thought he was joking, and weren't drive-bys supposed to be in the open street in sketchy neighborhoods, not in posh board rooms in uber-swanky megatowers?

I was looking right at her when the laser blast hit CC President Gem in the chest and blasted her body back across the room. The culprit was Mr. Treasurer and then he tried to shoot me too, but I ducked down again. I didn't know if the CC president was dead, but her aide definitely was. Ms. Akarui lay on the ground beside the table. Someone shot her, but it wasn't Numbers.

One group of board members was shooting at another with laser guns. Again, I felt I was in a video game as sections of reality were rising, falling, and moving to help board members dodge laser fire. I peeked up again. Mr. Atila saw my head sticking up from the table, smiled, and quickly shot at me. He missed as I jerked my head back down. So he was with Numbers.

If it had been a skit on a comedy show, one might have laughed. Board members of opposite sides shooting laser pistols at each other. I realized the left side, which I was on, was the president's faction, and the other side was controlled by Numbers, the Treasurer. More than a few board members were wounded or dead and on the ground.

I peeked up again, because Atila made me nervous. He wasn't the hide-behind-the-chair type. He was an attacker, and I was the one person in the room without a gun. Atila was reaching into the air and I didn't need to wait to know what he was retrieving from some invisible compartment.

I knew what Atila was going to do with his long laser machine-gun. He was going to jump on the table and shoot me first, then everyone else in

Gem's faction. I could see it in his eyes, the damn vampire-looking crazy maniac. He was going to kill me.

The board chairs were big and heavy, like solid rocks on the ground. All except the one that I had brought with me from the reception area. Mentally, I was transported back to when I was a kid playing sports. You got to a certain age, and you wanted to play baseball, not so you could hit the ball out of the park, but see if you could swing and knock the pitcher's head off. You wanted to play soccer, not to kick the game-winning goal in the net, but to see if you could kick the ball into the goalie's nuts. As Dot and I were learning from Cruz, Jr., kids could be the most wicked creatures that required constant surveillance and confinement when necessary.

It happened in slow motion. Atila jumped from the ground for the table. I flipped my chair in a quick round-robin motion he didn't see coming. He yelled as he dropped his machine-gun rifle to cover his head. The chair hit him right in his legs, knocking him off balance. His upper torso went forward, his lower torso swung back. The sound of his head and shoulder hitting the edge of the table as he fell was like two hovercars crashing. It was a miracle he wasn't dead instantly. But I could be a teleporting ninja too, like Cruz Jr., even crawling on the ground. That long laser machine-gun was mine. Atila stood up, and I blasted him in the chest and he was thrown back toward the wall. He disappeared through it, and then all we heard was real screaming. He was falling to his death.

I ducked back to the ground to avoid getting shot. "I'm really sorry about this, Ms. Akarui, but I have no choice," I whispered as I lunged at the dead woman.

I used her as a human shield as I charged Numbers. He wildly fired at me as he tried to back up. When he turned to stop himself, I threw Akarui's body at him. He blocked her, but I kicked him in the head. I'd never be a martial arts expert, but street fighting wasn't about form or excellence. It was about surviving anyway you could by doing as much damage to your opponent as you could. He too was gone through the wall, taking Ms. Akarui's body with him. Again, we heard screaming.

I never waited even a second. I was shooting my way to Madame President, taking as many of the Treasurer's faction along the way as I could. Then Gem's faction started shooting at me!

The floor exploded in laser blasts as it became transparent. On levels below us, corporate soldiers were shooting up, seemingly at all of us. Above, the ceilings also became transparent as corporate soldiers wearing jetpacks were jumping from many stories above and dropping toward us.

I fired at everyone to keep them away. They all dove for cover.

I reached the CC president. She was still alive, looking up at me from the ground. There was a big black mark in the center chest area of her kimono dress.

"Ms. Gem, we may not get out of this. What do we do?" I asked.

"Grab me and jump."

A normal person would have wondered, pondered, maybe asked a question or two, or hesitated. Working street detectives in Metropolis weren't normal. I scooped her up in my arms and jumped through the wall with lasers whipping past us from the boardroom, above and below, having no idea where I was jumping to.

Nothing was real. I couldn't even tell if we were falling down, or we were stationary and the walls were moving on their own past us and the bottom floor to us. I'd never experienced such a thing. Nothing you saw in front of your eyes could be trusted. Then suddenly everything changed again, and we were on the ground in the wide-open lobby.

"Get us outside," she said to me.

As I helped her to her feet, I could see she was bleeding badly from her wound. Out the main glass lobby doors I led her, the same way her aide had led me in not too long ago. The stone-marble plaque (PECUNIA EST RADIX OMNIUM BONORUM) outside the main giant revolving door entrance now seemed grotesque to me.

Suddenly, she stopped and grabbed me under my arms, startling me. Up we went into the air the very moment some kind of projectile landed where we were and exploded. So the Council of Corporations had missiles too. Ms. Gem's kimono dress doubled as a jetpack and we quickly rocketed around the side of the megatower. We were high enough up in the sky that if she had let me go, that was the end of Cruz, Metro P.I., but I was never worried or scared.

She set down in one level of the parking bay. It wasn't as large as the others I'd seen, so I assumed it was for something other than hovercars. As far as the eye could see were hovercycles—very expensive, high-end ones.

I helped her sit down on the ground. She didn't look good at all. Pale, clammy, not good.

My head jerked up when the air exploded with sirens. I'd never heard sirens so loud.

"We have little time," she said.

"What just happened?" I asked her. I knew she had used me for something other than simply hiring me.

"That, Mr. Cruz, was an attempted coup."

"Is that how you transition power between board members at the Council of Corporations? Ever heard of elections?"

She smiled. "This is the Council of Corporations, Mr. Cruz. I didn't become its president through elections. I never expected that I'd leave through elections either, but I'm not dead yet."

"I know you used me for something with them. What did you use me to do?"

"I had to draw them out. Now you can do what I hired you to do."

"Which is what?"

"Find and destroy the object. I know you'd never find it and give it to me. I had planned to have you find it, and we'd take it from you."

"Did you now?"

"That part of the plan is over. Based on what they tried to do, I clearly underestimated them. I will focus all my energies on maintaining my presidency from them and the others."

"Who are these others?"

"There are many 'others.' The ones I'm talking about you need not concern yourself with. They are my problem. The ones who are your concern, I'm going to going to lend you one of my operatives to deal with."

"What are you talking about?"

"There's no time. You need to get off the premises now. Steal one of the hoverbikes. Here."

She pressed a black dot on my wrist. "Take any of them. How is your memory?"

"I'm not senile yet, if that's what you're asking, but don't ask me to remember the entire encyclopedia from A to Z."

"The number I'm going to recite is the most important one you'll ever have to remember. If you remember it, you may succeed in finding the NeuroDancer device."

"NeuroDancer stole it from you, didn't she?"

"Psi-tech is the next race among the superpowers. Memory uploading, erasing, editing, expanding, sharing, and the coveted mind control. You don't think a dancing stripper invented it herself. She didn't just sleep with men."

"The Council was the source all along."

"We were its thief all along."

"And she stole it from you. What's the number?"

"Find the courier who delivered your non-disclosure agreement. He has something for you. The number I'm about to recite is twenty digits. Remember."

She slowly uttered the number string. I focused on every digit despite all the noise from the surrounding sirens. By now, they filled the sky with flying androids looking for us. I repeated it perfectly back to her.

Two minutes later, I blasted out of the parking bay on a Mach-13 Sinistro hoverbike. The Council's swarm of flying androids, drones, and hovervans were fast, but not faster than that bike. With my racing skills and knowledge of the hovertraffic flow and the surrounding city, I lost them all within ten minutes.

PART THREE
My "Crime" Crew

Chapter Thirteen
Phishy

That Mach-13 Sinistro hoverbike was one fine bike, and I hated hoverbikers. But just because I hated the morons who rode them didn't mean I hated the machines. Unlike most hoverbiker owners, I actually knew how to ride, which I had done extensively on secret, out-of-the-way lanes to truly understand aerodynamics when I built my Ford Pony. If my Ma and Pops knew I was racing hoverbikes at three hundred mph, I'd be posthumous Cruz the kid, not living, breathing Cruz the adult. I was sad I had to dump the Sinistro into a river accessway. In a city where it rained all the time, Metropolis had a network of underground rivers most people didn't know about. I was aware of them because I had the joyous occasion of almost falling into one a long time ago when I was a kid.

I had to assume that the hoverbike could be tracked. Even if Metro PD couldn't, the Council of Corporations would certainly be able to. It came from their headquarters building. I walked the dark, grimy streets of Wharf City, one of those low-life districts frequented by more of the criminal class than the normal people. I was alone. No vehicle, no omega-gun...

"Hey Pops, are you lost or something?"

Wharf City had a wide variety of sections: The practically a-ghost-town section of mostly commercial warehouse real estate, the seedy dance club section with scummy hotel rooms by the hour section, the high-end business district with offices, restaurants, and retail. I was in one of the in-between areas and, as luck would have it, a trio of street punks spotted me. I'd spotted them a block away, hanging out in the corner, a dark corner conveniently situated between two neon-lit establishments. But I saw their shadowy figures. When I passed them, I could make out their flapper hats and chia-pet bubble-coats, which were standard dress for the low-level street gangs in this part of Metropolis. Within the same hour, I went from the uber-wealthy Aurora Borealis with its corporate gangsters to Wharf City with its low-end street gangsters.

Now, the three "kids" were slowly following behind me.

"Hey Pops, can we help?" the lead one said, half-laughing.

I knew the second I stopped, they might draw on me. Wannabe gangsters and real ones looked exactly the same in this part of town. I didn't have my omega-gun, but I still had Atila's laser-machine-gun under my slicker. I turned and already began firing. If I'd wanted to hit them, they'd all be on the ground instantly. I wanted to scare them away, and that's exactly what I did. They ran so fast that they had reached the end of the block and disappeared around the corner in seemingly under a minute.

Good. I could think in peace about how I was going to handle my "swan song" case without ending up in the morgue in my nice new black suit and hat.

#

The Council had done some extensive profiling on me and likely had been watching me ever since the conclusion of my NeuroDancer case. They'd know all my frequent haunts in Metropolis, but I needed to resist the urge to go to places I didn't know. My frequent haunts were that because I knew the place, the people, the people knew me; they were places that gave me the home advantage, not the Council. I remembered Madame President's spoiled elitist comment: she'd never even fly over the places I called home. So the Council may know all my hangouts, but they didn't "know" them. I couldn't go back to my Liquid Cool offices, so I'd have to turn one of my hangouts to my temporary base of operations. I'd need my "people."

First would be Phishy. I laughed to myself that Phishy, of all people, would be my first hire on this Mission Impossible case. I'd finally reached a 24-7 convenience market where the college kid cashier was behind a six-inch bullet-proof, laser-resistant glass and if you made said cashier nervous once, all he had to do was push a button and the entire store would go on lockdown with you trapped inside.

"All I need is a phone," I said with a slight smile. If I was stone-faced, they'd think I was a criminal. If I was smiling too much, they'd think I was some kind of psycho.

The cashier guy pointed. I went to the aisle dedicated to a vast selection of quick-phones. Not the product, but pictures of all their cheapy mobile phones. Press the picture and all the specs you ever wanted to know about the phone would display. All I wanted was the cheapest of cheap because I only wanted to make calls. Didn't care about the Net, playing games, taking pictures, typing documents, graphics manipulation, or any other nonsense.

"Give me ten of them," I said when I got to the partitioned register.

"Don't I know you?" the guy said.

"Yes, I am Cruz of Liquid Cool. Yes, I know I'm not wearing my tan fedora and slicker. Despite being in a nice black suit and hat, yes, I know I'm currently off my brand and it's confusing to the public and my fans. Yes, I will correct the situation at my earliest convenience."

The cashier guy laughed. "You really are a real detective. Read all that in my mind. You're good. Real good. If I know someone who needs a detective, I'll send them your way. Maybe, if I ever graduate from school and get tired of this dump, I can work for you."

"What are you studying?"

"Officially or unofficially?"

"Officially, means college and you're doing it for someone else, like family. Unofficially, means what you want to do."

The kid smiled. "You are the real deal. Parents forcing me to go to college for business management and economics. Told my dad to just shoot me and get it over with. But no college, no allowance, so that settles that. But unofficially, don't laugh—"

"I'm a detective who used to be a hovercar racer and restorer. Why would I laugh?"

"I'm an amateur magician."

"Really? What kind?"

"Illusionist."

"Well, isn't that interesting," I said.

#

Not long after my first major case, and especially after my Blade Gunner case, I realized I needed to have a network of safe houses around Metropolis that I could use whenever I needed. Well, I needed one now, and that's why I was in Wharf City. Warehouses for hire by the month in the Wharf were always available and one of the two calls I made from one of my new quick-phones was to a real estate office that not only had I done business with before, but was also a very satisfied client—an infidelity case that led to divorce which led to the guy receiving very large alimony payments. The main thing was I knew I could trust him, and the Council likely wouldn't even know he existed. His business wasn't rich enough to be a member of the Council of Corporations.

The second call was to Phishy.

I waited outside in the shadows not too far from the warehouse. I wanted a warehouse rather than business offices because I wanted the farthest line of sight of everything around me as possible.

I told Phishy that we'd be "undercover." Clearly, that word meant something very different to him. I heard the music blaring from his hovercar ride from far off. Why were they playing Portuguese tango music so loudly in a district where no one speaks Portuguese and no one listens to tango music? Were they asking to get shot by one of the friendly neighborhood street gangs? I knew why they were doing it. Portugal had won the World Cup, but these idiots seemed to be unaware that the area was filled with fans, or fanatics, of the losing countries. Yes, they wanted to get shot.

The black hovercar descended right where I told them, so at least he got that part right. The front passenger window rolled down and there was a smiling, metal-mouth, gangster wannabe with bright neon tattoos all over his face staring at me. Neon tattoos were permanent and common among youth, gangster, wannabe gangster, and non-criminal alike. Cruz Jr. and Kat would never be getting any tattoos ever in the Cruz household. Dot and I already told them we'd scrub them off with a Brillo pad if we ever caught them in their "later" years.

"Please, turn that music down before we all get shot," I said to him.

"Portugal won the Cup!" the young man yelled. Another young man in the driver's seat, wearing a floppy hat, laughed. He, too, had a face full of neon tattoos and a mouth full of glowing metal. Replacing your good lower half of your teeth with metal that glowed any color you wanted was another gangster-wannabe practice.

"Yes, but turn it down anyway. And who are you?"

"We, old man, are the chauffeurs."

I'd already heard the passenger door opened before he popped up, trying to scare me.

"Cruz, you're back!" Phishy yelled, with his hands outstretched.

Actually, I hadn't seen Phishy in person since before my UFO Case, even though I spoke with him on the hoverplane, and he did help me in wrapping up that case.

Phishy always wore a dark-colored vest and pants, with some off-white, long-sleeved shirt extravaganza with colored fish all over it. This time I was seeing him with a new light-colored jacket with fishes all over it.

"You're not talking me out of it this time, Cruz!" he yelled.

Then it began. Phishy spinning around in the alleyway, doing his chicken dance. I'd managed to bypass it for a little while, but this was how he greeted me with some dance jig. I had to wait until he had sufficiently amused and tired himself out. The two gangster wannabees in the hovercar were laughing hysterically at the free show.

"Are you finished, Phishy?"

He stood up straight and smiled. "I think so."

"No, encore, encore!" his two gangster wannabees yelled, hanging out the windows.

I could have killed those two then if I had laser beam eyes. Phishy did it all again, spinning around with even more craziness.

When he was done with his dance, I had him immediately send his drivers away. I didn't want no fake gangsters around us. Phishy excluded, I needed serious people around me. Phishy did his hand slaps with them and the two rocketed out of the alleyway for the freeway.

"Gangster drivers, huh?"

"No, Cruz, they're not real gangsters. They're rappers."

"Not fake gangsters, but pretend gangsters, who get shot all the time by real gangsters. Well, they're gone now."

Phishy didn't hang with real criminals. He was a street hustler. A little non-narcotic running here, a bit of courier work there, whatever scam he could get into to bring in some extra cash. Nothing illegal enough to get him a solid prison stint, but always at the level where if he got caught, he'd only have to pay the fine and be on his way, not even a blot on the record. Cops and courts couldn't be bothered with street hustlers working non-violent, low-money scams. In a vile world, you had to set your priorities properly.

He was also a registered gun dealer, and he was the one who "acquired" my Up-Top omega-gun. How he got such a weapon from the off-world colonies, or maybe even Mars. I still didn't know to this day, but I was glad he did.

Phishy had an aversion to the hardcore criminal world, every bit as strong as me, but he maintained a knowledge of the players and he kept his ear to the streets. That was his great value to me as a working street detective. Anything worth knowing, Phishy would know about it, or who to go to find out.

"What's the undercover job, Cruz?"

"Is that you being undercover, Phishy, with gangsters drivers blasting crazy loud music from your vehicle to attract the attention of all the neighborhood street thug class?"

"No, Cruz. We were blending into our environment."

"Blending?"

"Yeah."

"Portuguese tango?"

"Blending."

"Whatever, Phishy."

"What are you wearing?"

"Not you too, Phishy. A man can't change his look?"

"Yea, you said we'll be undercover. I get it, Cruz. It's your disguise."

So Phishy considered my wonderful new black suit and hat a disguise. I was getting depressed.

"Phishy, we have work to do. A lot of work, so let's get to it. Get on the phone and get our Sidewalk Johnny Brigade here. I want to do a briefing in ninety minutes."

"Briefing?" Now that got Phishy's attention.

"Yes, briefing. For the new case."

"New case? What's it about?"

"You'll know at the briefing. So get them here."

"Great, Cruz. I'll get them here. You can count on me."

Phishy was already on his phone, talking. I made my third call as I led Phishy off the street to the back door to our new warehouse headquarters.

Chapter Fourteen
PJ

I'd rented a warehouse in the city before with Wilford G. in my A.I. Confidential case, but it was common practice for the Feds when coming into a specific municipality. Rent or commandeer temporary property for a base of operations for the length of the case until they rounded up all the bad guys for prosecution. I was putting a different spin on it. Rent a temporary base of operations to solve the case while fending off both known and unknown bad guys. Whether anyone would go to jail was highly unlikely, even though said bad guys would do all kinds of illegal things to get at me.

"Who did you call?" Phishy asked me while we surveyed the empty offices in the warehouse.

I liked the setup. The warehouse exterior shell was at least seven stories. Inside, there were two stories of offices in the center, like giant building blocks arranged in an S-formation. Massive open space inside and there were only two sets of entrances on either end, north and south, and not including a fortified giant sliding door for hovertrucks on the western wall.

"Muscle and weapons," I finally replied.

"Muscle?"

"Don't worry, Phishy, you know her."

"You mean PJ!" He started laughing.

PJ was definitely muscle with her cyborg arms. She wasn't called "Punch" for nothing.

She also arrived with gangster wannabe drivers in a big hovervan. I don't know what it was with the both of them. Phishy's were Portuguese speaking. PJ's were, of course, French-speakers. Phishy's were rappers. PJ's looked like real raw boxers or martial arts fighters. Well, she needed them and put the two big men to work.

While she had them moving furniture into the warehouse, she carried in four very long and heavy duffel bags. She didn't even wait for direction, making a beeline for one office on the ground floor. Those duffel bags were like cat-nip to me and I followed her like a zombie. Phishy was following both of us.

"What's in the bags?" he asked.

"Never you mind," PJ snapped.

Duffel bags full of weapons. I felt like it was Christmas and Santa brought all the coolest toys for me.

"What's that?" PJ asked, pointing to Atila's laser machine-gun strapped over my shoulder and hanging down, muzzle to the ground, under my slicker.

"Someone lent it to me," I replied.

"That's a long-nosed machine gun. Why would someone lend you that?" she asked.

"He won't need it anymore."

"So why did I need to bring all this?"

"PJ, I said we need our weapons here. I didn't know you were planning to outfit the entire Metropolis National Guard."

"National Guard," she scoffed. "We probably have more guns than those idiots."

"Be nice, PJ. It's community service, like jury duty."

"That's right. I hate jury duty! Do you know I got summoned again? I've gotten summoned two times already this year, and it's January. What's wrong with them? There's fifty million people in this city. Why are they picking on me?"

"I got summoned too," Phishy said.

That was all I needed—the PJ and Phishy show.

"With all the people in this city, I shouldn't be summoned again for fifty years. What's going on? Why are they picking on me? And I'm a felon, so I can't serve. Why are they bothering me? I get there and then I get excused. Have they ever heard of computers? Why don't their computers talk to each other? PJ is a felon so can't serve on jury, so don't bother her. Simple. What's wrong with them?"

I just let PJ rant with an occasional assist from Phishy as I examined all the bullet guns, laser guns, laser rifles, stun grenades, laser-tipped knives, and laser samurai swords in the duffel bags.

"What is this, PJ?"

"You know what it is."

"PJ, why am I pulling out an RPG from this duffel bag?"

"RPG," Phishy said with a big "let me see, let me see," smile on his face. "What does RPG stand for again?"

"Rocket-propelled grenade," PJ answered. "If you don't want it, leave it there," she said to me. "But don't complain to me if we get overrun by criminals and we need missiles."

"We can keep it," I said.

"That's what I thought. You didn't want my grenades, but didn't they come in handy against those attackers in the office?"

"PJ, you're keeping live grenades in your desk drawer."

"Where else will I keep them? I need them handy. Like my laser rifle. Close by. What good does it do me keeping them in a locked safe? That's stupid. Attackers come, you need to defend. How stupid is it having to run to some safe to get your weapons? They'd shoot you in back, laugh, then take your guns and safe with them with all your weapons inside."

"PJ, if I ask you a question, will you promise not to punch, Phishy?"

"Punch, Phishy?"

"Punch, me?" Phishy had a shocked look on his face.

"One one thousand," I said. "Two one thousand—"

"Oh, mon Dieu, I forgot the ammo!"

"Yes, PJ. We have no ammo."

She started laughing. "All the ammo is in the safe."

"Yes, PJ. Hilarious."

#

PJ had to leave with her two guys. They had unloaded all the furniture. I wasn't going to say anything at all when she came back. I had to let Phishy be Phishy, and let PJ do her thing, which was front of office. This warehouse was going to be the Liquid Cool office for a little while.

She returned less than an hour later with not one but a few backpack safes. Her two helpers each had one strapped to their backs. She marched them into the office we'd dubbed the Weapons Room.

After speaking all kinds of French, ninety percent of which was probably slang, her men were gone. In moments, just as she had created in the lobby of our Circuit Circle office tower, she had another pop-up reception desk set up. She had her mobile computer, phones, mini-refrigerator, and coffeemaker (for her, not me). Already she was going through all the voice messages. My VP of Client Services was workin'!

Chapter Fifteen
The Mick

I was back out in the dark alleyway as a Let It Ride Enterprises black hoverlimo descended to me from the sky. Their look was unmistakable, even before seeing the neon "Let It Ride Enterprises" letters on the sides. When a rear passenger window lowered, the well-dressed, portly, blue-eyed Irishman reached out and handed me a small silver case.

"Thank you, Mr. Mick."

"You're very welcome, Mr. Cruz," said Run-Time's VP of Covert Operations.

"Mr. Run-Time had me make the inquiries you requested."

"What did your contacts tell you?"

"Mr. Run-Time told me you're working for the Council of Corporations. That strikes me as an odd partnership based on your previous dealings. May I ask who hired you?"

"The President of the Council of Corporations herself, Ms. Gem."

"Then I'm sorry to have to inform you that your client is dead."

"Ms. Gem is dead?"

"A Council press release came out an hour ago stating that the Council President had died in a freak accident with more details to follow after appropriate family members are notified."

"Who is Ms. Gem's replacement?"

"Next in line would be their Senior Executive Chief Vice President."

"Mr. Atila?"

Mr. Mick looked surprised. "How do you know Mr. Atila?"

"Mr. Atila will not be assuming the role of the Council's next president."

"Why is that, Mr. Cruz?"

"Because he's dead."

"Dead? How do you know that?"

"Because I'm the one who killed him. He shot at me after Mr. Numbers shot Ms. Gem."

Mr. Mick struck me as having the ultimate poker face, but his expressions were changing by the second. "You didn't tell Mr. Run-Time any of this."

"I was on a quick-phone. Not a lot of time to talk."

"Mr. Cruz, maybe you should step into the vehicle for a quick talk because it would seem my latest information is not the latest. Also, Mr. Run-Time should be fully informed."

I stepped into the hoverlimo and sat across from Mr. Mick.

"First, tell me what your sources told you."

"I haven't been able to reach any of my sources at the Council headquarters itself, but those at the nearby Opus Fields said there was some kind of major shootout yesterday and the entire district is under lockdown. Their police have shut down all sky traffic into and the airspace above the Aurora. Their building security has been dramatically increased—human and android. Should I jump to the conclusion that you were part of that shootout?"

"The Treasurer shot the president. Then her people started shooting at his people, and then Mr. Senior Executive Chief Vice President tried to shoot me, so I threw him out of the building after I shot him and Mr. Treasurer too, after I kicked him."

"You killed two Council senior board members?"

"It wasn't my fault. They shot my client and tried to shoot me."

"But you didn't know your client, Ms. Gem, was dead."

"She was wounded badly, but I got her out of there, and she helped me escape the premises. She was alive."

"Then, despite the press release, she could still be. We should always view press releases from the Council of Corporations as calculated propaganda."

"Isn't that what a press release usually is?"

"If your client is dead, what do you plan to do?"

"Nothing changes. I've been paid and have a case. I'll continue on, and only Madame President can fire me."

"Fortunate for you, but the Council may take a different view."

"Then the clock is ticking. Can you keep me updated on the Council?"

"Could I coax you into telling me what the Council would hire you for?"

"Sorry, Mr. Mick, client confidentiality. If you hired me for something, I wouldn't even tell Run-Time about it."

"I'll keep you updated on everything. Is this going to be your new offices for the time being?"

"Until this Council case is resolved."

"Then enjoy your weapon and case, Mr. Cruz."

"One other question, Mr. Mick. The board members were talking, more like arguing, as if I wasn't there. Who are the 'others'? They seemed very concerned about them. Some of the board members seemed afraid of them."

"We have a Council of Corporations, Mr. Cruz. Other regions on the planet have theirs."

"How many others?"

"Besides Metropolis, five."

I sighed. "Six times the evil."

"That's one assessment. One that I don't disagree with."

Chapter Sixteen
Sidewalk Johnny Brigade

Now, I was understanding the argument of the CC Board. The Council of Corporations had a collective agreement with their global counterparts not to pursue the NeuroDancer object, but all of that had changed. Did I really set all this in motion with my secret project with Spiders?

Finally, they arrived—sidewalk johnnies. Phishy was a street hustler, but the real life of Metropolis streets were sidewalk johnnies, and occasional sallies. Homelessness had been eradicated long ago, like polio and cancer; housing was mandatory for all, even for those without a legacy. Sidewalk johnnies lived by day on the streets—hanging around, watching trouble, causing trouble, hustling, looking for a hustle, but doing little of anything meaningful. Sidewalk johnnies and sallies all had a "turf." For most, it was a street, street corner, or alleyway, and they never ventured very far beyond it. They congregated, watched, chatted it up, sat around, smoked, joked, disappeared to the bathrooms when needed, or disappeared to their sleep shack for a few hours—and repeat. They were harmless.

Phishy was in his element. He greeted all of them as they arrived at the warehouse, saying hello to friends, slapping a high or low five as he went along. All I heard was laughing, joking, and loud talking as they arrived in waves.

When I came out of the offices and walked to the growing crowd of johnnies, they all got quiet as they watched me. Most of them were wearing tan fedoras and their faces said it all. I had to get right up to them for them to realize it was me. But when they did, all I saw were smiles as they greeted me too—thirty of them, with more arriving.

Phishy wasn't a solo act. With his sidewalk johnny friends, I could extend my street intel network. That's when I formed my Sidewalk Johnny Brigade. I created it. Phishy managed it. Besides the intel, we could count on them for other jobs like this one.

That's when a few sidewalk sallies arrived and threw a wet blanket on the whole thing. The main one was Sidewalk Sallie herself. She wasn't smiling at all.

"What's wrong, Sallie?" I asked.

"I hate the new look," she said.

"What's wrong, Sallie?" I repeated.

"Word on the street is that you double-crossed the Council of Corporations when you were at their headquarters and stole something from them," she said. "There's a lot of money floating on the streets for info on you."

Phishy and the johnnies watched for my reaction.

Of course, I was cool as a cantaloupe. "When has the Council ever told the truth? More importantly, when has the Council ever put the word on the streets, our streets? They probably can't spell the word 'streets.'"

The johnnies laughed and all their attention shifted to the sallies.

"Cruz, this sounds like a dangerous gig you got us on," Sidewalk Sallie said. "We're not corporate soldiers, cyborg soldiers, or samurai soldiers. We're just johnnies."

I held up my hand with a fat wad of cash. All their eyes locked on it. I threw it at Phishy, who snatched it out of the air as if he had a bionic hand of steel. I'd seen it before, anytime I gave him physical cash. He had a look. It was like when I threw a piece of chicken to this feral cat as a kid. The cat pounced on that piece of meat as if it had never eaten before and had this expression, accompanied by a low, guttural growl. The piece of chicken was in a death-lock in its mouth, and if anything came near it, even its mother, it would scratch its eyes out. Phishy's face looked like that. Hustlers and johnnies preferred the physical cash to the digital kind.

"Phishy will manage the payouts," I said. "Simple jobs here. Sentry duty to keep a presence and eyes on our exits, offices, and alleyways. We're going to install external surveillance cameras everywhere, so I'll need eyes on all of it.

"Other job is to keep the street intel flowing on everything the Council is up to, and they're up to a lot. There will be a lot of noise out there. The Council will flood the street with garbage. We need the real bona fide intel, so you'll have to work your network.

"I'll be out working my case, but I'm bringing in a few heavies in here too who can handle a gun for protection. You got PJ over there in the corner who can shoot, too."

Everyone turned to look and wave at PJ ignoring us all as she worked her phones and typed who knows what on her keyboard. Johnnies called out "hellos" and she shooed at us with one hand. We all found it funny.

"Do you need backup out there, Mr. Cruz?" one johnnie asked.

"No, I'm going to have a driver with backup, so I'll be fine. I need you all to keep this place secure and processing the work. This is our temporary Liquid Cool offices, and I don't mean temporary turning to permanent. I mean temporary, as in wrap this up as quickly as possible to get back to normal."

"Tell them about the briefing, Cruz," Phishy said.

I smiled. "Yes, when we have the full team at the warehouse, we'll gather and I'll tell you all what it's about. So you'll know facts from lies."

"We'll be ready, Mr. Cruz," a johnnie said.

"I know you all guys and gals will. Cameras are on their way, and Phishy, let's get some food and beverages in here for people."

The johnnies nodded to that. I was going to pay them and feed them. Sidewalk johnnies weren't known for strong work ethics besides hanging around, smoking, and joking. But my Sidewalk Johnny Brigade was different. They were workers, and that's what I needed.

Chapter Seventeen

Quix

PJ was managing the "office" and Phishy was managing the sidewalk johnnies. I was ready to get to my detective work. Once again, I was in the same dark alleyway, but this time with a few chain-smoking johnnies around me.

The sleek hovervan descended. Quix immediately stepped out of the passenger side, as men jumped out of the rear doors of the vehicle.

Quix was another key person, along with Wize Gal, that I'd met through my posthumous mentor, Wilford G. Quix was an ex-Marine cyborg—short, bald, muscular, big leathery hands, an earring in one ear, part of his jaw and neck were metal, and he was wearing glowing yellow shades. He was a godsend because PJ was my muscle for when I was in the Liquid Cool offices, but I needed it in the field from time to time. Quix was that muscle.

"New hat," he said.

I didn't even answer him. I pointed to a lapel pin on his jacket. "Looks like another Portugal International Footfall fan. I'm meeting all of you in Metropolis in one day."

Suddenly, Quix's men began cheering "Portugal!" like crazy sports fans do.

"Thanks for that. We've alerted the entire Wharf City street punks that we are here and are fans of this year's World Cup winners," I said.

The men cheered again since they knew it annoyed me. All of them were big, tough, and likely ex-military, too.

Quix pointed to the five of them that exited the hovervan. "They're your armed security, on loan."

I nodded in approval. "This is our new base of operations until I get this case settled."

The men looked up at the warehouse.

"Who are you tangling against this time?" one of Quix's men asked. "Because if it's Wharf City street kids, you don't need us," he said.

I looked at Quix and said, "He's the comedian on your team, right?"

Quix smiled. His teeth looked enamel for the bottom half, but the upper was metal.

"I'm tangling with the Council."

"Council?" the man asked.

"The Council of Corporations," I said.

The men, including Quix, got quiet.

"Don't worry," I said. "I know what you're thinking. That we could never have enough men. But there's one very important piece of information. My client is the Council of Corporations."

The men were at ease.

"Which faction?" Quix asked me. "President or Treasurer."

"You know about the factions?" I asked, surprised, but only for a second.

"Ex-military for hire are all one big happy family, Cruz," Quix said.

"The president," I said. "She was shot, and I got her out of there."

"You were there?" one man asked, surprised.

"Yeah," I replied, "to meet the board. Then the mayhem started when the Treasurer came in. He shot her. I kicked him out the building."

"How did you have a weapon in the headquarters of the Council of Corporations?" another man asked me.

"Boardroom," I corrected. "I didn't. I took it off the Senior Executive Chief VP when I kicked him off the three-hundredth floor too, after I shot him. But I threw a chair at him first to distract him. Then shot Mr. Treasurer and kicked him out, too."

The men looked at each other, then back at me.

"What?" I asked.

Quix smiled and gave me a big bear hug, lifting me off the ground.

"What?" I asked, as the other men patted me on the back and shoulders.

"You'll never know how many people wanted those two bastards dead," Quix said.

"Rest in hell, Cast and Atila," another man said.

"Then when I close this case, you can tell me all about the late Mr. Numbers and vampire-man Atila."

The men laughed.

"Cruz, you're always doing the right things in the wrong places for the right results," Quix said.

I turned to see that I had an audience behind me—PJ, Phishy, and other johnnies and sallies.

"Yes, my boss is very handy at killing the bad guys," PJ said. "You didn't tell me you kicked people out the window," she said to me.

I shook my head. "Not out the window, but out the building. I need an entire hour to explain that building. You've never seen anything like it before. The whole thing was like a changeable hologram in a VR simulation."

"A holo-tower," PJ said.

"What?" I asked.

"That's what it's called. A holo-tower. That's what you were in."

"People can move through walls, ceilings, and floors?"

"Yes," PJ said. "You should make the Liquid Cool offices into a holo-office."

I looked at Quix. "Let's leave right now before my employee takes all my money."

Chapter Eighteen
The Courier

Couriers were one of the most eclectic groups in Metropolis. Few of them were full-time couriers, most did something else as their main vocation, but all of them were full-blown adrenaline junkies.

I thought it would be a simple matter to find the courier who'd delivered the Council's non-disclosure documents to my Concrete Mama tower. But I learned—against my will—that most couriers at this firm never came into the office and their current address was not always up to date. So I had to track him down—like a real detective.

The young super-slim courier guy's name was Glider. All I had to do was a simple Net search, and I learned Mr. Glider was actually a world-famous parkour master. I never understood how jumping from high places like a monkey without equipment was considered a sport. With Quix at the wheel and me in the passenger seat of his sleek super-charged hovervan, we patrolled a part of Old Metropolis frequented by these parkour maniacs. Smaller and more slender mega-towers characterized the district—no higher than one hundred stories, very close to each other, and narrow streets and sky lanes between buildings.

Neither of us had ever seen what happened next before our eyes in our lives. A lone person sailed above us, jumping from one skyscraper down to the roof of another as he was jerking his legs around as if he were dancing in midair. Keep in mind, our hovervehicle was twenty feet in the air and stopped at a traffic signal.

"That man is a lunatic," Quix said. He jerked the wheel hard-right when the signal changed to jump into another hoverlane and to the building.

Parkour was legal if they did it no higher than ten feet off the ground, which meant that all the kids did it far, far off the ground and even from megatowers hundreds of stories up. A recognized sport of running and jumping from one point to another with no equipment while doing some gymnastic or artistic maneuvers. I always said that the Olympics went downhill centuries ago when they allowed parkour and curling.

I found the real-life flying monkey, Mr. Glider, on the roof, laughing it up with his juvenile delinquent buddies with bottles of alcohol in their hands and music playing from a single boom-box.

"Cops!" one yelled, as he took a position to actually throw his beer bottle at me.

Glider put a reassuring hand on his buddy's shoulder. "I know who he is," he said.

As I got closer, there were about a dozen of them, clad in skintight black body suits under their hooded slickers and clingy combat boots. None of them were older than twenty-five but, other than Glider, all of them had mean, grungy faces.

"This is what you all do during the day?" I asked.

"We do it during the night too, old man," one said.

"How stupid. I'd have some respect for you if you all wore base-jumping parachutes, but if you want to commit suicide, take some pills or something."

"You don't understand the life, old man."

"I'm not an old man, and I do understand the life. I was an illegal hovercar racer in my youth. Ask me if we wore seat belts? Oh yeah, we did. Safety, pal. The goal is to do it for life, not do it once and be dead."

"Okay, okay, everyone," Glider said to us, holding up his hands. "It's too early in the day for long debates. You all can do that on your own time. Are you here for something, Mr. Cruz?"

"If you recognize me and you're expecting me, then you can answer your own question."

"She said to keep it on me at all times, in case you showed up." Glider reached from behind his waist, did some fiddling around, and put a data disk into my hand. "Thank you, Mr. Cruz. Item delivered, and you've made me six months of wages."

He turned to his buddies, laughing and sticking out his tongue.

"Booze, booze, booze!" they yelled in unison.

My cue to leave. "Bye gentlemen," I said, turning and getting the heck off that roof in case stupid was contagious.

"Sure you don't want to stick around, old man, to see us cheat death one day at a time for life?"

I never answered as I opened the rooftop access door and disappeared back down to the penthouse elevators. As the door closed, I saw red and blue flashing on the wall. The police had arrived. They had bigger and badder criminals to deal with, but they'd warn the kids off. By now, the youth were running for the same door to get away (the police wouldn't chase them), so I double-timed because I didn't want to see them again.

#

The data disk Glider gave me was biometrically coded to my fingerprints. I didn't even want to know how the Council got my fingerprints. As Quix drove, I plugged it into a disposal laptop he had straight from the box.

"We're going to the bank," I said as I read the only file on the disk.

"Safe deposit box."

"Yeah," I said. "Madame President has left me something. Hopefully, we won't be playing games too much longer."

"We have company behind us." Quix was staring at his rearview display on the dashboard. "Two of them. Two that we can see."

"I know this bank. I have an idea."

The Emporium Bank in Silicon Dunes. Another uber-wealthy part of Metropolis. I'd been to Silicon Dunes before but never the bank. Quix illegally dove out of the hovercar traffic and shot over the bank. We saw them. It wasn't two hovercars following us; it was more like forty. Literally, most of the traffic behind us gave chase.

Quix gunned the accelerator and zipped around the corner. That's when I opened the door. I dove—like a real-live monkey and no equipment—from the vehicle into the bottom opening of two parking levels right across from the Emporium. It was only twenty stories up, so I was technically doing something illegal, but not so illegal that I'd get a summons if the police saw me, only a fine. Metropolis was like every other city. They didn't want everyone in jail. They needed people to pay fines too, to keep the city's bank account fat and City Hall happy.

Quix was already long gone as I ducked around a corner and raced for the elevators, hearing hovercars in the air giving chase. But I knew not all of them would be dummies and some of them would expect me to do what I did, and even a few would guess I was headed to the bank.

As I ran, I ignored all the well-dressed people watching me in their trendy slicker gear and colored glasses. I saw one cop glaring at me, probably had just gotten off duty and was debating whether to get involved in whatever I was doing. But running down a parking level for the elevators wasn't illegal yet.

I dashed out of the elevator capsule on the ground floor, which was directly across from the giant main entrance to the bank, which could have been renamed the Crystal Cathedral. It looked like a giant church made of crystal. I bolted across the street packed with pedestrians, and finally passed through the auto-opening main doors and stopped.

Immediately, security guards appeared. Two big cyborgs at first, then two more. Rather than walk up to the tellers, I'd kill two birds with one stone. I strolled right up to the security guard quartet.

"Gentlemen, I need to get to safe deposit boxes."

"Downstairs, sir," one of them said.

"Thank you, sir."

I dashed off again. One had to keep in mind that law-abiding people didn't run in Metropolis. Running meant danger. You were chasing someone and were a criminal. You were running from someone and were a criminal or a victim. Attention was what I wanted. The security guards would watch me, but so would everyone else—tellers, managers, customers, dogs, everybody. That's what I wanted. Because if I was being chased, who was chasing me?

#

The main banking teller floor was bright and busy. Down one level to the safe deposit area was dimly light and quiet. The sole attendant waited in front of the elevator as I stepped out.

"Sir," he said. He was an enormous man with an over-muscular upper torso under his suit.

I handed him my business card. "Cruz," I said. "You should be expecting me."

He extended his right hand, and the palm of the cyborg was a scanner. "Right thumb, sir," he said.

I pressed my right thumb on his palm, and there was a quick blue scanning light.

"Mr. Cruz," he said with a smile. "Welcome to the Emporium Bank of Silicon Dunes. A package is waiting for you, courtesy of the Council of Corporations."

The man led me to one of the small private rooms to wait. When he returned, he set a large safe deposit container on the table.

"Take your time. I will be outside, Mr. Cruz," he said and left.

I opened the container and inside was a silver disk, about twelve inches in diameter, with an analog keypad. I grabbed it and struggled to lift it. The thing was heavy, as if it were made of lead. How was I going to get the thing out of the bank?

I popped my head out of the little room and there was the cyborg waiting. "Excuse me, sir. Do you have any kind of sturdy bag I can have to discretely take the item with me?"

"I have something even better, sir," he replied.

The bank gave me a mini-hover case. It was like any regular briefcase, but no matter how heavy the object that you placed in it, the case weighed the same—zero.

When I returned to the teller lobby, it was a complete madhouse. Bank security had increased from four to twenty, keeping a growing army of cyborg and samurai suit soldiers at the main entrance. I hurried the other way with my briefcase, but the corporate soldiers had already seen me. Customers were all staring at me, along with bank staff.

"Is there a back way out of here?" I asked one of the bank managers.

"No, sir, there isn't."

"How do I get out of here then?"

"I'd say the same way you came in—the front entrance."

"Let me ask the question another way, since my client is the Council of Corporations and I'm working on their behalf. How do I get out of here, then?"

The man's demeanor completely changed. "No need to worry, sir. The Emporium Bank of Silicon Dunes offers complimentary private security services to your vehicle or home. We even have our own corporate soldiers for extreme circumstances."

"Sir, I'm not a man of big emotions, but I love this bank!"

Chapter Nineteen
Gem A.I.

The Emporium Bank escorted me to my vehicle with an army of their internal corporate soldiers armed with long laser rifles. Once inside Quix's vehicle, we blasted off for the sky freeway. One hour of driving away from where we needed to go at maximum speed, taking any in pursuit with us. When we entered one of the few hover-tunnels in Metropolis, that's when we exited under the cover of darkness. Quix continued onward while I secretly hitched my way back in another hovercar waiting with one of Quix's men.

When we arrived at the warehouse in Wharf City, it was nearly the end of the day. Sidewalk johnnies were hanging out at the entrances, along with two of Quix's heavies. They greeted me and let me know that the "day shift" had already left, including PJ and Phishy.

"Ms. PJ said that all your messages are waiting for you on your desk," one of the johnnies said.

"Thanks," I said, not knowing that I had a desk.

When I strolled in, with my briefcase in hand, I could hear the team of johnnies at the other end of the warehouse, laughing and talking. The lighting was dim, but I could see that PJ's area had expanded. There were quite a few cubicles. I'd have to wait until tomorrow to find out what she was up to. Opposite that, they'd created a break area with tables for eating, a full refrigerator, an alcohol bar, and cooking machines. I had an incredible sense of satisfaction. Back on my home turf of Metropolis and my entire crew of "partners in crime" for the case. Crazy maniacs beware!

I walked to the center office blocks, since, according to PJ, I had an office. Knowing how she thought, it would be on the second level and closest to her area, so we could easily yell at each other. That was exactly which one it was—top level, outer corner office, which also was one of the largest. They fully furnished the office with a large desk, chairs, mini-fridge, small table, and a small waiting area. She even had a buzzer wired up on the side of the desk. On the top of the desk were hand messages in PJ's priority system: the "hot" pile, the "hold" pile, the "hell no" pile, and a miscellaneous one. They'd have to wait. I pressed my buzzer.

It didn't take long for one of Quix's men to come running from the door with a bunch of sidewalk johnnies. I stood at the balcony looking down.

"It's okay," I said. "Just testing my new gadgets. Keep an eye on the offices. I have an important message to review."

"You got it, Mr. Cruz."

I returned to my second-floor office and closed the door. Compared to the resources of the Council, we were so low-tech that I didn't know whether to be scared or ashamed. Ms. Gem entrusted with this gadget, and Council thugs wanted to get it from me, assuming they even knew what she'd given me. I needed answers. Madame President was my client, but the one thing my NeuroDancer case taught me was that sometimes it was your very client who you had to worry about shooting you.

I typed my memorized twenty digits into the disk's analog keypad. I stared at it and wondered if something was wrong. There was no doubt that I memorized Gem's number correctly. Something was happening. I heard a faint hum, then the bottom of the disk glowed blue.

"Please, plug the device into multiple power sources!" a female's voice whispered from the device. It was definitely Madame President's voice.

One plug point popped open on the device, then a second and a third.

"I can't believe all this," I said, frustrated. We were in a warehouse, not regular offices. Plugging things into a power source wasn't the easiest thing to do.

It took me almost forty minutes to find power cables that could reach the power outlets at the warehouse's outer walls to my second-floor office. We needed so many extension cables, and I even had to send people to the store to buy what we ultimately needed.

I'd sat down and began plugging in the cables into the silver disk. With each one I plugged in, the disk glowed more and the audible hum got louder. Then came the last cable and the glow and sound ceased. What happened?

"Mr. Cruz," a voice called out, startling me.

I turned, saw a figure, and instinctively fired my omega-gun. I'd fired point-blank into the chest of Madame President, who was standing in my makeshift office.

My mouth dropped open. Did I kill my client?

#

Ms. Gem stood in front of my desk, facing me. She was wearing the same outfit as that day in the CC board room. A crimson kimono-style dress with a fat pearl necklace. She was unmoved by getting shot because I could now see my laser blast had gone right through her and impacted my nice, previously pristine wall.

"Just great! Look at it. My wall is ruined, and I just got this office."

"You don't seem to be too upset at shooting me, though," Ms. Gem said.

"Because you're a hologram. You're not real. You could have warned me. Street detectives don't like people sneaking up on them from oblivion."

"Yes, I admit, Mr. Cruz, that was a bit of a low, uncalled-for practical joke. But it is my programming. You can blame my creator when you see her."

"You are the operative she spoke of."

"I am, Mr. Cruz. Shall we get started or do you need time to calm your nerves?"

I smiled. "You can make jokes."

"I can do a lot of things."

"Do you possess the ability to link into any outside systems?"

"That, Mr. Cruz, would be very unwise. I am a self-contained unit whose only purpose is to provide you with the information and intel to fulfill your mission."

"My mission?"

"Should you choose to accept it."

I laughed. The hologram smiled.

"Well, I guess it's not the worst arrangement I've ever had to deal with. If you annoy me, I can just turn you off."

#

Metropolitans didn't like robots, hated androids, but feared AI, which had only worsened after my AI Android Case. Ages ago, every megacorps on the planet wanted their own hologram-projected AI entity when it was the stuff of movies and the tech was rudimentary at best. Thanks to off-worlders, the tech was now a reality, but few wanted AI entities running around at businesses.

I'd only seen holograms at amusement parks, and they were pixelated babbling babies compared to the Gem AI. But with the Council of Corporations, with practically unlimited wealth and resources, anything was possible. After all, they had the most sophisticated holo-building on the planet. I looked up holo-buildings. If PJ knew about them, I should, too. Others had holo-buildings; the Council had a three-hundred-foot holo-tower.

The Gem AI was a projection, but with a tight projection point. I spent a few minutes stepping in front of the disk to find it and was satisfied when she disappeared. I put my hand in front of the projection point and there was a piece of Gem AI on my hand.

"Tell me, Mr. Cruz. You are a grown adult, are you not?"

"Ms. Gem, I've never seen a hologram like you before. What do you expect me to do?"

"How long will your playing go on?"

"I'm finished now." I returned to my seat in front of my desk.

Gem "sat" too. The program could adjust and mimic interacting with its surroundings.

"My mission?" I said. "Detectives don't do missions. They work cases."

"Mr. Cruz, you were working it without a client, or even a case. That's a mission. But it's the same mission the Council has been on too for these years. We would like to know how you were able to make the progress you did."

"We?"

"My creator and myself."

"Consider it a trade secret, Ms. Gem. If I tell you all my detective secrets, you won't be amazed by me anymore. We can't have that."

"As you wish, Mr. Cruz. The man you hired, Spiders, was much more than the average scraper."

"Did he send your trackers on a few wild goose chases?"

"Yes, he wasted a considerable amount of our time. Very illogical and unconventional in his approach, which is why we know you hired him."

"Ms. Gem, I didn't hire Spiders to find the object. I hired him to make you think he was searching for the object. I hired others to search for it."

"Mr. Tag and his people."

"Not Tag. I've used him more than once before, so I knew you and whoever else would know about him. People you wouldn't know, and I'm not about to tell a hologram either."

"Mr. Cruz, we are your client."

"No, Ms. Gem AI. Ms. Gem, Madame President, is my client. You're her operative."

"An irrelevant distinction in this situation."

"Do you know what happened to your creator? Is there any programming within you that's even curious?"

"No, Mr. Cruz. Machines, physical, digital or holographic, don't possess feelings. I simply pretend to. But to answer your question directly, no."

"Your creator may be dead."

"I assumed that might be a possibility when you activated me."

"I will tell you what happened."

"Mr. Cruz, I don't care."

"I know you don't. I'm telling you for the intel you can gather and can assimilate into your programming to adjust any instructions you give me for the mission."

"Very good, Mr. Cruz. Proceed."

"We were in the Council boardroom. Around fifty people."

"The executive committee. Other board members attend in the chamber auditorium."

"The board meetings are broadcasted?"

"Of course, Mr. Cruz. To an on-site auditorium, to members around Earth, to members off-world."

"Are you serious right now?"

"Yes, Mr. Cruz. I'm not programmed to lie to you. You are our operative. It's very important to us that this mission is completely successfully. Much depends on it."

"Ms. Gem, they might have killed your creator at that board meeting. There was a shootout. People killed. Mr. Atila tried to kill me. I killed him and I killed Mr. Cast. He's the one who shot your creator in the chest with a laser gun. I rescued her from the boardroom and left her alive, but she could have still died waiting for help. Now, you're telling me that board members everywhere were watching the whole thing on TV."

"Yes, Mr. Cruz. Besides the fifty-member executive committee, the board comprises five hundred board members and one thousand auxiliary members."

"Do you understand what I've just told you?"

"That the council will have some executive board vacancies to fill."

I jumped up from my seat, mad.

"A joke, Mr. Cruz. You are a very conflicted individual. You dislike the Council, don't trust the Council, but are upset that members have died."

"Not died, Gem. Killed by other members. Does this happen all the time in Council board meetings? Half the members starting shooting and killing the other."

"Of course not. Though it has happened in the past in extraordinary circumstances. But please, continue your debrief."

I sat back down.

"Maybe you should get something to drink."

"No, I can drink some coffee later. Now I lost my thought," I said.

"Start at the beginning, when my creator brought you into the boardroom."

"That's a whole other story by itself with your holo-building. Mr. Atila, that bastard, called it 'shifting.' You all spend money just to spend it."

"What else is it for?"

"Anyway, we did the pleasantries and introductions. She informed them she hired me to get the object for the Council. That's when things went off-track. The other board members were shocked, angry, and a lot of them were afraid. Afraid of who? The others?"

"You've answered your own question, Mr. Cruz."

"She told them they needed to get the object before anyone else, forget any of the agreements they had with the others, because it was already on the market."

"This is new information for me. We had weeks before, but likely we only have hours."

"Hours? What happened to days? Between weeks and hours is days. We don't even get that?"

"Proceed with the debrief, Mr. Cruz."

"Isn't this funny? I'm briefing the client and I'm the one who's supposed to be hired. It was when she told them that the object was on the market, that feelers had been broadcast."

"Then what, Mr. Cruz."

"She said something like: we either let the others get it, another party, or we get it first. Oh, then she said something strange that made me think you and your creator were using me. She said I've been looking for the object longer than them, and I found it. 'He just doesn't know it yet,' is what she said. That's when the Treasurer shot her and all the violence began."

"This all was yesterday."

"Yes."

"Have you slept?"

"No."

"Then you should do so now. You must start first thing in the morning. It may already be too late."

"It's not too late."

Gem AI smiled. "My creator was wrong when she said you don't know you've found the object."

"Yes, she was. I know exactly where it is and who has it."

"Your scrapers could find all that out."

"They did."

"May I ask how, Mr. Cruz?"

"The 'feelers,' my good miss hologram, came from me."

I didn't think holograms needed time to think, but for a few seconds, this one did.

"You didn't expect that, did you? I embedded my tipsters into every network of illegal fences on Earth and Up-Top. NeuroDancer was dead, but not whatever device she was using to do what she did, nor whoever was helping her, probably under her mind-control spell too. I was going to get that device first even if I had to turn criminal to do it. None of you crazy maniacs are going to get your clutches on that thing. It is true. There is tech that no human should possess. Someone invents a time machine or matter dematerializer and I'll do the same thing with those."

"My creator was wise to hire you when she did."

"Was she?"

"You can't resolve this case without us."

"I was going to go to the police."

"Don't do that. You know that the police have restrictions on their actions that we aren't burdened with."

"Yes, that's what I'm afraid of."

"We also have resources we will make available to you that not even your friend Chief Hub of the Metro Police Department would do."

"That's the only reason I'm doing this. Why do you want me to be your operative?"

"We trust you, Mr. Cruz. We trust you to do the right thing more than we trust ourselves."

Strangely, I believed her. Madame President said the same thing to the other board members before the shootout. I wondered if they feared that more than the others.

"What's my next move then, Boss?" I asked.

"My creator told you the MK Ultra story, I assume."

"She did."

"You know that NeuroDancer stole the object from us originally."

"But you stole it from someone else."

"Yes."

"What am I being hired to do? Find the object, or find its creator?"

"You've already found the object."

"Yes, but you know where to find its creator. Sounds like a conundrum."

"Life is about risk, Mr. Cruz, as you well know. We have to choose wisely. Time is not on our side. If we lose them, we lose them forever. We can't go after both at the same time, and going after one means we're likely not going to obtain the other."

"Then the course of action is simple. Go after the object first."

"Even though we have lost the optimum window of opportunity to get the object."

"The window is still there. It just has to be big enough for my little pinkie. I can make it bigger from there. The object first."

"We agree. If we fail, some hope of finding its creator remains, however remote."

"Exactly."

"Where is your first stop, Mr. Cruz?"

"A place called the Naughty Room."

"The mission has been accepted and we can begin, Mr. Cruz."

"But before I go. I want you to give me the entire Council files on an organization called Gyndromeda."

PART FOUR
The Naughty Room

Chapter Twenty
The Day Crew

I slept in my office with my client. Well, I was sprawled out on my couch and Ms. Gem AI sat in oblivion with the flick of the off switch. We didn't have a safe, so there was no way I was letting the holo-projector out of my sight. My virtual client had lots of information to share with me.

The "day crew" had arrived. I could tell by PJ's awful French ska music echoing through the warehouse. Washrooms were never the best in warehouses, unless you paid big bucks for them. The one on the second floor of the block offices was adequate, but I had always been a low-maintenance kind of guy. Still, I would have to find a place to take a proper shower.

From the balcony of my second-floor level, I could see that Quix was back. He and some new men had the giant sliding wall door open wide enough for them to back in a hovertruck. The back opened, and they rolled off a massive safe made of black metal.

I got the steps to the ground level as they reached me.

"Your super-safe as requested," he said.

I smiled. I loved working with professionals. I'd told one of his men I needed the safe last night, probably half-asleep, and here it was. "Thanks, Mr. Quix. Looks too heavy for the upper floor, so have your men situate it in the office below mine."

"What are you putting in the safe?"

"My client."

His eyebrow raised. Then he smiled. "The men said you were talking to someone last night. Let me guess. A holographic entity manifestation."

"Is that what it's called? I just call it the holo-client and leave it at that. These Council people have all kinds of tech no one has seen."

"Imagine all the tech they have you've never seen, like everyone else."

"I don't want to imagine."

"I'll have all the cameras put in and finished today."

I nodded approvingly and handed him a money card. "I had the holo-client cut some more money loose for your expenses."

Quix looked at the two sets of numbers on the card and smiled. "I can see we're going to have a very long and productive working relationship, Mr. Cruz. I like clients that pay without me having to ask or beat up."

We laughed.

Quix and his men moved the safe into an office as I walked to the break area where Phishy was being Phishy. The center of attention, chatting it up with the sidewalk johnnies.

"Hey Phishy."

He turned, and a big smile came over his face. "Cruz!"

"No dancing, Phishy. We have work to do."

"What do you need?"

"Where's the sallies?"

"I don't know."

"I need them."

"I'll get on the phones."

"Also, when Quix has all the surveillance cameras up and the display banks up, you'll run the show there. Have our sidewalk johnny brigade eyes glued to the screens. I what to know if anything approaches us from land, air, or sea."

"Got it, Cruz."

He ran back to the johnnies, but turned right back around.

"Hey Cruz, when are you doing the briefing?"

"Before I leave this morning."

He smiled and then spun back around again.

I was walking to PJ's domain when I noticed that Phishy had spun back around again and was running to me.

"Yes, Phishy. What now?"

"I got some new merchandise for you."

"Merchandise? What does that mean? I got my omega-gun. That's all I need."

"What about—"

"Yes, I have my pop-gun too."

"Okay, good. I got some upgrade for your vehicle," he said with a wicked smile.

"The Pony? I'm not messing with my vehicle, Phishy."

"When you see this merchandise, you'll be messin' that Pony all over the place."

"I have no idea what that means, but okay, Phishy, I'm intrigued. But that will have to wait because the Pony will remain in storage. Not having my classic Ford Pony blown up by the Council of Corporations or anyone else on this case."

"Is it that dangerous?"

"Not anymore," I said. "I got my 'crime crew.'"

Phishy laughed. "Yes, you do. You liked my assist on your UFO Case."

"Yes, Phishy. Only you'd be friends with the world's extraterrestrial UFO spotters."

"They came through, didn't they?"

"They did, and you did too. Sidewalk sallies, Phishy."

"Oh, yeah." He spun around and ran to the break area.

You had to keep Phishy focused to get things done, or his scatterbrain would have him all over the place, not doing what you wanted.

I stopped. Now, I spun around for the break area. I had to have at least one cup of my silk coffee.

Chapter Twenty-One
PJ

When I reached PJ's area, I noticed her metal barrier encircling her desk with three big screens. Her phones, mini-refrigerator, and coffeemaker were hidden from view.

"PJ, who are all these people?"

The cubicles I'd seen last night now had college kids working at them on computers.

"They're part of the PJ Liquid Cool internship program. We need workers and you're too cheap to hire temps. So we have interns."

"PJ, why do we need interns?"

"You have cases piling up, so they can do pre-work until you can do the real work."

"I could continue this conversation, but I'm scared that I'll find myself in a verbal maze with no escape. I need you to do something for me while I'm out."

"Which is?"

"Call Dot."

"Why am I calling your wife? Shouldn't you be doing that?"

"I could, but she wouldn't be happy with me if she hears it from me."

"Hears what?"

"NeuroDancer, the conclusion."

"Yeah, she might want to kick you. So you want me to be the bad guy?"

"So I can be the good guy later."

"Okay. How much are you going to pay me?"

"I'm paying you now. And how much are all these interns going to cost me? They're not working for free."

"No, they're not. Liquid Cool is a high-class establishment. It has a street reputation to maintain. Okay, I'll call China Doll."

"And keep her away from here."

"I will."

"And don't tell anybody else. Not the kids. Not the co-workers."

"Secret. Like a secret agent."

"Yes."

"Has she seen you yet?"

"She will see me when I'm ready."

"In your new suit."

"Yes."

"That you will never wear again after this case."

"You are all giving me a complex and a headache. This is a fine suit and I don't know why none of you like it."

"Are you getting senile, too? We had this conversation before. You are upsetting the Liquid Cool brand. Brand is key to a business. Key!"

"Call Dot, PJ. I don't want her worrying."

"But the Council will trace the call."

"That's why we have the quick-phones."

"I don't have one."

"Phishy has them. He can give all that you need. But you only need one to call Dot, so only take one."

"Then destroy it after the call."

"Don't destroy it. We can swap out the components later. Just don't use it again. Create a 'don't use ever again' drawer. Put it in there—after you call her."

"What's the others been using?"

"I don't know. Ask them. They've all done this before."

"But I haven't."

"Didn't you all use quick-phones in your *Les Enfantes Terribles* punk-posh gang days in Neo-Paris?"

"No. We used payphones. We were a high-class punk-posh gang. Not low-lives. I have no previous experience with quick-phones."

If you can believe it, the meaningless conversation literally went on for another twenty minutes. All I wanted was to have her call my wife. Should have been a two-minute conversation max.

Then the trio arrived.

Chapter Twenty-Two
Sidewalk Sally Jane

The sidewalk sallies had arrived. Not the ones Phishy called, but three specific ones that I hadn't seen in years.

The late NeuroDancer had sent one of the deadlier killer robots right to my Liquid Cool offices. We defeated it—luckily. Then I went after her, with two sidewalk sally shooters, Sidewalk Sally Jane and Teal, to her pleasure penthouse hideout in Silicon Dunes. We'd thought we'd be surprising her, but she was waiting for us. But at the back of my mind, I knew she'd be waiting. Our dangerous game of counterpoint came to an end. Four people on the ground: my two sallies shot but alive, I was unconscious, and my arch villainess was dead.

Now my sidewalk sally shooters were back.

"Sidewalk Sally Jane," I greeted.

"You remember," she said.

Sidewalk Sally Jane was tall, buff, and brawny, the perfect female muscle.

"Teal and Indigo, right?" I said to the two others.

"Yes, Teal."

"Hello, Mr. Cruz," Indigo said.

I smiled. "My muscle and two shooters are back!"

They all chuckled.

"We knew we'd see you again, Mr. Cruz," Jane said.

"Where have you all been?" I asked.

"Traveling, family, and stuff. But when you're born here, you can't stay away from the city for too long," Jane replied.

"Metropolis does that to all of us."

"Yes, I always got a kick reading about one of your cases in the news. Good thing I'm afraid of flying. I definitely would be scared off after reading that UFO case of yours in the Middle East."

"You fly every day, Jane."

"Riding in hovercars doesn't count. Planes are a whole other thing. Never been and never will."

"Jane, you've been off-world," Teal said, slapping her shoulder.

"That doesn't count either. Rocket ships just go up. I won that in the lottery."

"You used your lottery winnings for a rocket trip?" Indigo asked.

"Why not? Not like I'd ever save for a trip." Jane turned her attention back to me. "Why'd you go so far away? Plenty of work for you right here in the city."

"You don't need to tell me. I'm staying put for a long time. How did you know you'd be seeing me again?"

"Whatcha think? The bad guy, or bad girl, was dead, but not how she did it. I knew you'd never let it go."

"I don't like loose ends," I said emphatically.

"He's psycho," PJ said from her desk. "Ask that guy who scratched his car years ago. He never lets go."

"I don't need that from you, PJ."

"I'm complimenting you, Cruz. You've efficiently channeled your psycho energy in a positive manner," PJ said.

"We knew you wouldn't let it go. We made Judy promise to call us if the time ever came."

"Did you now?" I said as I threw a glance at PJ. She grinned back at me from behind her desk fortress. "So I wasn't the only one playing the long game on this one."

"Glad you didn't wait too long to wrap this up," Sally added. "When do we get started?"

"Right now. Teal and Indigo, get some weapons. We have a fine assortment. What about you, Jane?"

"Prefer my hands, but everyone needs a little protection out there on the streets. I'll see if you have something small but effective."

"Good. We'll have one of the guys show you to our armory. I'll get our ride."

Chapter Twenty-Three
Charade and Burlesque

Quix was the driver again, with me in the passenger seat. Our three sidewalk sallies were in the middle seat behind us, now sporting dark fedoras courtesy of Phishy. A trio of Quix's ex-mercs sat in the back seats. The vehicle was new. I'd noticed that Quix had a different hovervan for each day. But he would not get any complaints from me with the Council out there. We were making good time on the freeway to a place called the Naughty Room.

"What's this Naughty Room we're going to?" Jane asked. "How can we be effective bodyguards if we don't have all the details?"

"Your bodyguard services will be different here," I said.

"What does that mean?" Jane asked me.

"You'll see," I replied. "Probably a lot more than you want to."

"What does that mean?" Teal and Indigo asked.

I'd been to quite a few shadow markets in my detective days, and before in my illegal hovercar racing days. The Shadow Market was the shopping center for the criminal class. You bought your illegal goods and took them with you at the same time. There wasn't a main Shadow Market, but "outlets" existed all throughout Metropolis, and they were constantly moving, not always successfully, to avoid the police or other criminal gangs.

Then I learned that the shadow markets had competitors too. One of them was called the Naughty Room. It was both elusive, exclusive, and unique.

"Oh snaps!" I yelled as I grabbed the steering wheel from Quix.

He slammed the brakes, and the women in back jerked forward. A few hovercars behind us could have slammed into us, but they slowed to a stop.

"What's wrong with you?" Jane yelled.

I saw the answer to the question for myself, and so did the women, who began laughing at the sights on the ground below.

"Quix, are you a thirteen-year-old?" Jane asked, laughing.

"No, I'm a man," Quix said, laughing.

We'd found the Naughty Room—a shadow market where clothes were optional, or, as I called it, the open shopping center for nudist criminals. They were outdoors, all activities happening under plastic canopies to keep out the rain, but plenty of heat lamps. Heat for all the naked nudist criminals everywhere. Lots of skin and bionic parts. Quix had temporarily lost his sanity because of a group of extremely buxom naked women, except for their long, neon wigs and glowing glasses.

I came prepared and reached into my jacket for my special glasses. Before I could put them on, Jane snatched them from me.

"What are these, Cruz?" She put them on, looked down, and burst out laughing.

"What?" Teal grabbed them and put them on. She also became a laughing mess.

"Cruz, you are so predictable," Jane said.

"Let me see." Indigo put them on and looked. She laughed even louder. "Where did you get these?"

Quix reached back with his hand. Indigo gave them to him. He put them on, looked, and ripped them off. "I don't want these."

"Give me my glasses!" I said and snatched them from him.

"Cruz, you are such a square," Jane said.

"I'm an isosceles triangle," I said and put my glasses on. "Quix, can you manage to take us down without crashing?"

"Sure you don't need Cruz's G-rated glasses, Mr. Quix?" Jane asked. "G-glasses for G-Man."

Now all of them burst out laughing.

"Yes, you can all laugh, but when you're distracted and dodging plastic boobs and limp penises, I'll be the one focused and ready for action. I am a recovering germophobe, you know."

My friends were laughing so hard that Quix almost crashed our hovervan again.

#

My special glasses actually came from a toy store. Dot and I had gotten Cruz Jr. a replacement toy for the one he broke doing his ninja assassin fighting routines. But I'd seen the glasses then and something told me they'd come in handy one day. They were augmented-reality glasses and you could program them to do anything. Distort everyone around you to make them fatter or slimmer, give them cat or dog heads (very popular), make people appear as walking glowing skeletons. There was no limit to what you could do. Well, I made mine superimpose clothes on every naked person I saw.

We strolled into the Naughty Room, which was actually the Outdoor Illegal Contraband Market complete with cigarette butts on the ground everywhere and the water reflected every color of the rainbow, meaning nasty. At least the nudist criminals wore shoes and socks.

"Cruz, I don't like this," Jane said. "We're not blending into the crowd."

"We stick out like a flaming neon thumb in the darkness. I know," I said.

By now, my mind had completely adjusted to the augmented reality of my glasses. I only remembered that everyone was naked around me when my three sidewalk sally bodyguards began giggling, or did a double-take, or shielded their eyes with disgusted expressions.

"Who are you?" a large man said as he blocked our way.

"Get out of my way," I said.

"Why aren't you dressed for the market?"

"Oh, that's clever. I wear clothes when I step outside, you barbarian. Get out of my way, so I can shop."

"I say you and your friends are cops. You smell like cops."

"We're not cops, so get out of our way."

"I'll have to scan you to make sure you're not carrying any weapons."

I flashed my omega-gun at him and the ladies flashed theirs.

"Yes, naked boy, we're armed, which is more than I can say for you."

He grinned, which meant he had a surprise for us. I just shot him in the foot and he went down, butt to pavement. We all heard a metal clang hit the ground. Invisible guns?

We were all surrounded by a lot of people pointing their hands at us. Also, I could see the merchants in the market gathering their goods and folding up their tables.

"What are you going to do?" Jane yelled at them. "Shoot us with an imaginary laser beam?"

I held up my hand. "Excuse my friend. She doesn't know about the Room and the strict security you have to protect customers. We have a rolling appointment with a Mr. Free."

One man lowered his hand. "Why didn't you say that?"

"Sorry, I didn't like the fact that we were being blocked and no one else."

"Why might that be, genius?" he asked.

I grinned. "We're wearing clothes. Yes. Sorry."

"Get these geniuses to Free so they can get out of here. I don't like the look of them."

Another man gestured for us to follow. Just as we turned, the other man said, "Hey sister."

We turned, and the man shot a laser beam from his finger and knocked Sidewalk Sally Jane's hat right off her head.

"Yes, I can shoot laser from my fingers," he said with a twisted smirk.

She grabbed her hat from the ground angrily.

We followed our escort into the market, with everyone watching us. Even I realized that coming here was a bad idea, but I had to play it out. I thought that until I saw a large blue tent. That's where we were being led to and once we reached it, several women stepped out—fully clothed.

"You," I said.

It was the same woman I'd seen in the alleyway that day when I first arrived at the Liquid Cool offices in my new black suit and hat. She was dressed in neon everything—hair and clothes—then changed into a gray slicker. Moments later, she was back to neon everything.

"Hello, Mr. Cruz. We've been expecting you."

"Have you?"

"I'm Ms. Charade."

"Where's Mr. Free?"

"I'm Mr. Free," she replied as a larger female stepped out too, dressed in dark clothes with a wicked grin. The same one I'd seen in the alleyway with the neon woman.

The women moved close to us to keep us from drawing our weapons on them.

"Obviously, an alias to lure you here," she said. "This is Ms. Burlesque."

"Yes, I've seen you before, too. I didn't have time to return the middle finger," I said.

"You made all this so simple for us, Mr. Cruz? We waited such a long time to meet you. I've waited. Mr. Cruz, NeuroDancer was a member of our organization. We take the killing of our members seriously. You killed her. We're going to kill you, finally, at long last. No. We'll do so as NeuroDancer would have done. We'll make you kill your friends, then yourself."

"You didn't really bring the device here?" I asked.

My sullen poker face never wavered, but the buoyant, self-satisfied air of triumph vanished from their faces. They wondered for a moment, who had ambushed who?

Ms. Burlesque yelled out something. The blue tent collapsed, and we found ourselves surrounded by a virtual army of face-tattooed women in blue, pointing laser guns at us.

PART FIVE
Milky May and Gyndromeda

Chapter Twenty-Four
Peanut Gallery

Before the sidewalk sally trio and I could leave our warehouse HQ for the Naughty Room, or anywhere else in Quix's latest hovervan loaner, I had to give my briefing. The Sidewalk Johnny Brigade probably never uttered the word "briefing" before in their lives, but thanks to crazy Phishy, all of them were eagerly waiting as if I was going to do a Phishy chicken-dance and laser gun-juggling act performance for them.

"Do you have visual aids?" PJ asked me from my desk.

"Aids? Why do I need visual aids? I'm just talking."

"People retain more information when they receive information visually and verbally rather than just verbally."

"Is that so, PJ? These are sidewalk johnnies, PJ. They're all about the words so they'll handle the lack of fancy visuals just fine. Like they do every day on the hustle."

The Sidewalk Johnny Brigade, including several sallies, Quix and his men, PJ and all those interns—I still didn't know what she had them doing—were all gathered around. I'd found my spot between PJ's domain and the office blocks. Phishy was like my emcee enforcer because he got all the johnnies to quiet down from their joking and horseplay.

"Cruz is giving the briefing," he scolded them.

Phishy seemed more serious about it than me.

"What's the case? Why are we in Wharf City in this warehouse? And why are we going to be here until it's resolved?"

Phishy's hand went up.

"Phishy, no questions."

"But you asked questions."

The crowd was serious, and now it was giggling.

"No questions, Phishy, because I'm going to answer them in my briefing, which is now."

"Oh, I get it." His hand went down.

"We're all here and will be here for the duration, because this case is dangerous. Normally, I'd never disclose my client's identity, but this is one time where an exception has to be made. We're up against the Council of Corporations."

I saw the nervousness in the faces of the johnnies.

"But my client is... the Council of Corporations."

Their nervousness was gone, but that wouldn't last long.

"I know what you're going to say. Cruz, it's still dangerous. But, as Mr. Quix can already attest to, having the Council as a client means everybody gets paid."

My Sidewalk Johnny Brigade applauded.

"What's the case? A corporate fugitive locate. Someone stole a piece of proprietary information from the Council and they feel I'm uniquely qualified to find this 'rabbit' for them. Find the person, get the information back, maintain their trade secrets, get a fat bonus to be split among the Brigade and associates."

More clapping, but this time PJ was leading the chorus.

"There it is, team. While you hold down the fort, our fugitive retrieval team of me, Sidewalk Sally Jane, Teal, and Indigo, with Mr. Quix at the wheel, we'll be on our way," I said.

My team and I would be off for the sky freeway to the Naughty Room.

Chapter Twenty-Five
Gem AI

The night before I may have gone to bed to sleep, sprawled out on the couch of my upper block office, with my "client" turned off, but there was no way I was getting any sleep. The paranoia of either the Council of Corporations enemy faction forces or any of a dozen other parties storming our Wharf City warehouse or even blowing it up from the air was like a giant hippopotamus sitting on my chest with its big butt, slowly crushing me to a pulp. I was getting no sleep until I spoke with my client again and got all the facts I needed now, not in the morning.

I returned to my seat behind my desk after I activated the projector. Gem simply appeared in the seat in front of it in the same crimson kimono-style dress, same fat pearl necklace, same hairstyle, same composed demeanor, but with a slight smirk.

"My chronometer indicates I wasn't off long. Insomnia, Mr. Cruz?"

"Council files on this organization called Gyndromeda," I said.

"I have to insist. How did you become aware of this organization?"

"Some time after the NeuroDancer case, an inquiry was made about hiring a hit man to go after me. Imagine that. Someone wanting to hire a hit man to remove Metropolis of my wonderful presence."

"You put out feelers to find out who they were." Gem AI had answered her own question.

"With all the crazy maniacs out there and all the ones I sent to prison or the morgue, of course. Wouldn't the Council do the same?"

"I take your point, Mr. Cruz. We'd do much more than that. For someone in an auxiliary law enforcement profession, you are very adept at maneuvering through criminal circles. And please don't use your tired line that you were an illegal hovercar racer."

"How would you know it's a tired line?"

"Illegal hovercar racers don't know how to put traces out there on the street, the nether-net, and elsewhere to gather intel with no trace back to you or to do so without other parties knowing about it, even the Council. Must be all those criminal case files you like to read before bed. You could be a very good criminal, Mr. Cruz, merely say the word."

"I have a supreme power that prevents me from crossing over to the dark side, ever."

"Religion, Mr. Cruz? An ironclad code of conduct among the local street detective society?"

"Mrs. Cruz, Cruz Jr. and Kat beating me up."

Were holograms supposed to laugh? This one did. "Please continue, Mr. Cruz."

"The inquiry was made by someone who claimed to be with an organization called Gyndromeda. I never heard of it, but that meant nothing."

"So many secret megacorps out there, Mr. Cruz, on Earth and off-world."

"Yes, my Blade Gunner and Digital Samurai cases showed me that. Anyway, I began looking into this organization."

"Gyndromeda is a long-time international organization of female espionage agents."

"Spies."

"They work for megacorps, both legitimate and the more sinister ones out there in the shadows. They remain well connected and had a reputation for efficiency and trustworthiness."

I smiled. "They stole it first, and the Council stole it from them."

"And NeuroDancer stole it from us."

"I don't understand how you'd let her get away with—"

"She used it on us."

"Oh."

"Yes, Mr. Cruz. 'Oh.'"

"You couldn't 'deal' with her because she mind-controlled you to prevent it. What did Gyndromeda do?"

"You mean what did we do to them? We destroyed their reputation. No megacorp would ever trust them again with any business when we let it be known they stole an invention for themselves we hired them to retrieve. All true, though we left out what the invention was. They tried to do damage control, but the Council of Corporations have the financially backed lungs to yell much louder than everyone else. They couldn't sue us, nor the reverse, so it's been a constant battle behind the scenes. But we have many such relationships."

"I'm sure. But how did you know about them? They made one slip-up with me. Using their real organization name rather than a fake one."

"Their slip-up came when you sent the late Ms. NeuroDancer involuntarily into the next plane of existence."

"Yes, it's called death. So they contacted you?"

"They didn't believe that you killed her alone. They were convinced we had a hand in it, too, and wanted us to know, directly, that we'd be included in their revenge."

"Revenge? So you've known about these people all this time?"

"We took steps, Mr. Cruz."

"Steps?"

"Keeping you alive, but I won't go into all the details."

"The Council protecting a small-time street detective from international spies. Should I feel special?"

"You should, Mr. Cruz."

"Do you know the membership of this Gyndromeda, its agents?"

"We know names, not faces. They're spies, Mr. Cruz. They change their appearance as easily as you change a hat."

"Names will do, for now."

"The Naughty Room. Will you go there tomorrow?"

"First thing."

"Gyndromeda will be there?"

"Yes, they will. I'm sure of it."

"Do you always play these kinds of games in your profession? Telling your enemies who want to kill you where to find you."

"You said it yourself: 'Life is about risk.' People who want revenge can be manipulated to do the most foolish things."

"You already been in contact with them."

"For a long time, Ms. Gem. Tomorrow the game ends."

"Are you telling me you'll have the object tomorrow, Mr. Cruz?"

"I trust you, Ms. Gem AI, but only to a point. Let's see what happens and speak again."

"Do you still plan to destroy it? There are those in the Council and off-world who'd give you anything in the world you desire."

I smiled. "The second I get my hands on the thing, not one piece, speck, or molecule will remain of it."

"Until another one is made."

"We'll deal with that after tomorrow."

"Even if we succeed, Mr. Cruz, another will inevitably reinvent the tech. Years, decades, centuries, millennia in the future."

"Good. Then that future Cruz of Liquid Cool and Gem AI of that time will do what has to be done."

Chapter Twenty-Six
Skanky Bandit

"We'll do so as NeuroDancer would have done. We'll make you kill your friends, then yourself," Charade had said.

I had my poker face on, but did she see me smiling inside? After all these years of planning and waiting, putting the pieces together, I felt like a kid before Christmas for the one and only year I believed in the worldwide, age-old lie about some fat guy from the North Pole named Santa flying around in an invisible spaceship delivering toys to good children. Well, the lie was good while it lasted and that year I waited in bed, unable to sleep, thinking about all the presents in boxes bigger than me with toys none of the other kids would have.

I never was at ease with the NeuroDancer case. The villain was dead, but not her abilities. Wilford G. told me that not all cases are wrapped up in a nice, neat red bow at the end. Ironic coming from him, since he had his own version of my NeuroDancer case he held on to for fifty years and came back from the dead to close. I was prepared to go as long as Wilford G. did, even longer if I had to, but I was going to get the late villainess's bag of tricks and throw them into a fiery bottomless pit. It wasn't lost on me that Madame President and her AI holo-double both kept calling it an "object" or "device." Logical, of course, but for all I knew it was a secret potion or magic dust. Her mind-control powers could be anything; I kept an open mind. However, it was likely a piece of tech.

Charade's reaction to my question: "You didn't really bring the device here?" told me everything I needed. NeuroDancer's device was within my grasp. I'd have it without waiting fifty years. Assuming I wasn't about to be gunned down by a female spy crew dressed in blue.

Two words: PJ. RPG.

This time, the mayhem was all part of the plan. PJ loaded it into the hovervan for us, in case we came across Council bad guys or anyone else. I wanted to be prepared for anything the moment we flew out of the warehouse.

I don't think the Gyndromeda spy-gals knew what hit them. Quix struck with textbook military precision. The missile from his (highly illegal) RPG crashed behind them and the explosion sent them all flying. Immediately, his three men in the back of his long hovervan sprayed laserfire from their weapons out open hovercar windows.

My sidewalk sally bodyguards were on the ground too, but they were fine. I gave Jane a thumbs-up and turned, leapt to my feet, and was gone.

"Where are you going?" Charade yelled from the ground with an almost hysterical, psychotic rage, almost about to cry.

She knew what she had done. She'd brought the device right to me.

#

I felt I was about to become one of those adults, always berating young people for doing something wrong, and then the same adults are caught doing the same thing by the kids. I'd chastised the extreme parkour flying monkey guys, and there I was shimmying up the pole of the Naughty Room's plastic commercial canopies. Then I threw myself onto the top of it and ran.

Charade and the others below probably were confused why I was running back the other way. Quix and his men had stopped their onslaught from their air-parked hovervehicle with perplexed faces. They were wondering where I was going. I was getting higher!

I jumped, scaled up the side of the adjacent building, onto the fire escape ladders, upwards, onwards, and onto the roof. Running on any roof, no matter how solid you thought it was, was never wise. People fell through solid roofs every day. I was wearing aqua-soled boots, but that didn't mean I couldn't slip, fall, and slide right off the roof. A fall off a five-story building could be just as deadly as one-hundred stories. More for the body bag, but you'd still be dead.

Only in Metropolis would the following happen: I'd heard the footsteps, turned and there they were. A whole punch of smiling and laughing kids. From their clothes, I knew what they were—parkour jumpers. I'd traded the extreme ones for the normal ones.

I jumped from one roof to another, higher roof and landed right in a puddle of water. The two kids had landed too, one on either side of me. They were splashed with water, but couldn't care less.

"The old man has some skills," one said. More derogatory labels from the youth of our age. I was not old.

A laser shot struck. The only reason it missed was that we all swerved at the last minute to go around an obvious hole in the roof, which meant the entire area around it was unstable.

"We're being shot at!"

When I stopped, turned and fired back, it was the person I'd expected to see—Charade. But I wasn't firing alone. The two parkour kids had joined me in our running gun battle and all three of us shot so many rounds, Charade literally had to dive off the roof to keep from getting hit.

"Let's go," I said.

Just like that, I'd enlisted two juvenile shooters. We jumped. Five stories to two stories. This one hurt. But I was smart enough to let myself roll (in my nice new black suit) then back on my feet. One kid did a forward somersault for his roll; the other did some kind of side cartwheel. But now, I had to run faster to keep up with them.

We heard laser shots again. This time to our left, from the ground. I changed running places with one kid from center to the outer side to peek over. Charade, Burlesque, and every one of the female spy crew in blue following. They saw me and fired in unison, almost hitting me before I dashed to the center of the roof.

"This is a tough one ahead, old man!" one yelled.

They laughed, glancing back and increasing their speed. I simply waved with a grin. Through and down. Through the open rooftop door and down the stairs.

I shot across the street just as the last female spy gal in blue passed the building, still chasing after my two former parkour shooters. She never saw me as I passed through the crowds. But someone did. I heard a yell.

The alleyway I took was long and winding, but I knew if I didn't get to the end quickly, I'd be a fish in a shooting gallery with nowhere to go. It didn't matter if I shot back. If they all shot at me, they'd hit me.

As I made it to the end, the barrage of laser fire showered the curving walls like firecrackers exploding on a Chinese New Year's night. I'd barely made it, but my destination was in sight. A single parking tower ringed in orange neon. But I knew Charade's vehicle and where it was too.

#

Sometimes good guys and bad guys think they're so clever in their battle against each other that they forget someone else might spoil the party.

I saw Charade's orange sports hovercar gliding out of the ground parking bay as I was running to it. The scrawny, punky-haired male at its wheel wasn't Charade. His eyes locked on mine and I could feel my anger about to go off. Was this a car thief? Was my grand plan, my operation, years in the making, being foiled by some skanky hovercar thief? No!

He gunned the accelerator and shot up to the sky as I fired my omega-gun with everything I had. Bullets, lasers. I was going to blast the engine off that hovercar!

I was so focused that when other laserfire began hitting the vehicle, still rising, I didn't even jump. Charade and company were next to me, firing all their weapons, too.

The front of the sportster crashed to the ground. I didn't even move to get out of the way. The sound it made on impact was like an explosion itself. But it wasn't the engine. In the air, the orange hovercar flew away, become nothing more than a dot in the hovertraffic until it was gone from sight.

"In that model, the engine is in the rear of the car," she said to me.

I shot an incredulous look and lost it.

"I know that! Now! Why didn't you get a normal hovercar with the engine in the front and the trunk in the back, like every other normal person in Metropolis?"

I was so angry at losing the NeuroDancer device; I didn't need to shoot them with my omega-gun. My glare was as hot as any laser. They wisely backed away from me.

That's when Ms. Burlesque snuck up on me and punched me in the head. It was the fault of my augmented reality glasses. The glasses not only put clothes on all the naked Naughty Room sellers and buyers, they "modified" anything out of the ordinary on clothed people. Here, I didn't know that Ms. Burlesque wore some strange silver conic bra outfit on top of her blue outfit. Had I seen that, I'd never have taken my eyes off her. Unfortunately, I didn't see the truth until they knocked my AR glasses off my face as I fell to the ground.

Chapter Twenty-Seven
Milky May and The Mother Ship

Metropolis had lots of hoverhotels. Home to the city's super-wealthy eccentrics, the leisure class set of old money. The mobile, floating residences of different sizes and configurations, hovering high in the sky, slowly circled the supercity in an endless loop. Back in the day when they were "new," the plan was for them to circle the globe. But ever-erupting wars in one region or another put an end to that grand plan.

I'd been in a few in my time on cases. As I sat in a plush chair fashioned to look like a giant open oyster, I stared out a multi-story bay window at a height probably equivalent to a five-hundred-story megatower. I was alone in the giant white living room. At least, I wasn't dead.

I could sense a presence and swiveled around in my chair. They'd entered through the single door in the room quietly enough. On one side was Charade, who'd been crying, her mascara still streaked down her face. On the other was Burlesque, with her silly brassiere outside her clothes look. Was her conic bra really guns, perhaps? There was no end to the variety of crazy maniacs I had to deal with in my detective life.

But all I cared about was the head woman who came straight down the center of them to me. She was the leader. Her elegant bearing, exuding self-confidence, and steely expression told me that. Dressed in a stylish one-piece plastic-like white dress, wearing black silky gloves and her wide hat looked like a shot of outer space filled with tiny bright stars. Her bleached white hair, in a tight ponytail (all these ponytails), went down her back. She walked around with me swiveling in my chair so that I always faced her. Her back was now to the bay window. Suddenly a dainty, plainly dressed fourth woman appeared. She was a servant with a crystal chair and set it down, then disappeared wherever she came from. I'd have to keep wondering because I wasn't about to take my gaze off the head woman. I knew she wasn't just the leader. She was dangerous. Like a lioness casually strolling around her prey, wondering whether to eat it or let it go.

She sat with complete calm. I was still angry.

"I'll talk first," she said. "I am Milky May."

"Of Gyndromeda."

She smiled. "I won't have to say as much, then."

"And this is the magnificent Mother Ship."

"There will be no rescue, Mr. Cruz. We found the trackers on your person, and the one in your high-priced gun," she said.

"I've been told quite a bit about your female super-spy ring."

From a place overflowing with nudists to one with women wearing the most expensive and elegant clothes, even Burlesque's ridiculous outfit had some modicum of class. But ironically, in this room, I was the one who was naked. I knew they were armed. My omega-gun was nowhere to be seen.

"What have you been told?"

"A secret organization of female spies catering to the most powerful and sinister megacorps on the planet and beyond. Why you discriminating against the men? Don't you like men?"

"No, I don't. My two parasitic ex-husbands are men."

"Surprised you'd let them stay alive. Must mean they're higher-ups in one of the powerful or sinister megacorps. You planned to kill me today."

"That may still be the plan, Mr. Cruz. You killed one of our members. We always avenge our fallen sisters."

"Go ahead. Only one of us is employed by the Council of Corporations. I'm told they also don't like you. Why am I here, Ms. May?"

"We need to consider our options."

I spun around in the chair to look at Charade. "A spy ring with lots of beauty but lacking in the brain department. You brought the device out of hiding, then let it get stolen."

"You don't know what it is, do you?"

I swung back around to face May. "I know it was in Ms. Charade's car. That's all I needed to know when I stole it. But a low-life car thief beat me to it."

"He outwitted the both of you," May said.

"Are you suggesting, Ms. May, that your minion, Ms. Charade, was operating off-script when she brought the device to the Naughty Room?"

"Ms. Charade, do not be too hard on yourself. Mr. Cruz has been manipulating you as long as we've been watching him. I believe I can guess how you came to know about us—when Ms. Charade unwisely looked into putting a contract out on you. You are very clever or very lucky or both. Very few people on this planet or above can best us."

"Please, the Council of Corporations has done so many times before."

"Are you their cheerleader these days, Mr. Cruz? All it takes is a couple of bucks to get you on their side? You know nothing. I've made my decision."

"Have you? Do I get to sit comfortably or out the window I go? I believe your fallen sister tried that on me—unsuccessfully."

"You will be our guest for a little while."

"A guest of Gyndromeda. What's wrong with Andromeda?"

"One is our name, the other isn't."

"Are you its founder? Super spy, female extraordinaire."

"Since your contempt for my organization is annoying me, I'll correct your misconceptions. In the world of corporate espionage, there are rules, codes of conduct, and consequences that we all live by. The professional spy must be able to leave everything they know behind at a nano-second's notice. That's the life. Or that has always been what we've been told. But what if one wants love, a spouse, a child, a family? I hear yours is growing."

"Leave my family out of this and any future conversations, Ms. May. What about love, family, and your female spy organization?"

"Do you know what happens to a spy in this business with any entanglements?"

"Entanglements? Is that your term in the business?"

"Termination, Mr Cruz."

"You can't be serious."

"I am very serious, Mr. Cruz. In the dark but very lucrative universe of criminal corporations, they own you. That's the trade-off. Power and wealth, but you must be a solo entity for all your days. That was not acceptable to me, nor to many others. I saw an opportunity, a new market for professionals in my way of thinking, and I created the solution. I wanted a child, and no megacorp was going to tell me otherwise or threaten me. Gyndromeda was born. The universe for the baby or family-minded female spy. You can't image the radically family-unfriendly mentality in the modern megacorporate world."

"Spy during the day. Mommy at night. Why are you telling me this, Ms. May? Because really I don't care. And there's no way you'll convince me that NeuroDancer was a member of your professional female spy ring."

"She was my sister!" I heard from behind me.

I know Charade expected me to spin around again in my chair, but I threw myself forward as I kicked the chair back. She high-jumped over the chair to get at me.

"Stop, Ms. Charade!" May yelled.

But it was too late. Charade and I were in a real knock-down, drag-out fist fight with plenty of karate kicks.

"Stop them!" May yelled.

The fight was a lot of action and show, but unproductive as hell. Neither of us landed any actual blows on the other. When Burlesque grabbed her to hold her back and some other woman pushed me back, all we were doing was breathing hard.

"He tricked us. He made me bring it to the market," Charade yelled.

"Yes, Ms. Charade," Ms. May said. "You thought you were luring him into your death trap, when it was him manipulating you to bring it to the Naughty Room to steal it right from under our noses. He even knew the color, make, and model of your hovercar. Too bad, Mr. Cruz, you didn't know that its engine and trunk are at the reverse ends of other vehicles. The trunk had a metal case containing the device. You might have pulled off your gambit after all, but then we would have shot you dead."

"Not with my team. They were ready for you," I said.

"We knocked you out and brought you here, didn't we? Where's your team? Mr. Cruz, we've been doing this a lot longer than you. Regarding your team, do you always travel with RPGs in your hovercar? Not even your law enforcement will allow you to get away with that."

"If the Council of Corporations can have hovercraft with pulse lasers that can level megatowers, we'll carry a spare missile launcher to shoot their craft out of the air."

"I can't argue with that logic. Ms. Charade, stay away from him. Mr. Cruz, sit down before I change my mind about you."

A few more finely dressed woman had joined us, not one of them wearing blue like at the Naughty Room.

"Let me introduce my colleagues, Mr. Cruz. I have a feeling you already know their names."

"Don't let me spoil your fun, Ms. May—introduce away."

"Keep in mind, we use code names in the organization."

"Code names? Gangs call it street names," I said.

"We're not a gang, Mr. Cruz."

"You're criminals like them. What's the difference?"

"You'll soon learn there's a big difference. The one who restrained you from Ms. Charade is Ms. Mellow Drama. Here is Ms. Sugar, Ms. Spice, Ms. Exotica, Ms. Stiletto, and Ms. Trophy Wife."

Every one of them in a white business suit with tight-fitting pants or skirts. Lots of gaudy gold, platinum, or diamond jewelry. Lots of cleavage. All wearing different flamboyant styles of hats, except for Charade and Burlesque.

"All sexy mothers," Ms. Trophy Wife announced, smiling. "Do I have time to pick up some stick-on nails?" she asked May.

"When will lunch arrive?" Ms. Sugar asked. She was the slimmest of the bunch. "I'm so hungry my stomach is eating itself."

"Yes, where's lunch?" Ms. Spice chimed in. "I hope they didn't mess up our orders again."

Suddenly, the women erupted in chatter, all talking over each other. I needed to figure out how to get off the Mother Ship before I volunteered to take a header out the window.

#

So much tech around me. The bay window was not glass or any other transparent alloy. It was a force wall. Pure energy. Only the uber-wealthy could afford it, but even if the average Metropolitan could, we'd avoid it. We wanted tech that even if the electricity stopped flowing, we wouldn't be sent back to the prehistoric ages. All I had to do was walk through the bay window-force wall onto the balcony.

From the palatial balcony, an amazing view overlooking the supercity. The hoverhotels were like a massive train crawling through the sky around the edges of the city. The openness of outer space not too far above. Staring at the ground fathoms below could make you weak in the knees.

The balcony was where the servants waited. Out of sight and out of mind, but always close at hand. Hovertrolleys filled with bottled water, glasses, and ice behind them. The nine women were dressed simply in white, with the addition of white gloves. Their hair styles were neat, short, and normal. My kind of people. Middle class, not booshy.

"How do you like working for Gyndromeda?" I asked the same woman who brought Ms. May her chair.

"I enjoy it very much, sir," she replied.

"Do you know what we're waiting for? And don't say lunch."

She smiled. "I'm not sure, sir. I believe guests are on the way."

"Guests?"

"Yes, sir."

"Mr. Cruz, don't bother my servants," Ms. May appeared through the force wall and handed me a photo. "Get Mr. Cruz's order for lunch. He'll be eating with us."

"Yes, mistress," the servant said.

A flood of memories came to me when I saw it was a digital photo of the late NeuroDancer.

"Don't be too angry with Ms. Charade. She loved her sister. We all did. Gyndromeda is like a family," May said.

"Why didn't you ever use the device again in all these years?" I asked.

She laughed. "You know the answer, Mr. Cruz. Everyone was watching. To use it would have risked exposure and death. We had to wait."

"Use it on me first. Then what was next?"

"Why do you care, Mr. Cruz?"

"Rule the world like NeuroDancer planned?"

"She was ambitious, wasn't she?"

"That's one word for a psycho megalomaniac."

"Please don't let Ms. Charade hear you call her sister that."

"Her fans still mourn the anniversary of her death to this day, all around the world."

"She was a celebrity. People like worshiping celebrities."

"Didn't you have any growing up? Perhaps, watched on the TV that you admired?"

"No, we didn't have any TV devices in the house. My ma told me TV rots the brain, so I never got into any celebrities."

May held back a laugh. "Too bad we didn't meet a little sooner, Mr. Cruz. Would you like this copy for your 'Wall of Fame' in your Liquid Cool offices when you reopen?" May asked me.

"Thanks, but I have to decline," I said.

May took it back then crushed the digital photo in the palms of her hands. When she opened them again, all that was left was a thin black hairpin. In mere moments she wrapped up her ponytail into a bun behind her head and kept it in place with the hairpin.

"Will others be joining us for lunch?" I asked.

"Possibly." May walked back through the force wall into the residence.

The servant handed me a pad. "You can choose your selections, sir."

"Can I ask you a favor?"

"Yes, sir."

"Do you know where my gun is? I feel lost without it. It's a detective thing. Do you think you can ask your mistress for me? She'll listen to you."

"Sir, I'm supposed to get your lunch order, not guns."

"But she'll be open if you ask for me. She doesn't trust me. I bet she doesn't even like me."

"Don't say that, sir. My mistress is very hospitable to all her guests."

"If she would just trust me and bring me in, I could help. We need to get the device before they find out. I just feel so naked without my weapon. We could get attacked."

"We are very secure here, sir, but I'll see what I can do."

"Thanks."

As the chief servant walked back into the residence, two others came over to me. One gave me a glass of ice while the other poured the water. I thanked them.

"Why do you feel we could be attacked, Mr. Cruz?"

Ms. May had returned to the balcony with all her other spy mamas glaring at me. The chief servant sheepishly waited behind them.

"Where's my gun?" I asked.

"You don't honestly expect us to give you a loaded weapon," she said.

"You're all armed, and I'm sure you have plenty of guards nearby, so what does it matter? I want my weapon back now. Then we can stop playing games and get to work."

"No one's playing games here," Ms. May said to me. "We're waiting for guests."

I walked past them to the chief servant. "Ms. Milky May, can we stop playing games now? Send your actresses home, give me back my gun, tell me what guests you have coming, then I'll tell you what guests I have coming."

Her subservient look vanished from her face. It was like a complete personality transfer between the two groups in the blink of an eye. "Go get Mr. Cruz his gun," the real Ms. May said to the fake one.

Chapter Twenty-Eight
Female Force

Games. Among the hustlers on the street, there was a concept called "the endless con job." Everyone's scamming everyone else for so long that at some point no one remembered what's real, what's not, or even what the purpose of it all was. Well, I was certain of my immediate purpose: find and destroy the NeuroDancer device. The Council of Corporations planted the seed that it was a "device" or "object." Gyndromeda went further in reinforcing the notion by claiming it was in a metal box in a trunk of a hovercar—in other words, portable. As I was certain of my ultimate purpose, I was also certain that all I'd been told could be lies. None of them wanted me to know what the actual mechanism of the late NeuroDancer's mind-control abilities were until the very end. But the endless con job often meant that sometimes you conned yourself into not knowing which way was up or down. The Council, or at least Gem's faction, wanted me to destroy it. Gyndromeda's goal was as yet unclear. But they at least gave me back my gun.

"Do know the original story of the Andromeda myth, Mr. Cruz?" the real Milky May asked me.

"But you're Gyndromeda."

"Yes, but everything is a derivative of something else."

I had the pleasure of being taken on a tour of the Gyndromeda's hoverhotel headquarters they called the Mother Ship. She'd led me through the penthouse residence to the elevators, with the other real members of her group following. The first stop which was a vast room that reminded me of retro switchboard offices. We stood on the railing of the upper level, looking down at the lower level. As far as the eye could see, there were women in business attire in large office pods on phones and computers. A ruckus of activity everywhere.

"Andromeda was the daughter of royalty. Her queen mother bragged to all that she was far more beautiful than the sea fairies, the Nereids. She angered the gods. So the god Poseidon sent a sea monster to obliterate their kingdom. To save all, Andromeda's dear parents, the king and queen, had their daughter chained to a rock as a sacrifice to the monster. In the end, the warrior Perseus rescued her. Are you here to save us, Mr. Cruz?"

"I'm not marrying you and I'm not interested in ruling your super-secret female spy ring with you."

"You know the story, then. Our take on the story is that Gyndromeda is the warrioress. She alone saves the kingdom from the sea monster and, for her bravery and self-sacrifice, the people and the gods reward her."

"I like it. Has a witty, megalomaniacal undertone to it. Fits with your organization's brand identity."

"What you're seeing, Mr. Cruz, is our version of MI-6 or the CIA or DGSE." May said the last acronym with a French accent. "Nations need these services, so do megacorporations. They have security needs too. An external apparatus beyond the reach of any internal politics or manipulation, but principled, dependable, impressive, merciless. Spies for hire."

She led me down the corridor to look through a glass wall to another section that looked like a control center with large hover display screens hanging above tables of female agents, all wearing holo-glasses. The screens were real-time maps of locations all over the world.

"In our business, we identify civilians who we can enlist in our operations. NeuroDancer was one such civilian. Normally, such a high-profile person would be completely unacceptable, but in her case, it was the opposite. Her contacts throughout the corporate and political world were extensive. A call from her opened doors at the highest levels that would take us months to infiltrate. But she was a civilian operative, not a professional agent. Sometimes operatives can go astray, as happened with her. One day she went rogue, cut off contact. Agents we sent to retrieve her never returned. Agents we sent to do more also never returned. When we started hearing the rumors from insiders, we learned what had happened. She had acquired a device from a small unknown research megacorp and, as the saying goes, her quest for world domination began."

"May, may I ask a question?" I asked.

We'd reached another hallway—white exterior, shiny faux white-wood floor.

"Of course, Mr. Cruz. You're our guest. You can ask us anything."

"First, you were an organization bringing universal family leave to evil megacorp spies. Now, you're the MI-6 for hire for evil megacorps. What's the truth?"

"Truth, Mr. Cruz? The truth is whatever you want it to be. One or the other, both, or neither. You decide. Truth is always about what you choose."

"Where I come from, truth is much more simple. Santa Claus is not the truth. Ma and Pops sneaking around at midnight dumping toys under the tree is the truth."

"In my world, simple doesn't exist. Blacks and whites don't exist. An ever changing rainbow of grays is our world."

"Why did you waste time with the earlier simulation? You extensively profiled me."

"We did, Mr. Cruz. Anti-authority, anti-elite, anti-wealth—"

"Hardly. I got a family, employee, business, and classic vehicle to support."

"Pro-Average Joe and Jane, always in the underdog's corner or for the victim. We believe in testing all scenarios, Mr. Cruz. Begin with the most basic and work from there. You have well-developed street smarts, and you've taken federal profiling courses yourself. What have you gleaned about me?"

"I thought we agreed not to play any more games."

"We agreed to a truce, nothing more. The game never stops."

"I asked your faker, so I'll ask you. Why am I here, Ms. May?"

"I told you. We're waiting for our guests. And we're waiting for yours."

"What about the device? Are we not going to retrieve it?"

"We are, Mr. Cruz. No doubt about it. But what is foremost in my mind is why you allowed yourself to be captured by us."

"Why did you capture me and bring me here then?"

"For the same reason, you have your people holding out at that Wharf City warehouse. This is our base of operations that we can defend. When do they get here, Mr. Cruz? If you weren't so deceptive, we'd have left by now."

"You know who the car thief is?"

"There was no car thief, Mr. Cruz. You know that."

"Who then?"

"We're not finished with the tour, Mr. Cruz."

"You're not finished with the stalling and games?"

"You're a master at games."

"In the next simulation will you all say you're actually aliens from the planet Venus, and NeuroDancer planned to mind-control Earthers in an unauthorized attempt at world domination, and you're here to make sure the device is retrieved and never allowed to get into non-Venusian hands? Also, I know NeuroDancer had no sister, or any siblings."

"You're a natural. You should write all our scenarios."

"The fakes, your doubles, you sent to the Naughty Room were in case you were ambushed? But not by me, others."

"Others?"

"Just a scenario?"

"I told you. Perspective and perception are fluid."

"At least you didn't say they're relative, so you're not a college graduate."

"I've graduated from many colleges with many degrees, Mr. Cruz."

"No, Ms. May. There's a difference between those of us who get certified in a specific tangible discipline, like you and me, and those who get some general studies degree regurgitating words like 'relative' and 'self-actualization.' Perspective and perception aren't relative."

"Aren't they? One day all you were was a laborer, restorer and racer of classic hovercars, then you said you were a street detective and you were. If I didn't know it is as fact, I'd say you were really a secret agent with a unique and unusual cover story."

"Well, maybe I am. My pops is a kendo master, and I caught my ma a few times with a hidden little gun in her little purse with the candies she likes to eat."

"One day, you were a slave to your OCD hyper-germophobic episodes. Today you're married, with children, and quite the diaper changer. Perceptions and perspectives can shift all the time, even between truth and lie."

"Despite what you say, I don't like games."

"Those of us in this business like living in a puzzle inside a conundrum, inside an enigma. We've escaped the boring life of the masses."

"Personally, I've always preferred the boring," I said, and turned my attention to the other women behind her. "One of you give me your lipstick. Come on. I know one of you has one."

One of them reached into her jacket and threw me her gold lipstick pen. "Which one are you?" I asked.

"Ms. Burlesque," she replied with no emotion.

I stared at her for a moment with a smirk. The real Ms. Burlesque was a refined but plain Jane compared to the large, conic bra-wearing fake Ms. Burlesque. With the lipstick, I drew a complete circle on the floor. When I was done, I stepped into the pinkish circle.

"Okay, we're ending this. This is the Truth Circle. You step inside and you can speak the truth only, unconditionally, without qualification, without hesitation. I'm ready. What about you?"

Ms. May just stood there. I couldn't believe what I was seeing. She seemed genuinely uneasy, as if she felt if she stepped into the circle and lied, she'd be struck down by a bolt of lightning from the cosmic gods.

"Ms. May, I'm waiting."

"What form will this truth-telling take?"

"What's wrong with the simple Q and A approach? I ask a question. You answer. You ask your question and I answer. And so on."

"No," she said emphatically, holding up her hand, pointing. "One question only."

"One question only?"

"Yes, Mr. Cruz."

"I consider that a cheat because you already know my one question: if I have to choose from the many that I have. Agreed. Get in here."

"I can answer from here."

"No, Agent May. From within the circle. You could pretend uneasiness or you could have some strange secret phobia that prevents you from lying inside a circle. Come on in."

She joined me, not over three feet away. "Who goes first?"

"On the Mother Ship, the man, of course," I said.

"Typical."

"You can save your false female chauvinism for someone else. Most of the vicious criminals out there are men, but the ones that are female are as devious, depraved, and violent as the men. I wouldn't be surprised if you've killed more people than me, Agent May, but we can talk about that later.

"My question is simple: Where exactly, this very moment, is the NeuroDancer mind-control device, apparatus, or thing, and all its components, and any necessary auxiliary components, and in whose possession, this very moment?"

"Compound questions allowed, Mr. Cruz?"

"I didn't say they were disallowed. Well, Agent May? The answer is?"

"The device is in the possession of an organization called the Gentlemen Boys and is currently in an establishment called the Cat Walk."

"Is that the truth?"

"Only one question, Mr. Cruz. Did we legitimately capture you, or did you let yourself be captured?"

"Why did you waste your only question with that one? You know the answer is the latter."

"Shall we continue the Q and A?"

"That was my intention, but you said only one question."

She stepped out of the circle. "And that is how it will have to remain. Our guests have arrived."

"Too bad. We were just beginning to have such a pleasant conversation. But did they just arrive, conveniently waiting for us to have our conversation, or did they arrive a while ago and you're telling me now?"

"You know the answer is the latter, Mr. Cruz."

#

With the rest of her crew following, Ms. May led me back to the same penthouse residential space with its bay window. But the majestic room was far from empty. Inside, corporate samurai soldiers in shiny red, orange, yellow, and green suits filled the room. Their guns may have been concealed under their jackets, but the hilts of their samurai swords were in plain sight, strapped over their backs.

Of even greater concern was outside the room, hovering in the sky. Several hoverdirigibles, the same design as the one that buzzed my Liquid Cool offices that day when Council of Corporations President Gem visited. I knew I was only seeing a small fraction of their men and firepower.

The head man in the center of the corporate samurai soldiers was bald, wearing gold-tinted shades and dressed in a shiny white suit with gold pinstripes. All their eyes were on us the moment we stepped through the door.

"Who are you?" I asked.

"I, Mr. Cruz, am the new president of the Council of Corporations."

"No, you're not," I said. "Per the Council bylaws, there must be a full board meeting where nominations for any vacant office, including the president, are presented in a sanctioned motion. However, the formal election by hand vote cannot happen until the next scheduled full board meeting."

He pulled off his golden glasses.

"You want to be president of the Council of Corporations, but you don't even know your own bylaws."

The man had such a disgusted look on his face, as if he swallowed a bug. "I heard about you, Mr. Cruz."

"Did you? Why are you here?"

He smiled and put his glasses back on his face. "I'm taking you into custody, Mr. Cruz, for the assassination plot of President Gem."

"You have no authority to do anything on behalf of the Council, pal. In fact, I'm the only person in this room working for and on behalf of the Council of Corporations."

I looked at Ms. May. "When did they hire you?" I asked.

"Some time ago," she replied. "We are an organization for hire."

"You're working for the faction that tried to seize the power of the Council by assassination, and I'm working for its official governing body of the Council. All bases covered," I said.

"There is no official governing body of the Council outside of my group!" the man yelled at me.

"I hope you told the truth in the circle of truth," I said to her.

"I did," May replied.

I knew what was coming next as I could see the Council man turn to his suit soldiers to give the order.

I pointed to the sky. "My friends are here," I announced to him.

He didn't even have time to turn around.

\#

Neither of us were exaggerating when we each said we had "guests" on the way. The only issue was which of our guests were deadlier. Outside the Mother Ship, two factions of the Council of Corporations met. I had the unique, once-in-a-lifetime distinction of having the Council of Corporations trying to kill and protect me at all costs at the same time.

The first hoverdirigible exploded with enough force to put every one of us—me, Gyndromeda, the Council man and his suit soldiers—on the ground. The only good thing was that we weren't showered with glass, but the force wall was gone.

My stay aboard the Mother Ship had come to an end. As I hopped to my feet and bolted for the door, I thought: Gyndromeda should never had brought me to their lair.

Fear could be a very healthy motivator. I knew where I needed to be and my legs were moving as fast as they could to get me there. Many people didn't seem to know even in this day that explosions could disrupt normal hover-tech fields. No hover-tech and a hoverhotel becomes a hotel dropping to the earth at whoever knows how many miles per minute.

Another explosion rocked the building and this time it tilted, oh so slowly, forward and back. My senses screamed out that I'd better get to where I had to be—now!

I'd felt a presence before, but now I heard the running footsteps. It was like I was on the roofs of the buildings near the Naughty Room, but this time when I turned it wasn't two extreme parkour kids. It was all the "real" Gyndromeda women.

"You have parachutes," I yelled.

"Yes, we do," one said.

"But I don't have a parachute," I yelled.

"You didn't ask for a parachute. You asked for your gun. Typical man."

"That's not very helpful." I turned and with the flick of a switch on my omega-gun, I'd fired.

The explosive round blew the door away like nothing. I could see a clear sky ahead at the end of the hallway. We heard more explosions.

"Here!" one of them yelled as we all sprinted through the hole, one after another.

I turned just to catch a parachute pack from Ms. May.

"I'm not putting on a parachute from a stranger," I yelled at her.

"Then don't."

The end corridor opened out to another patio balcony. It was also the end of the Mother Ship hoverhotel. The building was descending slowing, but we all knew that was only the start.

"Self-destruct in five-four..."

"What the hell! Self-destruct? When did this happen?"

"One!" the computer voice echoed.

"Oh snaps!" I never had a chance to strap on my parachute pack as I dived over the balcony along with all the Gyndromeda women.

But they also had rocketpacks and flew away in formation. As for me, I plummeted through the wide-open sky. I turned to see the entire Mother Ship hover-hotel exploding, section by section, as a battle royale of hoverdirgibles blasted each other with laser cannons above the falling hoteltower. There was a final explosion and more than one of the hoverdirigibles was caught in the blast.

The heat and concussion of the blast almost knocked me out, pushing me away and spinning me around like a rag doll.

Lucky for me, I didn't need the parachute. I'd come into the Gyndromeda trap prepared, too. I was falling like a stone, but not that fast. Quix's mini-hoverjet reached me and pulled me into its cargo bay with two robotic arms.

PART SIX
The Dean and The Gentlemen Boys

Chapter Twenty-Nine
Flash

Quix and I both agreed. We needed to ditch his mini-jet and get to the Wharf City warehouse separately using other transportation. Metro PD wasn't stupid. A giant laser battle and exploding hoverhotels would bring an army of units converging from everywhere in the city. Metro PD also had its own surveillance satellites, so they'd identify and track every hovercraft in the area, especially those rescuing falling street detectives from said exploding hoverhotels. They'd certainly identify me and put out an all-points bulletin.

The skies were going to be swarming with police, media, and looky-lous. Whatever we were going to do had to happen fast. So I got to use my loaner parachute after all (but I checked it first, or had Quix check it). Quix and I bailed out of the hoverjet and let it crash into an out-of-the-way access point to one of the city's underground rivers. I was glad Quix had the contacts that let him ditch expensive mini-hoverjets with a "plenty more where it came from" attitude. I needed those kinds of friends.

Ms. May revealed she knew exactly where I was based. But I wasn't worried. If she were after me, she wouldn't have told me. I'd figure out everything when Quix and I got back to the warehouse HQ.

Owning any kind of classic hovercar was a lifetime investment far beyond the vehicle itself. Security always had to be top of mind, and simply landing and parking in the common streets was not an option.

I always used my best friend's company, Let It Ride Enterprises, for mobile car security. Most of the time, the guy who did that security was Flash. He had a light complexion with a ponytail and a small goatee. Flash was friendly, reliable, and took his job seriously. But I called him not for car-sitting security. He was a hovercar taxi driver, too.

Flash was one of the few people in Metropolis I knew who had a real life domestic robot in his home to do chores. His wife and kids loved it. Flash and I always ended up talking about it and he was always amused that I still expected it to attack him one day. He caught me up on its latest exploits. Then we'd starting talking about the kids. Then the wives, of course.

"Cruz, did you see the news?" he asked, coasting down the sky traffic lanes wearing his favorite yellow jumpsuit over his clothes and blue eyewear.

"What's going on?" I asked from the backseat in the seclusion of the hovercar's tinted wraparound windows. I was also glad it was raining again.

"A proverbial world war near Crystal Cliffs. News said two unknown megacorps started firing at each other in their hoverblimps. Blew an entire hoverhotel out of the sky."

"Really? The police have to do more to clamp down on all this wanton violence everywhere. They need to find everyone involved and put their butts in jail where they belong. People are raising families in this city."

"Tell me about it, Cruz."

#

Flash's Let It Ride yellow hovercab glided to my warehouse headquarters. But the alley was completely empty of all life.

"Hang above that door," I directed.

Flash always had spare quick-phones, so I dialed the office number and added the proper suffix at the end. PJ, of course, came up with the codes.

"Who's this?" she answered.

"It's me, PJ. I'm in the taxi outside."

The door opened and a few sidewalk johnnies peeked out.

I had my own standing tab with Let It Ride, so Flash was already paid with a tip, as always. We said our goodbyes, and I bailed from the hovercab and dashed into the building.

The door was closed for me and I found myself surrounded by a ton of people.

"Am I at Metro International? How many people are in here?" I asked.

But the one person I was looking for had already arrived too—Quix.

"What happened, Cruz?" Phishy asked me, genuinely concerned.

"He's here, so it was a successful op," PJ said with her arms folded. I noticed her team of college interns standing behind her had grown from the last time I'd seen them.

"I'd say we need to talk about today," Quix said, his own armed men standing around him.

"That we will do, but there's one person I need to talk to first."

Chapter Thirty
Gem AI

I sat at my desk with Ms. Gem AI in the chair in front of me. Same crimson kimono-style dress, same pearl necklace, same hairdo, same attitude.

"When were you going to tell me you'd also hired the Gyndromeda organization?"

"Why would I need to inform you of something you already know?" she said. "Besides, the Council has never believed in putting all its faith in one basket."

"I fail and others can still do the Council's bidding."

"Something like that, Mr. Cruz. Are you offended?"

"Not at all. Even so, you could have told me. If you wanted me to work with other operatives, I would have."

"Have you retrieved the object?"

"No."

"Then you will work with my operatives."

"Are there any others we should know about?"

"I am confident that you can complete the task with or without their assistance."

"Who's Fatherboard?"

"They are another corporate espionage organization for hire. Their specialty, though, is dirty tricks and black market trading. Undoubtedly, other factions within the Council hired them."

"Factions that may or may not have killed your creator, you mean?"

"The mission must go on, Mr. Cruz."

"This Fatherboard stole the object?"

"If Gyndromeda said they have it, then yes."

"Stole it from Gyndromeda."

"Yes?"

"You hired the people who had it all this time, are an adversary, had it stolen, and you hired them to help you get the object? Gem AI, I feel you and your confederates are trying to confuse me."

"No need to be confused, Mr. Cruz. The Council has always lived by the rule that today's adversary can be tomorrow's ally. Besides, we made them an offer they could not refuse—restore their reputation among the megacorp universe. They care more about that than money, though they are being paid exorbitantly for their cooperation and assistance."

"More than me."

"Obviously," she replied with a smile. "As for the object, had the object simply been destroyed, what would you have done? You'd continue to search for it all your years, as with all the other players out there. Becoming more desperate, dangerous, and more paranoid. You do not destroy an object of its magnitude in secret. You must allow others to take it from you. Then you seize it back and destroy for the entire world to see. Then it is over."

I watched my AI client with a bit of admiration. From her programmed perspective, it was the only course that could be taken, and I agreed completely.

"Then I will go seize and destroy it for the world to see. Will Gyndromeda be helping me or getting in my way? You're their client too."

"I know you pride yourself on your sidewalk johnny brigade and ex-mercs, but I thought an upgrade of your backup would be needed for this operation. Gyndromeda has provided such services for the Council in years past. They will do so for you here."

"An organization called Fatherboard doesn't elicit much concern in my book."

"I know you don't underestimate anyone, Mr. Cruz, and you shouldn't here. They look like average gentlemanly type businessmen, but every one of them is an accomplished killer."

"Like Gyndromeda."

"But the Fatherboard doesn't have you, so the odds are in our favor."

Chapter Thirty-One
The Gentlemen Boys

In the end, the all-female espionage organization would always sell their services to the highest bidder. They had loyalty to none, which to me meant they never could be really trusted. Someone could climb out of some deep, dark corner and throw a few more coins into the pot. Then the person who you thought had your back was now stabbing it. People like me, my best friend Run-Time, and Quix had a code that once we agreed to help you, then that was it. We had your back to the end. There was no being lured away by any amount of money by anyone. That's how it was supposed to be. That was the code of the decent, the code of the good guys. Without that, you were nothing but a mangy animal in the sewers.

One of the many amazing quirks of living in the largest supercity on the planet was that if you wanted to visit a different restaurant, bar, club, or shop each day for the rest of your life, you could easily accomplish it and never have touched even half the city. As a detective, I was always interested in what new place I'd set foot in for a case.

I'd never heard of the Cat Walk before and strangely when I looked it up on the Net, I easily found its address, but nothing more. What was the place?

When we arrived, the opaque one-story tall structure, unusual for Metropolis, stood on top of a hill. There was plenty of neon lighting, but none with its name. Quix descended and hovered just above the ground as I opened the door. Then a hoverlimo dropped from the sky almost on top of us.

My hand had already reached for my weapon under my jacket when its door opened. The original Gyndromeda women dressed in their revealing, curvaceous white outfits with stylish hats, and clear slickers over it all.

Ms. May—the fake one—walked to our hovercar first and leaned down. "We'll take it from here, Mr. Quix."

"Thank you, Ms..."

"Ms. Milky May. Mr. Cruz will be in our beautifully good hands with my team."

"But can those finely pedicured hands shoot a gun?"

"Among other things."

"I hope so," Quix said, unconvinced.

"Don't worry, Mr. Quix. We're professionals too."

#

Quix flew off in his new hovervehicle as the ladies and I walked to the main anonymous entrance.

"What is this place?" I asked.

"It a gentlemen's club, among other things," May replied.

"Other things?"

"Criminal things, Mr. Cruz."

I'd been in country club establishments before, but the place was unlike any I'd seen. We entered a long, dimly lit corridor toward a blue neon-light doorway. Once through, two attractive women in black evening dresses waited at a counter (the real Milky May and Charade). There was no recognition of any kind on their faces. They said nothing. One simply gestured for us to pass on by.

What we thought was a wall was really a dark curtain. I passed through first and there was our catwalk. An inclined ramp from the ground to a stage-walkway five feet up from the ground. However, the reason we stopped in our tracks was on either side of the incline were empty tables of well-dressed people. They looked like dining guests, but no food or drinks in front of them. They all watched us, nodding, simple smiles, nothing threatening. But why were they there?

"Go through," one of the counter women said.

I was feeling brave. I led the way. At the end of a very long catwalk, much of it in dim light, curtains opened and an enormous man, almost busting out of his suit, stopped us with blue neon glasses.

A new woman stepped to him (the real Burlesque) and handed me a blank playing card with a suit of spades. "Your complimentary membership card, sir."

She handed blank playing cards to each of the women—all of them with the suit of diamonds. "You can all go through," she said as the large man stepped aside.

Finally, the inside establishment looked like what I was accustomed to seeing in a country club. Velvet ceilings and floors, marble walls with expensive paintings, people and landscapes—all from the history of Metropolis. Members were in their areas of choice: reading areas, sitting areas, dining areas, bar. It was all men with waitresses buzzing around in black evening dresses. Signs indicated the restrooms, private phone pods, poker tables, saunas, massage parlors, energy massage parlors, and quiet rooms. The establishment was only one story from the outside, but now inside we could see the elevators to its many lower levels. Such clubs were often where real business occurred in business and politics.

Another woman approached me. It was the real Ms. Sugar. "May I help you, sir? Who is your party looking for?"

"The Dean," Ms. (fake) May answered for me.

"Follow me then," she said.

#

An elevator took us to the very last floor in the bowels of the establishment. I had the fake Gyndromeda with me, but the real Gyndromeda all seemed to be bona fide employees of the establishment. Working right under the noses of their rival organization. Brilliant. But did the Gentlemanly Boys really not know who they were?

In my training as a police intern back when I was a high school kid, they drilled into you that when you knock on the door or buzz the ringer, you never stand in front of the door, always to the side. The same went for an elevator. Stand to the side. The elevator door opened, and we were instantly riddled with lasers. It didn't matter I was at the side because the lasers bounced off the walls and ladies to hit me and knock me out cold on the ground.

#

The ladies had convinced me of their grand plan to get the object. They assured me I was in charge and that, no matter what, it would be turned over to me per our client. Whether I believed that was another story. What I believed was that they knew every inch inside the Cat Walk, where the object was and how to retrieve it. We wouldn't need to storm the Gentlemen Boys' lair. We'd just stroll in the front door and steal it back before they knew what happened. I asked how. They said, "watch the professionals at work." Then we all got laser-shot in an elevator.

Someone was calling my name. That's what woke me up. I felt as if I'd been beaten up. That's what stun lasers did to you. At least they were the stunning kind, not the killing kind.

I looked up, seated in some chair, and saw that skanky car thief staring back. The grin on his face was from ear to ear. Unlike before, he was in a presentable dark charcoal suit. Gold bracelets and gold rings were on all his fingers, including the thumbs.

"Welcome back, Mr. Cruz. It is Mr. Cruz of the Liquid Cool Detective Agency?"

The man seated across from me reminded me of a college professor. He had the dark tweed-like suit, tie, crimson vest, and neon lined the soles of his shoes. "I don't think I've ever met a real-life private investigator before. But is this really the work for a private investigator?"

I was still groggy, but I answered. "Detectives do corporate investigations, too. A client may need to verify if a potential business partner is legit, investigate parties behind a smear campaign to ruin a megacorps reputation so that a libel or slander case can be mounted. Or more often, a detective is called in to investigate the loss or theft of proprietary secrets, products, inventions, items."

The man looked genuinely interested in what I was saying, as were the several men standing around him. They were all dressed similarly, except each one had a different-colored dress vest.

"Very interesting, Mr. Cruz. Thank you for the information. I don't think we have one member who's a private investigator. We need to remedy that. My manners. Mr. Cruz, I am the Dean. Pleased to make your acquaintance. Excuse me if I don't shake your hand, but once I start smoking my cigar, I put such pleasantries to the side. Are you a cigar man, Mr. Cruz?"

"No, sorry."

"Don't worry, Mr. Cruz. The effects will wear off shortly. We can simply chat until you're one hundred percent. Let me introduce my colleagues, from my left to right. This is Knuckle Duster, Neanderthal, Goon, Brute, and Dude. Collectively, we're known as the Gentlemen Boys."

"Pleasure meeting you. What is Fatherboard then? And this place?"

"Mr. Cruz, you've been talking to our rivals. Not even they know the truth, but I'll tell you, man to man. Fatherboard is a faction within the Council of Corporations composed of all megacorps whose primary business or services have to do with intelligence.

"As for the Cat Walk, you've heard of shadow markets?"

"Yeah, a shopping center for the criminal class."

The Dean looked at his men. "Are we the criminal class, gentlemen? Mr. Cruz has us all wrong. The Cat Walk is a member's only gentlemen's club for those who wish to always be kept abreast of what's available and attainable in the shadow market and ghost market universe."

"Where are the ladies? They're not here with us."

"No, Mr. Cruz. This part of the club is men only. The ladies are elsewhere. Would you be upset with me if I said we had disposed of them?"

"Why would you do that?"

"Because that's what they came here to do to us."

"Did they?"

"Mr. Cruz, we know a bit more about your visit than you might think. Intelligence is our chief commodity and we employ many operatives to gather it. Operatives, agents, and double agents, too. How else would we have known you and Gyndromeda were on your way to us? I bet you'll never guess who our double-agent is?"

"Spies, again."

"A very imprecise term, Mr. Cruz."

"Corporate espionage agent?"

"Better, but we work for governments too, unlike the ladies. Gyndromeda has always been very unwise in self-limiting their market."

"A female-only espionage organization and a male-only one. I don't believe in coincidences, so what's the real story, Mr. Dean?"

Dean took a puff of his cigar. "Isn't it obvious? We were married. Then we divorced. The organizations followed. Never go into business with a spouse, Mr. Cruz."

"If you say so. Why did you shoot me, anyway?"

"We needed to stop you from being foolish with the ladies. Until we could talk as men and set you on the right path."

"Which is?"

"You're never leaving this place with the device."

"Can I see the device? NeuroDancer almost killed me twice with it. As a victim, I should be able to see it once."

"Why not?" Dean said and stood from his chair.

"Why are we doing this?" one man asked angrily.

"Because he asked, Mr. Brute. We will indulge his curiosity. The Gentlemen Boys live to present the show with all the pizzazz. We are unique among the unruly mob for it." He turned to me. "Mr. Cruz, follow us and we can continue our talk."

As I stood, I could finally focus on my environment. We were in a cigar smoking room and library. The room looked like it was straight out of a Victorian museum recreation. I followed the men through the double doors to a hallway. Skanky car thief who Mr. Dean hadn't introduced or acknowledged followed behind me.

#

The "gentlemen" had their own red retro trolley, complete with its own tracks. We boarded the one-car transport and Dean got a kick out of yanking the pulley-activated "choo-choo" siren. The trip didn't take long.

As we neared the end of the tunnel, I could see men in white coats. We all jumped off the trolley and followed Dean into some kind of control room. The "scientists" I passed outside the door and those inside the room with all its lighted panels and displays, with buttons and dials, weren't like any scientists I'd seen before. Under their lab coats were expensive suits, and they wore the most expensive shoes like the rest of the Gentlemen Boys.

"The Cat Walk, Mr. Cruz, also has its own R-and-D department. Besides acquiring desired black market items for our clientele members, we have gotten into the business of being able to create highly sought-after items ourselves. Everyone is always seeking the next big thing in high tech."

The Dean moved to the front of the room and pushed a button. "Behold, Mr. Cruz."

The wall retracted into the ceiling. We looked down at a lower-level room with circuits lining the walls and ceilings, pulsating and flashing with electric power. But in the center was an armless upper torso model with tripod legs. The mannequin's head had giant eyes with oversized circular spectacles. The lenses weren't glass or clear. It was an off-white film with a single dot in the center.

I saw Mr. Dean press another button on the table panel at his side. And down below we could all see the spectacles on the mannequin spin. A line started from the dot and ran around itself clockwise, round and round. The center room also had the same disorientating optical pattern going round and round, spiraling out from the center to the outer edge, and starting again.

The Gentlemen Boys and the scientists all stared down at the device.

I glanced at Skank and his eyes remained locked on me. I leaned to him and whispered, "While the men play games, can I have something to drink? Maybe some snacks. What do you have?"

"Games, Mr. Cruz," Dean said loudly, turning to me.

"What's with all you spy organizations and the games?" I asked. "Mr. Dean, hello, the late NeuroDancer used the damn mind-control thing on me. She didn't have any deformed mannequin with stupid, mesmero-glasses like some fake circus performance trick at a kid's amusement park."

"You're right again, Mr. Cruz. You'd be surprised how many sophisticated people we've brought into this room. Every one of them would have given all the money in their accounts to possess what you've correctly identified as a fake. Let's show Mr. Cruz the real thing, since he passed the test and won the prize."

#

We left the room for the elevators. It was a vertical elevator, and this time it wasn't a quick trip. All the Gentlemen Boys joined their boss in smoking their own cigars. I glanced behind me and Skank still had his eagle-eyes on me.

When we stopped and exited into a large dim hallway, Mr. Dean walked to the wall and slid open a large door and we all stepped into a wide open space that reminded me of a warehouse. In fact, it was a giant storehouse filled with crates, but also plenty of suit soldiers armed with machine guns of every make and model. In the center of it all was Charade's orange sportster hovercar.

"Is this what you want, Mr. Cruz?" Dean said, admiring the vehicle.

I walked to it with Skank at my heels. "Is this the real one, or did you create a counterfeit?"

"No, imitation, Mr. Cruz," Dean said. "The genuine article."

"So this is the beginning. I was told it's called psi-tech."

"Psi-tech," the Dean repeated. "I like that name."

"Sounds cooler than mind-control tech."

"Yes, psi-tech it is. The beginning of a great new era."

"How does it work?" I asked.

"How indeed, Mr. Cruz. A device for mind-control in the body of a hovercar. Seems incredible. The megacorps, nations, and crime bosses all wanting to get their hands on this vehicle and what it contains."

"But how does it work?

"It is only one piece of the puzzle, Mr. Cruz. It's the amplifier. The end point of the device. The tip of the spear of the device is elsewhere too. This is the only prototype of the device anywhere on Earth or beyond. Sitting right here in my grasp. The power it represents. A device that can change everything. Turn the Gentlemen Boys into modern-day gods."

There was that psycho megalomaniac talk again.

"But don't worry, Mr. Cruz," he continued. "You'll see it all for yourself soon because we have to demonstrate the device and we'll need test subjects. You and the ladies will do nicely."

"I don't think you can do that, Mr. Dean. I'm allergic to mind-control. The late NeuroDancer used it on me twice. No, she used it on me three times. That's my full life quota."

"Mr. Cruz, you are completely correct. You've done your part more than once. Besides, if it wasn't for you setting these series of events in motion, we would have never been able to steal the device from all of you. Yes, someone else will do their part in your stead. I'll use it on the ladies and you can watch."

"Watch what?"

"Watch them kill you."

Chapter Thirty-Two
Get Cruz

While I was in the "belly of the beast" at the Cat Walk, my friends had just arrived at the Let It Ride Enterprises monolith office tower headquarters in Peacock Hills. This time it was PJ leading Quix out of the elevator capsule on the penthouse level to be greeted by its three finely dressed women seated at the vaulted main reception area.

"Good afternoon, Ms. Judy," the receptionists responded in unison.

She smiled. "You remember me? How can you remember me after all this time?"

"How many stylist cyborgs work for Mr. Cruz?" one asked rhetorically.

"Only one—me! Look at my buff bionic muscles."

Quix knew best to keep quiet and just shake his head as PJ began posing.

One of Run-Time's VPs brought them to his main office to wait. Up the steps to the private second floor of the penthouse level with its purple stone ceilings, white marble walls, and plush purplish carpets. The door to the spacious office at the very end of a long hallway was already open.

PJ admired the decor of ivory whites and smooth black metals when Mr. Run-Time arrived with Mr. Mick, his VP of Covert Operations.

"Judy," Run-Time greeted. He gave her a hug. "I know better than to shake those bionic hands."

"I punch. I don't crush people's hands." She gave him a devilish grin. "Well, sometimes I do if I don't like you."

Run-Tim shook Quix's hand. "You're the Mr. Quix I've heard about. Worked with Mr. Wilford G."

"The Man, yes. Nice to meet you, sir."

"What brings you two here?" Run-Time asked.

Quix looked at PJ. "Tell him," she said.

"Cruz may be in trouble," Quix said.

"Trouble?"

"He walked into a place called the Cat Walk with strange people and no guns," PJ said.

"The Cat Walk?" Mr. Mick asked to clarify.

"Yes," Quix said. "You know it?"

"It fronts as a gentlemen's club, but it's a shadow market. One of the more notorious ones. Why would Mr. Cruz go in there unarmed? Everyone else is."

"Is this still his Council of Corporations case?" Run-Time asked.

"Yes," PJ said. "But it's really still his NeuroDancer case. The sequel."

"The sequel no one asked for," Run-Time said.

#

Run-Time was one of the good guys in the megacorporate world, but that didn't mean that he didn't have the tech, security, and firepower to equal or surpass the bad guys. Let It Ride had its own paramilitary command center on one of its floors, where everyone had gathered with displays of satellite aerial feeds of the Cat Walk building and surrounding areas. Mr. Mick had already assembled an assault team of heavily armed corporate soldiers, ready and waiting in the hallway. Quix used a secure phone to line up a team to rendezvous at the Cat Walk. PJ just wanted the biggest weapons Let It Ride had to lead the combat ingress herself.

Run-Time planned to go too, despite objections from Mr. Mick.

"Mr. Run-Time," a voice of one of the main receptionists came over his new wrist communicator.

"Yes, ladies?"

"Mr. Run-Time. The police are here."

Everyone looked at each other.

Run-Time changed the display feeds to the external security cameras of Let It Ride headquarters megatower. Several large black police hovercruisers hung in the air, encircling the penthouse level.

They went back up to the penthouse lobby reception area. As soon as Run-Time, The Mick, PJ, Quix and other staff stepped off the elevator capsule, they were face-to-face with a virtual army of police. All clad in silver-and-black body-armor with PEACE in big bold white letters on the chests, and wearing their black visored half-helmet. But in the center was the chief of the Metropolis Police Department himself.

Chief Hub stepped to them. The six-foot tall, musclebound, veteran officer had dark hair, a thick mustache, and dark green eyes. He was not smiling. "Whatever you are planning, you are to stand down immediately," he directed.

#

Run-Time had that charm to deal with politicians and the city's business elite. He reconvened back in the Let It Ride command control center with the Chief and gave him control of their satellite display feeds.

With the chief directing the city feeds by barking orders at a Let It Ride staffer, they had a broader view of the area around the Cat Walk. Black police hovercruisers were everywhere, converging on the establishment.

"What's happening, Chief?" Run-Time asked.

"You all have stumbled onto an ongoing operation," the chief answered. "The raid is moments away."

"But Cruz is inside," PJ said.

"We know," the chief said. "The place has been under round-the-clock surveillance since yesterday. Major Organized Crime has had it under surveillance for months. This is a multi-agency operation. No civilians allowed. Even those that generously contribute to the Police Nonprofit Fund."

"Understood, Chief," Run-Time said with a smile. "We were only going to rescue a friend in need."

"That might have been the intent, but with the hoods inside that place, I don't know how you would've been able to do that without a massive shootout. So ladies and gentlemen, we'll save you the need to call the police by going in first."

"There's more intel you might need, Chief," Quix said.

"Mr. Quix. No need. We've had surveillance on Mr. Cruz, the cyborg secretary..."

"I am the VP of Client Services," PJ corrected.

"And the rest of you for days. You don't really think Council of Corporations hoverships have an all-out laser battle above my city and a hoverhotel explodes in the sky and you and Cruz can fly away in that unlicensed, hence illegal, mini-hoverjet of yours. You're not in the military anymore, but I see you still have the 'toys.'"

"You were busy," Quix said, shrugging his shoulders.

"We were busy watching you. If I didn't need Cruz running around, I'd have arrested the lot of you. Anyway, you all are staying here. Watch it on the TV here in comfort, but you're not leaving this building until it's over."

"Chief, if I can ask, how did you get onto this?" Run-Time asked. "You said you've had many of us under surveillance for days."

"Don't you know?" The Chief seemed genuinely surprised.

"No," Run-Time said.

"Cruz. He called me on my private line."

"My boss called you," PJ said.

"You activated this kind of operation for Cruz?" Run-Time asked.

"He didn't have to say much to me, Mr. Run-Time. All he had to say was two words."

"NeuroDancer."

"Mr. Cruz, to my surprise, my pleasant surprise, understands the stakes better than my bosses. We've been working this case as a team from the start."

"I thought he was being incredibly reckless and stupid," Quix said, "when all along he had the best backup money can't buy."

"A street detective with some potential, wouldn't you say, Chief?" Run-Time asked with a smile.

"Some potential, but let's get to the end of the day first. Few things are more dangerous for cops than raiding the stronghold of a den of criminals with international and off-world connections."

"But you have the element of surprise," Quix said.

"Do we?" the chief asked. "They got exterior surveillance satellite feeds of their building and the surrounding area, too."

Chapter Thirty-Three
The Puppet Master

The Dean smoked his cigar with a sickly self-satisfied look. I stood facing him like a prisoner waiting to be executed, with all the other Gentlemen Boys around me, wishing and waiting for me to try something.

We'd moved from the warehouse to an adjoining empty room, except for several desks of different colors and styles against one wall. From the marks on the floor, crates had been stored here before.

"Is this how you imagined this day would happen for you, Mr. Cruz?" Dean asked.

"Day isn't over yet, Mr. Dean," I said.

"You're correct, Mr. Cruz. Any famous last words?" He turned to his men with a laugh. "Always wanted to say that!"

"I doubt I'm the first."

"No fear at all?" Dean asked as he took another puff. "Most people start to cry or tremble at the end. Not you."

"Since I can't get something to drink or snacks, let's get on with it."

"In the Cat Walk, we aim to please. Let's get on with it, indeed."

The Gentlemen Boys moved much closer to me on the other side. Dean fiddled with his tie. "Gentlemen, I shall return shortly with the ladies, and the experiment can begin."

The Dean turned and exited out another door while we waited.

I turned to the others, focusing on Mr. Brute. "Are you gentlemen really that stupid? He already has the device. He's going to use it on all of us! We're the experiment."

"Shut up. It's in the hovercar," one of them said. "We know what it is. You don't."

"Brainless, she used it on me three times and none of those times was there any hovercar around."

Brute grabbed me around the neck and shoulder. "Your mind games won't work. The vehicle has a special ray gun that shoots its beam at victims, and it makes them susceptible to any suggestions."

"You really are stupid. If your boss told you that—"

"He's not our boss," Brute corrected.

"He's lying to you. It's not in the hovercar. She controlled the device's powers, not some accomplice bumbling around in a hovercar at some distance far away. She had the power right with her at all times. Your Mr. Dean already has it. Well, don't ask me. Ask Mr. Car Thief. Ask him if he delivered a metal briefcase from the trunk to your Dean."

Brute stared at me, but I could already see he was wavering. The gentlemen slowly turned their attention to Mr. Skank.

"He's lying!" Skank said. "There was nothing in the case but money. Dean showed you."

"Gentlemen, Dean said he had an insider in the Gyndromeda organization, right? He's the insider!" I yelled. "Gentlemen, this is your last chance. Dean comes back and I'm dead, fine. But what happens to you? Mind slaves for life. He can make you jump off a building too, shoot yourself with your own gun, even rat out all your secrets, including the ones you don't want him to know. Ask the car thief. He's in on it."

The criminal class. Governed by suspicions and paranoia even among the hardest, tightest crews. I added the last spark.

"What's taking him so long? Is he walking to the Siberia Ice Colony and back?"

The first shot popped in the blink of an eye as I dropped to the floor. It was now the second time I found myself in a shootout without my omega-gun or any weapon at all. Unlike the Council of Corporations boardroom, none of the shooters had any immovable tables, massive chairs, or "shifting" tech to hide behind. This was a violent, raw, bloody gun-battle in close quarters and over as quickly as it had started. I was afraid to move, but I had to because the Dean would be back.

I jumped to my feet, ignored the pile of bloody bodies around me, grabbed one gun, then another, and was about to jump. I heard the sound and shot the car thief in the head before he could fire at me. Another Gentlemen Boy was about to shoot me and I hit him in the head too as I jumped on one of the desks at the other end of the room and up. Having done similar work in my Liquid Cool offices, I'd become an expert on real solid ceilings versus fake ones that were made to hide all the wires. Metropolis was an analog, wired city.

I'd moved so quickly up and through the ceiling tiles into the darkness, I was like a cat burglar. The real ceiling was about three feet above me, and there were both vertical and horizontal metal beams above and below me. But I wasn't there to hide, then explore. I was there to hide and watch, which I did though a small crack I created by shifting one tile slightly forward.

Again, I ignored the pile of bodies and kept my eyes glued on the door Dean had exited out of.

I held my breath. The door slowly opened.

I saw nothing for some time, then a hand with a gun appeared. The Gyndromeda women, the fake ones, entered the room with guns in hand. A couple of them checked each of the men, bending down and placing an index and middle finger on the side of their neck. Two others went to the other door and opened it.

One gentleman was alive, but then the women shot him in unison. It was uncanny how they all moved as one. The two women who checked outside the room came back in. They all looked around as if waiting for instructions.

Mr. Dean entered the room with his own gun in hand, but something was off about him. His cigar was gone, and he moved slowly, almost like a robot. I quickly counted the women. All nine accounted for.

I finally noticed a shadow of someone else standing in the hallway out of my bird's-eye view sight. Unfortunately, it wasn't enough of a shadow for me to tell if it was a man or woman. Then the shadow moved back as if whoever it was sensed me.

Dean looked up to the ceiling first, then all the women. I felt a knot in my stomach. The mind control tech was real, and it was back. A new puppet master had emerged. They all stared up at the ceiling, scanning and listening.

I had two guns, but not my omega-gun. There were ten of them, and an unknown person who I didn't know if they were armed. Also, right next door was a storehouse filled with an army of corporate samurai soldiers, so if, by some miracle, I could get the drop on the mind-control zombies, I wouldn't get past the army. No real Gyndromeda backup, no proper weapon, no options. The shooting would begin soon and I'd be completely exposed.

I didn't care about killing Mr. Dean at all. I cared a lot about not killing the ladies, who were under the mind-control spell. No good options at all.

Dean and the women raised their guns to the ceiling in unison. Here it comes, I said to myself. But I could still see a piece of the puppet master's shadow at the open door to the inner hallway.

#

I threw the gun so hard, as if I wanted it to break through the wall in the ceiling crawlspace. I don't know what it hit—it was all darkness for me except for my tiny ceiling peephole — but the gun set off an explosion of noise. It was like the sounds of buckets of metal, nails, bolts, and screws falling. The mind-zombies swung their aim to the opposite side of the wall, and let loose with their laser guns.

Crashing through the ceiling wasn't the smartest move, but it was the fastest way down. All I had was one gun, but I made it count. I strafed them with laser fire. That was the best I could do to incapacitate rather than kill. The sound of plopping down on corpses almost made me have a complete germophobic relapse.

The shadow was gone!

I heard someone running away. The ladies and the Dean didn't appreciate my altruism and still tried to kill me with laser-fire as I grabbed another gun to give chase. I immediately stopped, turned and fired at them to stop their barrage, and kicked the open door of the inner hallway shut. And stopped!

My posthumous mentor, Wilford G., had told me that sometimes the bad guy will get away. I had almost forgotten that I was far from alone in this case. I likely saved my own life by not walking through that door to give chase. I'd underestimated NeuroDancer once, despite the warnings from my instincts.

"You lose, Cruz," a bloodied but smiling Mr. Dean said to me from the ground. I didn't know if he'd returned to his true self or was still under "the spell." "You'll never get out of here alive."

I stood up and shot him. "You talk too much," I said. I'd shot him in the shin so the pain would keep him occupied.

"What are you waiting for?" he yelled at me.

I saw moving shadows outside the door to the outer hallway. I sighed. Here comes the corporate soldiers.

"I'm waiting for the spacemen."

The Dean, by day's end, was going to wish I shot him dead.

Nothing could prepare for the feeling. Unnerving, weird, violent, serene. The ceiling broke apart above our heads as an invisible force pulled them up. Pieces of the walls, the desks, doors, then us. It sucked me up into the sky, floating up. As I rose into the sky, I saw the magnitude of what I'd set in motion. Dozens of police heavy cruisers, dozens of hoverdirigibles, and directly above Up-Top flying saucers. The beaming tech of Up-Toppers still amazed us Earthers. They really could levitate any person or thing from the ground into their spaceship hovering above in the sky. Completely illegal, unless the governing Earth authorities granted the permission, which in this case, was the Metropolis Police Department, and they had.

Every patron of the Cat Walk, every suit soldier, the ladies, the former Gentlemen Boys, the real Gyndromeda ladies (who I noticed were all dead), unfortunate pedestrians around the building at the time were sucked up into Interspace Police flying saucers as wide as any large Metropolis megatower.

I saw her.

The person I'd been scanning the sky for. The puppet master. A petite, purple-haired woman dressed in white like an evil angel. Had I seen her before? There was no doubt she knew me by the way she glared at me. Never blinking, never looking away. She stared at me with burning hatred. She tilted her head forward in my direction and mouthed the words: I WILL SEE YOU AGAIN.

I shook my head. We both knew it wasn't true.

Where the pulse blast came from, I didn't know, and probably never would. The ball of yellow light hit her and incinerated her instantly. I heard the explosions first and when I looked around, floating in the air, I saw what looked like drones being shot out of the sky.

My eyes were heavy, and I closed them. I wish I could have said it was over, but only part of it was. The last chapter of the NeuroDancer case had ended, but the sequel case hadn't even begun.

PART SEVEN
We Don't Like Mad Scientists For a Reason

Chapter Thirty-Four
Chief Hub

There was a time when even driving by Metro General Hospital would have triggered one of my OCD episodes. In Metropolis, it was where every potential patient was taken, unless you were wealthy or politically connected. I still had some familiarity with the place from my hovercar racing days. More than a few drivers crashed into a communication or light pole, and this was where the ambulance took them. In my detective days, I'd been a "guest" a few times and here I was again, though I was completely fine. Spacemen had sucked me up into a flying saucer. Their teleporting beam tech wasn't painful at all, and once aboard, the spacemen were very hospitable and even offered me some snacks.

However, the Cat Walk was no longer in existence and neither were most of the surrounding streets. I'd been in the company of the "nice" spacemen, but as my first and second high-profile cases showed me, "not-so-nice" spacemen had lasers that could literally blow up a terrestrial building from space.

The identity of whoever vaporized the woman who wanted to be NeuroDancer's successor might never be known. And I didn't care. If capturing her wasn't possible, then obliterating her and everything in the Cat Walk and around it was the only way to make sure whatever "the device" was would never be possessed by any member of the human race, earthbound or Up-Top. My mission was completed for me by others.

I was taken to the hospital for observation. Those captured by Metro PD, the Council, and the spacemen would be held at non-medical facilities for a lot more than observation and wouldn't be allowed to leave for a long time.

"Are we getting rid of the suit yet?" Chief Hub asked.

He'd strolled into the open door of my hospital room without a sound. Outside my room, they had stationed officers. I'd been lying on top of the bed in all my clothes, with my black hat tilted down over my closed eyes. The plan was to get some shut-eye.

"Not yet," I answered, removing my hat. "Soon though. Is it over?"

"Our plan worked," the chief said.

"Good. Years of waiting and planning, but at least, I didn't have to wait fifty years like Wilford G. to wrap up my ultimate loose-end case."

"Is that why you let him rope you into his obsessed-over Venn case?"

"I helped him because he was my mentor and the Man. And he was right."

"Let him rest in peace."

"That I will. Do we know who she was?"

"Someone does, but not me."

"Chief, what does that mean? You're the head of the largest police force on the planet and have every clearance that exists."

"You'd think so, but the Metro PD is being left out of this one. The main thing is that it's over. No one got the mind-control tech."

"Which was our plan?"

"I'd say you deserve a brief vacation for your troubles."

"Chief, we tried that, remember?"

"Yeah, didn't work out so well for either of us. You got to visit the Middle East, though."

"I'm not leaving Metropolis for a long time. The wife and I will wait until Cruz Jr. and Kat are old enough to get the hell out of the house and start earning some money to pay us. What did my parents-in-law call it—generational dividends?"

"My wife and I waited until all the boys were old enough to join the force."

"You can send your officers home."

"That I will. The doctor has cleared you for release."

"Is there something we don't know about the spacemen's levitation beam? It doesn't cause cancer or sterility or something?"

"Maybe you'll glow in the dark."

"Don't tell Cruz Jr. that. We're finally getting him out of the teleporting ninja phase. I don't want him stalking spacemen and asking them to turn him into a glow-in-the-dark boy."

Chief Hub shook my hand. "Go home, Cruz. The NeuroDancer is over."

The chief had barely left the room when I heard the loud chatting of PJ and a lot more people coming down the hall toward my room.

"Chief, where's Cruz?" I heard PJ ask outside in the hallway.

Chapter Thirty-Five
Face

The crowd coming down the hall wasn't just PJ, but it was an entire army of sidewalk johnnies and sallies. The warehouse headquarters had been closed down and the Liquid Cool officers were back in action thanks to PJ. Phishy was out in the field. Quix was on another job. I had lunch scheduled with Run-Time for the real behind-the-scenes scoop on the Cat Walk affair. One thing with sidewalk johnnies is that they brought their own fun—sandwiches and booze in tiny glasses for all to celebrate the end of the case.

But it wasn't over.

After enough time had passed for conversing, joking around, eating, and drinking, I handed my note to PJ. I told her to read it at the office and that was that. She'd handle everything needed while I was away. When the crowd returned to the office or the streets, I'd be going my own way for some simple, long-overdue, shoe-leather detective work.

#

I haven't seen Face for a while. My wife worked at Eye Candy Image Salon in Paisley Parish. She was the second in command there to the longtime owner, Prima Donna, the Matron Queen of Metropolis fashion. Prima was the one who first introduced me to Face. For Prima to refer business to a bald man definitely meant he was good at something. Image salons didn't want the follicly-challenged anywhere near their business. One doesn't make money off bald people. In premiere salons, hair was what ruled.

He picked the place because I didn't want to go to any establishment connected with me. I hadn't been waiting long when he came in through the door with a black briefcase in each hand. He was wearing a dark turtleneck outfit and flat cap on his bald-as-a-melon head. The diner establishment had private offices on the two floors above. Such places were popular for the business set and were very much like one of my favorite diners, the Wet Cabeza. This place was called the Hole in the Wall Block. A classy, upscale diner where the waiters and waitresses wore uniforms a cut above most places. Food was good, but we didn't come for that. The quirk about these establishments was that food and drink stayed on the dining level only. Above floors were for business. You could order drink service, but that was a separate and extra service.

After tangling with international spies, I thought it funny I was about to use the services of a person who'd fit right into their world. In fact, I really didn't know what Face did for a living.

"What do you do for a living?" I asked him.

"Mortuary services," he replied as we went up the stairs.

I wished I hadn't asked the question. A guy who does perfect disguises for people sounds cool. Fixing up dead people for funeral services doesn't. But with all the mayhem in Metropolis, someone had to attend to all the badly damaged corpses with skills. Face had the skills.

"What will it be this time, Mr. Cruz?" he asked.

Chapter Thirty-Six
The Street Hustler

Every so often, I leisurely drove through the city. No destination in particular, just driving for hours. But when I wanted to get an even better feel of Metropolis, nothing replaced just putting on the aqua shoes, wrapping myself in a nice slicker, and walking. From the street level, the utter magnitude of Metropolis could be perceived, or a fraction of it. The supercity occupied a region nearly twice the size of almost all others in the nation, hence its power.

My Sidewalk Johnny Brigade, through Phishy, was a treasure trove of intel for me. The street often knew things days in advance of any megacorp or government-intelligence gathering division. How they did it, no one could say, but knowledge passed through the street like electricity surging through wires and circuits. If one knew how to tap into the street, learn its players, and make them allies, a private detective could run circles around even the uber-wealthy, thousand-person detective firms in the supercity.

Sidewalk johnnies were worldwide. I had my crew in my part of Metropolis. There were many more in the city, with their own streets and corners. In the light drizzle, I made my way down narrow streets filled with dark-slicked pedestrians with the glowing eyewear, some with neon umbrellas.

Sidewalk johnnies were the happy-go-lucky bunch I worked with. But in this street were the more criminal sidewalk johnnies, or more accurately, street hustlers bordering on street thugs. There was a clear distinction between street hustlers and street gangs, but only the street-wise knew, and you got that from experience.

Hidden under my black slicker, my hand gripped my omega-gun. I wouldn't be going into any future situations without being armed again. Being in a shootout without a gun was one sure-fire way to get a one-way trip to the morgue. I wasn't interested in trying out body bag attire.

The street hustler I was meeting came through many levels of contacts. The street had its own way of communicating info to interested parties. A chain of contacts could be dozens, hundreds, or thousands of people, but the info would always get through. It was better than the post office.

I'd told the street I wanted to know when my "mark" was on the move, and I didn't care what time of day or night. Also, I was willing to pay good money for the tip. Since I was a frequent customer that others on the street could vouch for, my job would get priority. The street rewarded longtime customers, and especially prompt paying ones.

There were parts of Metropolis that really were "neon jungles." Buildings lined with neon edges, glowing light posts, flashing text and video image signs. But all jungles had their animals. The little street hoods sat on a main corner between two large neon lampposts. All wearing hooded slickers, glowing colored glasses, and glowing cigarettes in their mouths. None of them were older than their twenties. At the moment, every eye was on me as I approached them.

Street hustlers had their own inner radar. They could sense fear, danger, and cops. None of those vibes came from me. I stopped and simply waved for one of them to come to me. A younger one popped and walked to me. I handed him a card. He had to pull down his neon glasses to read it, which I thought was stupid because it meant he was wearing it to look tough, not to actually see.

"Follow," he said, and was already three steps ahead going down the street.

I was in the company of a great conversationalist.

#

The more we walked, the darker, grimier, and wetter the landscape got. We were still in the retail section of the district, but whenever the neon signage of the businesses disappeared, it meant whatever goods or services they were providing were none of the public's business. The police couldn't be bothered with these low-life criminal districts unless there were gang shootouts and bodies dropping everywhere on the concrete. Districts such as these had turned keeping a low profile to an art form.

My silent, hooded escort stopped and just pointed. With that, he was gone. I was approaching a lone shadow. I reached inside my slicker and put on my night-glasses that turned night into day. The street hustler was already grinning and pointed to his almost identical pair on his face.

The foot traffic on the street was almost nonexistent. In the distance, I saw other shadows with their own corners staked out. Part-street hustlers, part information-brokers, all of them.

"You're Cruz's guy?" he asked.

"I'm his guy."

My disguise included a black bowl-cut hairdo, mustache, goatee, fake scar across one cheek. Matched well with my black suit, hat, and slicker. Face wanted to give me silver choppers too, but that was a bit much. Regardless, I wouldn't have recognized myself.

I didn't even wait. I pulled out his cash for the information he hadn't even given me yet.

He smiled and took it. "How do you know I have the info he wants?"

"If you don't, he'll come looking for you. And he won't be alone."

"No need for that. Don't want Cruz on my trail. He's not scary and all that, but his friends are, especially the cops."

"What do you have for me to give him?"

"Tell Cruz to hurry. I doubt the man will be there long."

"He's making a run for it?"

"That's what my people say."

"Anyone else looking for him?"

"I haven't had other inquiries, but that doesn't mean anything and all that."

"Cruz, put a tip in there for you. For the next time."

The street hustler looked at the cash bundle more closely. "Tell your man, Cruz, that this is one corner king that welcomes long and mutually productive business relationships. Maybe I'll send him a tip or two to keep my services top of mind."

"He'll appreciate that. Have a good night."

"You too. Stay dry."

Leaving a business deal with a hustler was always the most dangerous time of street work. My hand never left my gun under my slicker. After money and goods had exchanged hands was when the unscrupulous, or stupid, might try a double-cross. But again, I had a solid rep on the street, and even though he didn't know it was me, it extended to intermediaries. I was a frequent customer, paid promptly, and, as the hustler said, had lots of scary friends.

Chapter Thirty-Seven
The Passenger

I was one of the few people in Metropolis who'd seen a part of the supercity locked down twice. That's exactly what they had done as I passed the district on the sky lanes with heavy hovertraffic. Every exit to the district where the Cat Walk used to be was still closed. In the sky was a full-scale "red-and-blue siren party" from the lights of police hovercruisers hovering in the air for miles around. The craft in the air and ground weren't just police, though. I saw people on the ground in hazmat suits. I knew anything inorganic down to the molecule would be thoroughly inspected or destroyed. It was the only way for all the powers of Earth and Up-Top to be sure that the "object" was gone forever.

The safe with my "client" was already at another location but nowhere near my Liquid Cool offices. Quix had been at my side, but warned me. I understood his suspicion. Hologram or not, she was still part of the Council of Corporations.

"She wouldn't bother blowing me up," I said.

"I'm glad you're so certain about that."

"To the Council, we're not worth the trouble, the effort, or even the energy. Remember, Quix, our lowly feet have actually touched the ground of Free City."

He laughed.

Before I turned her on, I'd already expected what was about to happen. I pushed the button and expected nothing. No Gem AI appeared. We could hear gears grinding, then came smoke, then the large disk burst into flames.

"Interesting," I said. "A self-destructing holo-projector."

"More than a little nothing."

"The Council doesn't leave their tech around for us lower species to get their paws on."

Madame Gem and her Gem AI wanted to help me destroy the "device," but turning over its creator was another matter. It would all start over again, even worse. Everything done would have been for naught. The Council was not about to help me stop the next chapter of NeuroDancer before it started. But I'd set my plan in motion years before.

#

Metropolis was a supercity that was once been a megacity. We called that original center Old Metro. It was the main stomping ground of my posthumous mentor Wilford G. Like the greater city; every nation, language, and dialect represented on the planet, just different ones from those I was accustomed to.

One had to marvel at good street intel when it all came together. My journey began with Phishy, then to other sidewalk johnnies in my part of the city, then an endless chain to my final street hustler to hand over my wad of cash.

My Let It Ride taxi descended from the air to take a space near a smallish motel in a heavily Polish speaking area. For some reason, there were a lot of dogs running around and I saw more than one cat in a window in a residential tower across the street. Dogs and cats. I wonder if they had the isopods crawling around too.

The hotel was old. Fake palm trees bordered the walkway to the main office and the ground-floor rooms looked ancient. I never trusted places where, when you opened the door, you were outside. I didn't want any unwanted strangers knocking on my door or stray animals peeing on it. Being a street detective didn't mean I lived in the gutter and didn't have class.

For the moment, I was on a typical stake-out. I had the driver-side window down just a crack to hear voices of people hanging out or walking down the street. Music played in the distance from one of the residential towers. I leaned back and got comfortable.

I had it all planned. My Let It Ride hovercab from Run-Time. My disguise. I made my call. A male voice answered.

"Your hovercab is here outside."

"You're early," he said.

"Traffic's light, sir."

"I'll be out. Almost done packing."

"I'm right outside, sir."

\#

The man only had a single suitcase. He didn't even let me get out to put it in the trunk. All he did was a gesture for me to open it, and he did the duty himself. I let him get in and comfortable before we ascended for the hovertraffic freeways.

"What's your name?" he asked.

"My name's Mr. Incom," I answered.

"How long have you been with the cab company?"

"Been with the company fifteen years."

He grunted to himself, satisfied, and rested his face on the back seat as close to the window as he could get. The man wore dark clothes with his hood tightly around his head. His face was unremarkable—like an Average Joe. Even his glasses were average and forgettable.

The freeways in Old Metro were wider but always had far less hovertraffic. If I'd been born or lived here, I wouldn't go anywhere near Metropolis Proper. At the moment, there were more hovertrucks visible than vehicles.

The megatowers were smaller in this part of the city but possessed all the neon flash as the rest of Metropolis. A police cruiser raced by in the opposite direction of the sky freeway. I'd glance into my rearview mirror to see what was behind me, but also to catch a look at my passenger's sad face against the window.

"How long do you want to drive for, sir?" I asked.

"Until you run out of fuel."

"That's a long time, sir."

"It's all I ask. Since this will be my last. My last of everything. I want to sit here and enjoy it."

"Happy to do so, sir."

The back wasn't bright enough to see clearly, but the man looked to be crying. My preconceived notions of the man were so far away from what I'd held in my head over the years.

"You're trying to understand me," he said after a long silence in the vehicle. We'd been traveling about twenty minutes but were still in the same district of Old Metro.

"Not really."

"Is Incom a real person?"

"Just an alias I use sometimes. Doesn't mean anything, really. Pulled it out of the air one day."

"Did you think I'd call?"

"Didn't matter to me either way."

I heard his loud sigh as he stared out the window again.

"I've had over five years to figure out who you are," I said after a moment.

"Did you?"

"Yes, and no. But you know what that means. Your whole life is an alias."

"You think I'm a criminal."

"I don't know what you are, but creating a mind-control device should be criminal. Did you create it for yourself, or was the plan to sell to the highest bidder?"

"You think I'm a criminal? We created it. A group of us."

"MK Ultra."

The man's head lifted from the window. "Excuse me?" The look on his face and the way he reacted made me think the phrase meant something different to him than what I knew it was.

"A walk down history from a former client of mine," I said.

He slowly leaned back.

"Did I say something wrong?"

"No. I mean, most people don't know the history, know any history. Forget it. I was not expecting a cab driver to say that. A program from centuries ago. In a way, you're right, though. We created our own version. A group of us."

I hadn't asked for his life's story, but I felt it coming. It was like the man was giving his last confession to a priest.

"There were forty of us at the start," he said. "Scientists from many specialties. It may surprise you, but we stumbled upon creating the device. Like most inventions, an accident. But we quickly realized what we had done and spent a considerable amount of time discussing our course of action."

"Keep it for yourselves or sell it."

"You're under a false assumption. We didn't create the device for a megacorporation and have it stolen by an individual. The device was for the government. We were under contract. But its invention was an accident. We were working on another application."

"What application?"

"If I told you, you'd laugh. How something so innocuous could become the device. We set out to help people. I laugh at that today. No need to tell you what our original intent was."

"What happened after you invented it?"

"What was inevitable? Members of the team stole it first. Then a megacorp stole it from them, killing many of us doing so. Then we found out another person stole it. I knew it was her the first time I saw her at a concert. A singer-dancer had our device and there was nothing to be done."

I glanced in the rear-view mirror to see him staring up at me.

"What did you do then?" I asked.

"I disappeared. My remaining colleagues did not. They tried to reason with our employers, and they disappeared."

"Couldn't they build another device?"

"No, they couldn't. I'm sure they were tortured horribly by our employers and others to realize that. Their mutilated bodies turned up at regular intervals until I knew I was the only one left. I'm the only one who knows how we invented it."

"You could become the wealthiest man in the universe."

"No, I couldn't. That was never a possibility. I'm a scientist, not a criminal. We—I cared about the work, not financial compensation. I didn't know where to keep myself alive. But all I could do was hide and watch."

"Watch for what?"

"Watch you."

"You've been keeping up on my cases."

"I get an email digest of everything having to do with you and your detective agency weekly."

"Weekly? I don't make news weekly."

"You'd be surprised. Most of it is recycled information, but there is something. I knew I had to wait until the right time."

"Like someone finding NeuroDancer's device."

"That was my only chance to escape. While all the attention was on retrieving it, I'd made my move. Get another new identity and escape somewhere where no one knew me and I could live off-grid till my dying days. But the world isn't as big as you think when you don't have money."

"So true."

"I thought I had more time. But the device was found and destroyed. You were at the center of it all. I thought I had more time. I'm not what you expected, am I?"

"I always keep an open mind when it comes to crazy maniacs."

"No fangs, horns, or the cloven hooves you'd expect."

"Funny you say that. I actually had a psycho with fangs try to shoot me. A board room, no less. Got himself kicked him out the three-hundredth-floor window for his effort."

"You've gone to far more exciting board meetings than I've ever been to."

"Council of Corporations."

"Of course. My chief tormentors." His face was once again resting on the window as he stared out at the sights zipping by outside.

"Your group should never have done it."

"It was an accident, I said. We had no evil intent."

"What did you think would happen with such a device?"

"I was naïve."

"Not the word I'd use. More like mad."

"I didn't know."

"Why invent such a thing and throw it into the world?"

"That's a simple question. So we could say we did."

"That's no answer. Why would you invent such an inevitably evil thing with no regard to how it would be used?"

"The scientists who invented the first atomic bomb asked themselves the same thing."

"This is potentially far worse than that."

"You mean I am."

"You're a real moron for such a smart man."

"And now I'm going to die."

"Is that your plan?"

"Why did you track me?"

"I could ask, why did you call me?"

"How did you know? Tell me that one thing."

"NeuroDancer didn't create the device. She was smart too, in her evil way, but she was still a singer-dancer. She got it from someone else. That meant an inventor. If I were her and there was an inventor who could create another device, what would I do?"

"Kill them."

"Yes. Or keep them on hand to maintain the original device. But first you find them."

"But you couldn't find someone who doesn't exist."

"You don't exist to me, but you exist to others who know who you are. A top-secret scientist in either government or megacorp conglomeration. As I expanded my network of associates over the years, I was able to expand my search for potential scientists. You got your emails about me. I got emails about dead and missing scientists. I couldn't search confidential or classified circles, but others could on my behalf. They didn't even have to know why, just be thorough."

My passenger nodded. "That's how you found me. You learned of one dead colleague and that led you to another, then the rest, and me."

"The one unaccounted for."

"Very creative of you. Must have taken years."

"It did. Then I put out my notices."

"Why would you ever think I'd respond to such a notice?"

"If you were being hunted, you'd still keep yourself informed. Corporate news. Government news. Here and around the world, and Up-Top. My only hope was to find a piece of information related to the device and that only one of its scientists would know."

"And the people who funded it."

"That couldn't be helped. I needed to get your attention. Get you to make the first move and once you found out it was from me, you'd reach out."

"Very risky."

"Risky for both of us. But as you said, you have no money. The device destroyed, and all the hunters would devote all their attention to finding the creator of the device."

"I so wish I could go back in time," the man said as he began sobbing. "You have to help me. I have no one. No one at all."

"But there remains a problem."

"The knowledge of the device in my brain. If I can convince you that there is no possibility of it ever being created again. If I could do that?"

"I've thought about this a long time. What would I do if I ever met you?"

"Kill me. Is that what you've been fantasizing about?"

"It's no fantasy. Do you know what's happening right now to the district they found the device in?"

"I know. I watch the news."

"They vaporized the woman who wanted to be the next NeuroDancer with all her powers."

"You're a good guy, though."

"Aren't you the bad guy?"

"No. It's more complicated than that."

"I'm not into scientific amorality when the lives of my family, my city, and my planet are at stake. You are a walking world war, you are."

"I've had years to think about me, too. I understand the stakes. I'm not good or bad. I'm just a man, a single solitary man who hasn't been able to sleep for years, terrified that I'd be snatched out of my bed by forces who also don't consider themselves good or evil. I have what they want and they'll keep me alive and torture me to get what they want. To live, I can never create another device. That's the bargain. I want to live. Can you help, Mr. Cruz? Please help me."

PART EIGHT
Operation Starlight

Chapter Thirty-Eight
Officer Break and Caps

6:30 a.m.

In my Buzz Town business tower on Circuit Circle, I was like any sidewalk johnny, corner king, or street gangster. I knew my turf better than the back of my hand—every floor, every hallway turn, every sound, which is why I was always content walking around without bodyguards. The temporary warehouse base was gone, and I was back in my Liquid Cool offices. But I didn't come out of the elevator on the 100th floor alone. Flash was with me, but not as muscle. Besides giving back his loaner hovercab, he'd man the front office until PJ arrived. It was a rare day when I got to the office before PJ, and this was one of those days.

However, I had my first scheduled visitors for the day and they were already waiting outside the office door.

Officer Break and Officer Caps—who I privately called Ebony and Ivory without their knowledge—stood in the hallway clad in their Metro PD silver-and-black body-armored uniforms with the word "PEACE" in big bold white letters on their chests.

I called the two veterans officers my "buddies" because we had a history that went back to my first days as a detective. Buzz Town and Rabbit City (where I lived) were both part of their beat, so they were literally our local cops. While most policemen couldn't wait to get off beat work for Homicide, Vice, Sex Crimes, White Collar, or anything else, they both preferred the grunt work. It was early morning for most Metropolitans, but for the street cop on duty, there was no such thing.

Flash knew them too, like most Let It Ride employees. Run-Time was a major donor to the Police Charity Fund. He greeted the officers before they turned their attention to me.

"Cruz, what's with the new clothes?" Officer Break asked.

"Don't you start too. Don't you like the new look?"

"No."

"Caps, help me out here."

"I don't like it either," Officer Caps said.

"Cruz, Cruz, Cruz. You leave Metropolis and we read about you in the news. You come back here and there you are in the center of the news," Break said.

"Playing with spacemen as an entire building is obliterated from space. And there's Cruz," Caps said.

"It's not my fault that crazy maniacs won't behave themselves in my company. Officers, you said the chief had something for me."

Officer Break pulled the disk from a chest pocket. "The chief said you'd want to see this."

"What is it?"

"Internal surveillance tapes of the establishment formerly known as the Cat Walk," Break said.

I took the disk stick. "Thank the chief for me. I'll watch it right away."

"You might be able to thank him yourself today."

"What's the occasion?"

"We'll let the chief answer that," Break said, "and one word of warning, Cruz. Be on your best behavior."

"I am intrigued, Officers," I said.

"You have a good day, sir."

The grinning police officers strolled past us for the elevators.

I looked at Flash. "Let's open up and get some work done."

"How much are you paying me again?"

"You've been hanging around PJ too much, or is Phishy to blame?"

Chapter Thirty-Nine
The Liquid Cool Crew

6:40 a.m.

I'd wondered what happened to the real Gyndromeda women. The plan to waltz into the Cat Walk to find the device was primarily theirs. As I stood at my desk sipping my silk coffee and watching the vid disk play on my tabletop screen, I learned the women had not abandoned me after all.

The women in their evening dresses had gathered and made their way to the subterranean elevators. Who knows how long it took for them to infiltrate the criminal base of the Gentlemen Boys? I was told it was the life of spies. Secret identities. Agents, double-agents, an odd triple-agent on decades'-long deep cover. I surely couldn't live a fake life like them, but there were plenty of others who would relish working the dark world of megacorp espionage.

The sad part was that the Gentlemen Boys knew the women weren't loyal, longtime employees in their posh evening dresses. When they exited the elevator, that's when the women pulled their guns, provocatively hidden on their bodies—thigh-high gun holsters under their dresses or from their bra—and gunned down two bodyguards. But the Gentlemen Boys were waiting for them around the corner. They jumped out and mowed them down with some nasty laser rifles. It was painful to watch. One espionage organization had literally eliminated their rivals. The women would never know, but I knew that the Gentlemen Boys got what they deserved not too much later that day. The Dean's fate was probably worse than death.

I had no illusions about Gyndromeda. If they were working with the Council of Corporations, they likely were bad guys, too. But they were my bad guys, and they were living up to our bargain to come to my aid. The act cost them their lives. The very operation cost them their lives. That was the world of espionage in the shadowy universe of secret organizations.

Flash, drinking his coffee, stood right next to me. "Rough, Cruz," Flash said to me in a sad tone. "Walked right into the murder ambush."

"But I got them to gun down themselves."

"Gun down themselves? How?"

"Words."

"Words?" He smiled. "Criminals need to watch out for you, Cruz. I thought you only gunned down criminals with your gun. You can make them shoot each other with words, too. I'd say I'd like to see that trick, but I really don't."

We heard the bell of the front door opening.

"Who's in here!" PJ's voice. "I'm armed with big weapons! I'm talking about my bionic arms and not my two laser rifles in my hands. So stay where you are!"

I looked at a laughing Flash and said, "My employees."

#

Flash spent some catching up with PJ, but had to get back to his real job. Then the French retro-disco was playing with PJ's bionic fingers typing at hyper-speed. I stepped out of my inner office to behold the scene for myself. One, two, three young interns sitting in my office waiting area on the purple couches also tapping away. They were nicely dressed and wearing tan fedoras.

"PJ, who are these people?"

The kids stopped and looked at me, smiling. They stood up and immediately walked to me to each shake my hand.

"Nice to meet you, Mr. Cruz."

"A pleasure, Mr. Cruz."

"Glad to be here, Mr. Cruz."

I looked at PJ behind her workstation, behind its metal barrier.

"They are the Liquid Cool college interns."

"Why are they wearing tan fedoras?"

"Speaking of tan fedoras, where's yours? We spoke about this already. You are upsetting the company brand. You are confusing the customer. If management will not maintain the brand, then its staff will."

"I am wearing my black fedora, but when I do return to my tan fedora, I don't want any other people in this office wearing tan fedoras."

"That's better. Team, our plan is working. Keep wearing your hats every day. It's called subliminal suggestive marketing. The target audience, in this case one person, sees the product all the time on model-like interns and at some point must comply and copy."

"PJ, when did Liquid Cool get interns in the office?"

"They started when we had our warehouse operations."

"PJ, how much are paying these college interns of yours?"

"Mine? You're their employer. I'm just the manager. But they're interns. They're here for college credit."

"What does that mean?"

"College credit means the college pays them."

"Why would a college pay them to work at my agency?"

"Cruz, get with the times. That's what an internship is. Colleges pay students to get on-the-job experience. Internships are a big deal. You have to be approved. I applied last year, and they approved us this year." She gave me a big smile.

"So all those interns you had working at the warehouse and these kids here are being paid for by the college, not me?"

"C'est exact!" she said.

"That's correct," I translated. I smiled, then turned to the kids. "Welcome to the Liquid Cool Detective Agency."

The front door was thrown open. "Cruz!" Phishy yelled as he jumped in.

I ran back into my inner office when I saw him begin his chicken-dance.

Chapter Forty

Phishy

My main appointment would arrive soon. Officers Break and Caps were right. The chief was on his way but with even bigger VIPs. PJ had gone through all our priority messages, and it was the first one she called out to me. Soon she'd have my desk flooded with messages in "hot" pile, "hold" pile, "hell no" pile, and "miscellaneous" priority order.

When Phishy finished his socializing with PJ and the interns, I pulled him into my inner office.

"Phishy, I got a big project for you."

"Project?" I had his attention.

I sat behind my desk, and he was still following me. "Phishy, are you going to sit on my lap? Get on the other side and sit down."

He laughed and ran around to a seat in front of my desk. When he was down, I held up my index finger.

"Phishy, I need you to focus."

"Focus?" His look was a combination of concern and curiosity.

"I'm going to give you a tablet. You'll read the message, then push the button."

"Push the button?"

"Yes, Phishy."

"Why?"

"It will delete the message from the device."

He looked worried.

"Phishy, it's a 'your-eyes-only' document. This will be a secret mission."

"Secret mission?" He was smiling.

"Read, delete, and run. Read the message. Delete the message. Run out of this office and secretly get your mission done."

"I'm a secret agent!"

"No, Phishy, you are a Liquid Cool associate on a secret project. But it's a secret."

"Oh, yeah. I won't tell anyone."

"Secret, Phishy. Means only you can know."

"Yeah, I got it. I won't tell anyone."

After I turned it on and opened the document, I handed him the tablet from my desk. He had the screen close to his face, as if he was preventing someone else from reading over his shoulder. He read as I watched. I just sat there. Why was he still reading?

"Phishy!"

"I'm almost done."

"Why are you still reading? It's two sentences, not an epic fantasy anthology. What are you doing?"

"I'm reading it, so I don't forget it."

"It's two sentences."

"Okay, I got it." He looked up, smiling, while he reached out to hand me the tablet.

"Are you forgetting something, Phishy?"

"I am?"

"Read, delete, run."

"Oh, yeah." He pulled the tablet back and pushed the on-screen button. He watched the on-screen effects as the document was "shredded" and "vaporized." "I like that, Cruz. You have new software."

"Yes, thanks to PJ."

Phishy sat there, looking at me. I sat there looking at him. I liked Phishy, but these were the antics I had to deal with.

"Phishy, aren't you supposed to be doing something?"

"Am I?"

"Read, delete, run. We did number one and two already."

"Oh, yeah!" He jumped up from his chair, laughing. "I'm off for my secret mission, Cruz."

"Secret means not telling anyone, Phishy."

"You got it, Cruz."

Phishy ran out of my inner office. However, before he left the offices, I heard him being Phishy again.

"PJ, I'm on a secret mission!" he yelled.

"Phishy!"

He was gone out the main door.

Chapter Forty-One
The Mayor

When I was on the illegal hovercar racing circuit, I never placed even in the top ten percent—always in the top twenty percent. No one ever paid attention to that second tier, but that was all I wanted. Those in the top ten percent had to deal with the drama, racing politics, money temptations, the crime world, and the unrelenting pressure of staying at the top, which caused more than a few to crack up on the circuit or sadly even commit suicide. But those of us in the next tier were just as good as them. We just didn't have the drive, or like me, were smart enough to know we didn't want the hassle. We just loved the speed and the fun of racing. They could have all the rest. Both the top tenth and next tier were better drivers than the other eighty percent on the circuit. That meant than we all were better drivers than all of Metropolis with its fifty million people plus. I'd never get a trophy, but I always was a winner.

Liquid Cool would never be the top detective agency in Metropolis. That distinction would be for the booshy, private investigation megacorps with offices across the globe and Up-Top. Some wealthy clients and other megacorps wouldn't think of hiring a detective firm with only one principal. Some wouldn't go near an agency that hadn't been around for at least a decade or two, or was a generation firm that had existed decades or centuries, which in Metropolis were many. But I'd already made a mark in the city, which most of those legacy firms could never say.

However, I quickly told anyone that you had to work your butt off to get to even that second racing tier. My national vocational listing before becoming a street detective was "laborer." Most laborers were lazy. I'd be the first to agree. But not me. I'd always go the extra mile to achieve. I'd go another two miles. Few could out-work me. That's how I got started in the detective business to begin with. I walked the streets, megatower to megatower, floor by floor, office by office, to get new business.

There was another needed ingredient, though. I needed to get there first. Many wondered how I did it so often, but I was always like that. I hung up my illegal hovercar racing shoes to become the best hovercar restorer out there and I did, even though the pros in the business were twenty, thirty, forty years older than me. I was good and fast, but I got to things first. Any latest gadget, paint color, accessory, tech, I always knew about before the others because I got there first. When I did my shoe-leather soliciting for business as a new detective, what I needed was for people to take a chance on me. The only way that was going to happen was if I knew the case, and solved it, before I even got it. That's really how I got on the map. One happy client told his friends. She told all her friends, they told all theirs and the rest was history. Clients came to me. It'd been years since I had to do shoe-leather soliciting again. But I did it before and could do it again, if I had to.

When my seven a.m. appointment strolled into my Liquid Cool offices, I already knew what it was about because I'd already been there first. The world focused on the mind-control device. But this case was never just about the "device." To really end the case, it would ultimately turn to its creator. Madame Gem and Gem AI thought they were the only ones who knew who he was. They were wrong.

#

7:00 a.m.

The door opened, and the show began.

The office's security lights flashed red. One corporate soldier, then another, stepped in wearing dark shades with their dark suits. I gave PJ the signal, and she temporarily turned off the visual alarms so there were no more flashing red lights on the ceiling. Our scanning arch embedded in the main doorway alerted us to weapons and cyborgs. Both of them looked at me, PJ, the college interns, and around the main office. One stepped in further and looked into my inner office, then he whispered into his palm communicator.

In came the mayor of Metropolis with a full entourage of staffer sand aides. Mayor Likegate had been Metropolis's mayor for over a decade now. He was always the slickster-in-a-suit—black hair, clean-shaven, pearly teeth so shiny that you could bounce a laser beam off of them. I stayed away from politics as much as I could. That was my best friend, Run-Time's, specialty. However, I'd had my run-ins with the mayor over the years, both good and bad. And, of course, his eye immediately caught the photo of himself with me on the wall in the waiting area where the interns were working.

PJ called it my "Wall of Fame." Framed pictures of me with famous clients and VIPs, including the one with me and the mayor. PJ entertained waiting clients with a picture tour down memory lane. I had to be a legit detective, they'd say. I was shaking hands with the mayor of the supercity.

Like any political creature, he knew I was watching him looking at the picture of us on the wall, turned around, and smiled at me.

"I almost didn't recognize you in the new suit, Mr. Cruz," he said. He walked to me with his entourage right behind him as if they were all attached to each other with invisible string.

"Good to see you, Mayor," I said as we shook hands.

"I knew we'd be seeing each other soon."

"Oh, Mr. Mayor, don't neglect meeting my Liquid Cool staff. Current and future voters, all of them."

That look came over his face, like when I waved a wad of cash in front of Phishy. I said the magic word "voter" and it was as if I'd hypnotized him. He introduced himself, smiling and laughing and shaking hands with PJ (who later kicked me when no one was looking) and the three college interns.

Then came the stories. Politicians always had some story, often ending with a moral, witty or fake profound saying. They had one for every day of the year. I'd always imagined that they had memorized them before they left home each morning. His entourage of staffers, aides, and even his two suit soldiers were hanging on his every word. I could have thrown up on my new black suit.

Then the "grown-ups" entered the room. The Feds came in next, dressed in black suits. As I watched the seven of them, I looked down at my own identical black suit and instantly became less enamored with it. Another Fed came in by the name of Pike, who I hadn't seen in years. Chief Hub came in afterward on his own.

"Cruz," he greeted. "Got my tape?"

"Thanks, Chief. Wished it had turned out differently for them."

"You say that now," he said. "People like them. Friend today, enemy tomorrow."

"Mr. Pike, isn't it?"

"Yes, Mr. Cruz. Nice suit."

I said nothing.

"Everyone, we'll all be meeting in Mr. Cruz's office," the mayor announced. "Won't be long."

Any politician that said those words "won't be long" always met the opposite. But his entourage knew that better than me.

Chapter Forty-Two
X-Branch

The mayor and Pike took turns with the useless small talk. We were obviously waiting for at least one other person. When one of the mayor's security guards opened the door of my inner office, I knew the person had arrived. On cue, the chief rose from his chair and walked to my lounge area to grab an extra one to set in front of my desk.

He introduced himself only as "X." Another black suit, black shirt, black shoes wearing government bureaucrat. The suit fit him nicely, but his balding fat head flowed out from his collar. He wasn't a bureaucrat. He was much more. I could tell by the body language of deference all the other men showed him from the moment he stepped into the room.

"Any coffee or tea?" I asked. He held up his hand to object. "They didn't want anything either."

"Shall we get started?" the mayor asked.

We all got comfortable again in our chairs.

"Do you have any idea why we might be here, Mr. Cruz?" Pike asked.

"No," I replied. "I'm intrigued by Mr. X, though. What division do you work for?"

"You wouldn't know it," the man said.

"Is it X as in X-Branch?"

The man's eyes narrowed as he stared at me. He glanced at Pike and the chief first, then the mayor. A smirk hung on the mayor's face.

"How does this man know of X-Branch? Or is he guessing in the dark?" Mr. X asked.

"X-Branch is the city's own secret intelligence division."

"The mayor of Metropolis didn't learn of it until his second term. The chief of police only because he has the highest clearance and needed to know. How would you, a civilian, know?"

"I was a police intern."

"Police interns don't have security clearances. No, Mr. Cruz, you need to do better than that."

"When I was a police intern, my mentor was Compstat Connie."

"The now-retired head of the Metro PD CIC. Yes, Ms. Connie would share that with her star mentee. Mr. Cruz, I must implore you never—"

"You don't have to read me the official secrets acts. The chief can attest to my ability to keep secrets."

"Yes, you're right. Take no offense."

I was still not happy that the Crime Information Center (CIC) of the Metro Police Department was no long run by my former, very much alive and kicking mentor, Compstat Connie.

"No, sir, it's far more than that." The man clasped his hands in his lap and leaned back in his chair. "X-Branch currently is a kind of United Nations of intelligence services. A long time ago, a scientist contacted the National Patent's Office. I will not tell you what he invented, but I will tickle your imagination a bit by saying it would have changed everything on this planet."

"Like hovertech," I said. "But I suspect in a malevolent rather than benevolent way."

"That potential was inevitable. The scientist never got to register his patent. He never got to do anything. He disappeared along with his invention and business."

"Who killed him, Mr. X? Is that what you were about to say?"

"That is unimportant and unknowable, so far removed in time from the events. The intelligence services on Earth and off-world felt that, for the collective good of humanity, we should monitor all new and potentially new inventions in the world. Not an exact science, but the attempt through an informal association of nations and off-world colonies."

"I thought you were a professional organization. Sounds like you're nothing more than a members-only club for the globalist intelligentsia. Hold on a minute."

I pressed the intercom button to PJ's desk outside. "PJ?"

"What?" her voice answered.

"I used the word 'intelligentsia' in a real sentence. Isn't that French?"

"Non. That's a Russian word," her voice echoed.

"Okay, well, it still counts."

"You're getting smarter. Smart businesspeople have big vocabularies."

"They do. Bye." I hung up. The men in the room were, of course, far from amused. "What can the Liquid Cool Detective Agency do for you, gentlemen?" I asked.

"The scientist is 'on the market,'" X announced.

"What does that mean?" I asked, sitting up in my chair. "What scientist?"

"I'm using small words, Mr. Cruz. The meaning is clear. What scientist might we be talking about?" X said.

I stood from my chair and walked to my bay window. The sun was actually peeking through the overcast sky.

"This never ends," I said, looking at the chief when I turned back around.

"I know," he said.

"How do you know this?" I asked X.

"How do you think, Mr. Cruz? Certain unknown parties are 'selling' him to the highest bidder. The deepest, darkest, most secret criminal channels are on fire with the news."

"Selling him? Selling a person, a human being? I know I'm a G-rated kind of guy, but isn't that dark even for us?"

"G-rated, you?" the Mayor said with a laugh. "You shoot people."

"I'm a licensed private detective, and I never shot or killed anyone who didn't deserve it. Why are you upset by that now? You gave me an award, and isn't that you manhandling me for the cameras in the picture outside on my wall?" With the mayor sufficiently silenced, I returned my attention to Mr. X.. "I can't believe you're telling me the scientist inventor of the device we worked so hard to erase from existence is 'on the market.' Like he's some inanimate object," I said.

"On the criminal market, you can sell anything. They still sell human beings on planet Earth, despite it being a crime in every nation on the planet and off-world. Criminals do as they please, as evil and dark as they wish," X responded.

"I appreciate you all telling me this and upsetting me, but what does this have to do with me?"

The mayor stood from his chair. "Mr. Cruz, we are here to hire you to take no action. We know you'd find out, and that's why we came here to tell you preemptively. But there are forces far greater than the both of us handling this."

"Why would you think I'd do something?" I asked.

"You have a reputation."

"Reputation. You make it sound like I'm stumbling around jumping into trouble. I'm a licensed private detective and got involved in this business because Ms. NeuroDancer came here. She came to my offices. I didn't go looking for her. The crazy maniac villainess hired me. I got involved again because the Council of Corporations hired me."

"Okay, we got the message," the mayor said. "Clients hired you. You went out and detected. We're here. Clients to hire you, and we're hiring you to do nothing."

"But what would I do?"

"Do nothing?" the mayor repeated.

"I wouldn't do anything because there's nothing for me to do."

"We'll pay your fee outside," the mayor said.

"It's your money to burn."

Pike, the chief, and Mr. X all stood from their chairs too.

The Chief just looked at me with a smirk. "Aren't you going to ask how much we're paying you?"

"I'm sure it'll be fair," I said.

"I will be far more than fair," Mr. X said.

"With all of you here, it must be a huge operation. What's it called?"

"Operation Starlight involved the authorities from Earth and off-world. Do not intervene," X said. "That name I gave you is also classified."

"I know. Official secrets act."

The men simply turned and walked to the door. No shaking hands or goodbyes. I followed them out into the main area. The mayor's entourage had been sitting on the floor, working on their mobile phones and collapsible tablets. They got to their feet as the mayor walked to PJ behind her desk and handed her a card.

"Full payment."

A smiling PJ stood to take the plastic card. "Thank you, sir. Do you need a receipt?"

"Send it when you can. Mayor of the City of Metropolis. You have my contact details."

Politicians, Feds, police, and entourage filed out of my office. I walked to PJ's desk and touched the buttons so that the feeds of the surveillance cameras showed on her monitors.

"Isn't your computer at your desk working?" she asked. "Your domain. This is my domain."

I watched them get on the elevators and planned to keep watching as they made their way out of the building.

"What did they hire you for?" PJ asked me.

"To do nothing."

"What? What kind of case is that?"

"It's a ruse. They really came here to find out if I'd get involved."

"And, will you?"

"Of course, I will."

"Do they know that?"

"Of course, they do."

"What did they pay you for then?"

"PJ, people like this throw around money all the time. They don't care."

"Well, money is money. It goes into the bank account and there will be no refunds."

Chapter Forty-Three
Mr. Seraff

"What are you up to, Cruz?" PJ asked as she popped into the doorway of my private office.

"Why do you ask?" I said from behind my desk on my computer.

"You came into the office before me this morning. You sent Phishy out on a secret mission. We had the mayor and the chief of police here and that strange man. Guess who's coming later?"

"Another surprise guest?"

"Guess?"

"I'm not good at guessing, PJ."

"They don't live on Earth and fly around in flying saucers."

"Spacemen? Spacemen are coming here? Who?"

"You know who. He's been here before."

#

I called him the Spaceman, but his name was Mr. Seraff. All Up-Top people were space people. Mr. Seraff was born in the space colonies, as opposed to the Lunar Colonies or Mars. He strolled into the office in his typical all-white outfit. I always suspected the people Up-Top dressed in white just to be the opposite of us, Metropolitans. However, he came with his own entourage of other spacemen.

He was with Interpol, or they reported to him. Back in the day, the International Crime Police Organization (they dropped the Criminal from their name after a major scandal) was always handicapped because they could never supersede the authority of any country and had to be asked in. But when humans launched off Earth to populate space stations and lunar colonies, Interpol became the Interspace Police Organization. We had hover-vehicles; they had real spaceships. We had lasers; they could vaporize a building with a laser blast from orbit. Interpol were the police from Up-Top, Up-Top's FBI and CIA all rolled into one. Their authority superseded the city police and the Feds on Earth.

Mr. Seraff sat down in a guest chair, facing me, after I heard him share some pleasant conversation with PJ.

I shook his gloved hand. When we first met, I'd shaken his naked hand and with the lack of actual muscle strength, it was clear he was born in zero gravity.

"Mr. Seraff, what brings you to our blue planet?"

"I missed your sense of humor, Mr. Cruz."

"I thought I might tell you a story."

"Was your agency involved in the Alpha Ville business?"

"The Cat Walk, the Gentleman Boys, Gyndromeda. The NeuroDancer device. The death of the person hoping to be the next NeuroDancer. The Mayor, Chief, Mr. Pike, and Mr. X already stopped by. They wanted to find out if you were going to stay out of it all."

In less than ten seconds, he let me know he knew everything. "Mr. Seraff, I'm eager to hear your story."

"Let's move to your waiting area, away from the windows."

As I stood, I noticed something from the corner of my eye. I looked to see a real flying saucer hovering outside the bay window of my office. Great! The media would be snooping around the building soon if they stayed too long.

#

We sat in adjacent plush chairs in the lounge area corner of my office. The flying saucer had gone, so I felt relaxed again. But Seraff's tone was always relaxing. To me, he was straightforward. He held things back, but he didn't play games. As an off-worlder, he frankly didn't care about the machinations between people, agencies, and organizations of Earth. I appreciated that we Earthers all looked alike to him, but we thought the same of all spacemen, especially in their shiny white outfits.

"I'd say Mr. X left things out," he continued.

"Like what?"

"Starlight."

"What about their Operation Starlight?"

Seraff grinned. "Ironic they'd name this current operation by the same name. The nation that created this mind-control device named the project Starlight. I know the name was previously familiar to you."

"I knew the name, but no context. I was guessing."

"Then an excellent guess on your part."

"A nation, not one of the megacorps?"

"More precisely, an administration of a nation that is no longer in power. And before you get worried, that former administration no longer exists. The incoming administration saw to that, and before they could enjoy their good fortune, Starlight was stolen by one of those megacorps you alluded to."

"And NeuroDancer stole it from them."

"A very industrious woman. Exceptional singer and dancer too. Most Earth singers can't sing even a basic chord, lots of lip-syncing. She could sing, play real music instruments, dance, and was a tri-athlete which most people don't know."

"Also, an exceptional crazy maniac who wanted to 'rule the world.' Her words, not mine."

"That is all in the past, along with her device. What I can't piece together is how you could possibly find out the project name without knowing its existence?"

"I didn't. Any name that I came across in my deep search of anyone and anything related to her I publicized on the same dark Net. Someone always responds to an inquiry. Most is nonsense. But it was how people reacted to the simple posting of 'starlight.' That led me down a new path of investigation. Soon I found my way to the world of scientists with services for sale.

"Mr. X told me about an incident with the National Patent Office."

"Yes, that's all true. The members of this nation tried to sell outright the device back then and specifically used its name."

"They tried to sell the device on the dark net?"

"Yes."

"How is that possible?"

"Mr. Cruz, if you've spent any time in the virtual universe, you'll know that people are selling everything with claims of everything. I can buy a device to shrink me to one inch, another to grow me to tower over a megatower. You could buy a spaceship with a real faster-than-light warp drive."

I smiled at him. "You fell for it, didn't you? The fake laser sabers on the dark net, didn't you? Don't feel bad. Everyone does. They're so cheap, you say to yourself, oh why not?"

"Yes, Mr. Cruz, I gladly allowed myself to be duped in purchasing a fake purple laser saber. The point is, no one believed the claim of a mind-control device to be even remotely real, to the sad realization of the original sellers. Now every claim, no matter how outlandish, is thoroughly investigated, here on Earth and Utopia, though we know nearly one hundred percent of them are false. No one wants to let another NeuroDancer device slip through their fingers again."

"Which nation was it?"

"I can't tell you that, Mr. Cruz."

"You know which one, though?"

"I do."

"Why not say?"

"It's not fair to the nation, for one. Second, that knowledge would only encourage some person or organization to feel if they go to that nation that could somehow glean the knowledge from its people to create another device, which is not true at all."

"Meaning that others are already doing that."

"Meaning others have tried, but not Utopia."

While the Average Joe and Jane referred to off-world as Up-Top, Up-Toppers called their colonies Utopia.

"I fear the operation to seize the device has given people ideas. A device that can fit in a metal case that can fit into the trunk of a mid-sized hovercar," Seraff said. "Despite the original being destroyed, it must be possible to recreate such a portable thing."

"I believe that was all a ruse," I said, "as was the claim that a single hovercar was the device."

"I agree with you. We believe the device was many parts. The controller wore one part. The device itself was like a network of aerial satellites and drones."

"Sounds very logical."

"Yes, it does, which means we're probably wrong, too. The quest for the ultimate weapon in psychological manipulation and control will continue."

"Weapon?"

"Yes. Didn't you get the MK Ultra story?"

"From Madame President of the Council of Corporations."

"Only a nation could have created this or had it created it from the start. Governments want control, megacorps want money. Your late client, NeuroDancer wanted control, not money."

"And she got dead for her wrong thinking."

"Are you going to stay out of this like the mayor and Mr. X asked you to?"

"They did more than ask. They paid me too, which is the same as threatening me in this case. Let me guess, Mr. Seraff. You're here to pay me to do the opposite."

"You don't like loose ends, Mr. Cruz, and neither do we. Our objections once again align. You have always referred to this business as NeuroDancer. We have always called it the Starlight business. We want it ended for good. It was one thing when no one believed it to be real or no one knew it existed. Everyone knows now. Extremely powerful entities on your planet and off-world."

"Everyone that matters."

"Exactly. Starlight must never see the light of day again. We will hire you to stay in the game. We've seen you work enough times, so we trust your ingenuity and initiative. The scientist is a human being, and I am not one comfortable with the parable 'the needs of the many, outweigh the needs of the one.' But the parable is valid. If this is the last scientist of the Starlight project, he must die. Are you comfortable with that?"

"I'm an assassin now?"

"You could turn them over to the authorities. But you're intelligent enough to know that turning this person over to the police would have the same outcome. You have taken on the role before, when it was necessary."

"I was aboard a plane with two thousand passengers. We wanted to live, land the plane, and get home to our families. I'd have shot anybody. Any of us would have."

"Then the stakes are even higher here. Utopia will not allow such a device to exist on this planet, any more than one of your nations would allow another to possess it, or any megacorps to have it. The stakes are that much higher."

"Scientists are always causing problems. Like inventing the first atomic bomb."

"Yes, they can, when they're not curing cancer and hypertension, or inventing greening-micro-terraforming."

"Or hovertech," I said, smiling. "I agree. The stakes are much higher. You can hire me."

"Not a conflict of interest with your previous clients."

"They didn't hire me to stay out of it. They wanted to confirm with their own eyes that I'd do what they knew I'd do. Stay involved to the end."

"Good, then I'll pay your Ms. PJ outside."

Chapter Forty-Four
Wize Gal

Wize Gal wasn't exactly happy with me the last time we met, but I didn't have to wait to see her when I arrived at her casino-restaurant-club in my loaner hovercar. Since it wasn't the Pony, I gladly handed it over to the valet attendants. A waitress in a business suit escorted me through the high-stakes tables of poker, blackjack, and roulette; and cheering or booing people, watching their sports games or races on the large wall and ceiling monitors.

We reached Wize's grand office in the center of the establishment. Wize Gal sat at her desk doing calculations with multiple tablets.

"Still in your not-disguise, disguise suit," she said.

"Hello, Wize," I greeted and sat down.

"I guess apologies are in order," she said as she put all her work away in the side drawers of her desk.

"Apologies for what?"

"You were right, and I was wrong. You survived the Council and their case."

"My clients are always satisfied with my work. You can read all about it on Trusted Reviews on the Net."

"Why are you here again, C-Man?"

I smiled. "I need an attorney, or someone who can act in that capacity, so I'm here to hire you."

"What do you need legal assistance with?"

She got up from the desk and walked over to her office's side kitchen. I hadn't noticed that she had water boiling and was making herself some tea. "Do you want anything? You're a coffee person. Silk coffee. How do you want it?"

"Shaken not stirred."

She gave me a look with a smirk.

"What do you need legal assistance with?"

"Ever heard of a Nazareth?"

"Are you taking an ancient criminal history class in school? You mean the name for shadow markets of the past? A criminal market."

"More like a criminal auction."

She walked back to the desk with her tea and my silk coffee. She handed me the cup. "Cruz, why would a legal representative, highlight the word legal, be interested in a criminal, highlight the word illegal, auction of stolen goods?"

"I'm going to be a spectator and the buy-in is fairly high. A Bar registered legal representative is required to accompany and notarize the promissory note."

"Cruz, are you crazy? I thought you were crazy, and I was wrong, but I'm reconsidering. How much is the buy-in?"

"Five million."

She sat down in her chair behind her desk and push her cup of tea away from her. "Cruz, are we so rich these days that you can throw five million dollars away to be a spectator at a criminal auction? Watch, not buy anything?"

"It's an auction. You bid, not buy."

"I know what an auction is, Cruz. Why would I risk my legal certification for this?"

"You don't have to worry about that."

"I don't? The police tend to arrest people at criminal auctions."

"The police will be there too, to bid."

"Cruz, I am completely lost right now. You said a criminal auction?"

"Yes."

"Meaning illegal and filled with criminals?"

"Yes."

"Why would the police be there to stand side by side to bid with the criminals?"

"Because they want the featured item, too."

"Which is?"

"I probably shouldn't tell you that part. So, can I hire you for this?"

"No. The featured item is what?"

"The source of an invention that was destroyed."

"Cruz, this is still the same case. This is still your NeuroDancer thing. 'The source of an invention.' What does that mean specifically? A data disk with the information to construct her device would need a physical auction or a five-million-dollar buy-in."

I hesitated as long as I could. "Wize, the police will be there. The Feds. It's all covered."

She rose from her desk like a cobra. "You're talking about a person, aren't you?"

"Law enforcement will be there."

"But you just told me they'll be bidding for it too."

"Wize, the bottom line is this scientist cannot get into criminal hands. The authorities will either grab him for themselves or make sure no one else can. This is a public safety thing."

"Public safety? Are you a PSA spokesman now for the government? No, absolutely not. This is crazy, Cruz. I'm not going. When is this Nazareth of yours?"

"It's not my Nazareth. It's in three days."

"Five million dollar buy-in."

"Not my money."

"And what will happen there?"

"Criminals will bid for the featured item. Law enforcement will try to outbid them. Someone will win. Then what happens at the end happens."

"You mean an all-out bloodbath."

"Precautions will be taken."

"Why would you want to be in the center of this?"

"To end my NeuroDancer case finally, once and for all."

"But you did that already."

"Device, not its inventor."

"You have that Wilford G. look in your eyes again. This is insane."

"You don't have to stay. Just notarize and go."

"Notarize and go. And leave you there?"

"Yes."

"Are you bringing backup at least?"

"Of course. My team to back me up."

Wize stood there at her desk, looking around. Then she began pacing behind her chair.

"This is certifiably insane. Nazareth? This would be the biggest Nazareth of all time. Probably the last ever, too, if it ends the way I suspect it will. Cruz, what's going on? You can handle yourself in a shoot-out, but you never walk into one, not this. You're happy and smart enough to run away from them if given the chance."

"End my NeuroDancer business once and for all."

"You don't seem nervous at all." She had stopped pacing and watched me. "Why is that, Cruz? What do you know?"

"I know it will all be fine."

"How do you know that?"

"I just do. So have I hired my legal representative? We'll have to dress to impress, our best business dress."

"Will you be wearing that undertaker's suit?"

"I'll be wearing my tan fedora and slicker. What about you?"

She laughed. "Okay, I'm in C-Man."

PART NINE
The Man in the Tan Fedora Returns

Chapter Forty-Five
China Doll

Every time a Metropolis resident saw one, it was seen as a good omen. We called them vortexes. Wherever the rain came down between two city ground heat vents, it created vertical spiraling circles of water. They were fun to look at, and kids loved to run through them, pretending to pass through dimensions or time, like in sci-fi movies. Whenever I saw one, I was immediately drawn to it too.

I was in front of the famous Eye Candy Image Salon—my wife's place of work. I stepped through the Eye Candy door and was immediately engulfed by a multitude of fragrances. Clients packed the salon from opening to closing. Women came from every corner of Metropolis to be made to look like movie stars with its "fashion police" of makeup artists, hairdressers, manicurists, pedicurists, skincare techs, tattoo artists, wardrobe stylists, and even dressers to assemble their wardrobe, if needed. The establishment was owned by Prima Donna, the Matron Queen of Metropolis fashion, who still had the magic touch after so many decades and tended to their oldest and highest-tipping clients.

My wife, China Doll, was Prima's number one and boss in her absence. Like every other fashionista employee, she wasn't some by-the-hour laborer. This was a coveted and highly competitive career, and everyone who worked in the parlor had advanced degrees in beauty and skincare, fashion and styling, health, and nutrition.

The interior of Eye Candy was designed like a beehive, and every section was visible, because of its transparent walls, to every other section, except the break room, full body baths, and the bathrooms. Eye Candy was nothing but carefully coordinated chaos—women sitting on chairs getting their hair and makeup done in one section, their nails and toenails in another, facials in another, tattoos in another (always temporary to change according to current fashion trends), skincare consultations in another, and wardrobe style analysis in yet another section.

Prima saw me first and I could see her announcing my arrival to the ladies and men on the floor. Customers and fashionistas were all beginning to take notice of my arrival. Then I saw my wife China Doll's head pop up.

She went by China Doll, but women who knew her called her China; men called her Doll. Only her family called her by her real name—Dot. I saw her saying something to her client in the chair as she sprinkled a dash of glitter on her hair.

I patiently waited as she washed her hands, towel-dried them and walked to me. As always, from the first day I saw her those years ago at Phobias Anonymous Support Group—every piece of clothing, every accessory, and every piece of jewelry she wore were the trendiest and the most stylish. She always looked the way she turned every client who sat in her chair—"movie picture perfect." Today, she wore a peacock-patterned, luminescent light-green halter top with a black neck scarf around her bionic neck, a black belt and skin-tight pants, and light green heels. Her hair was tied back, with the ponytail carefully resting on one shoulder, and every finger had a colored ring, and each wrist had multiple bracelets.

"Cruz, why are you wearing Junior's suit?"

I gave her a perplexed look and looked down at my suit. "What do you mean? Cruz Junior is six years old. How could I be wearing his suit?"

"His suit in the future. When he's all grown. Only he wears a black fedora. Where's your suit?"

"That's why I'm here," I said with a smile. "May I see an Eye Candy stylist, please, miss?"

"That's misses to you, sir. I think we can help you out."

She grabbed my hand and pulled me to the floor. "Ladies, look who's here."

Besides Prima Donna looking like a queen in silver without the crown, I knew all of Dot's colleagues, who were all busy at work, but greeted me with hellos. There was Cyan, who had a million outfits, but all were the same color of cyan; Pinkie, known for her bright pink hair; Goat Girl, with a large ring hanging from her nose septum; and Lipps, who had quite the set of augmented lips.

#

I stood admiring myself in one of the eight-foot rectangular mirrors.

"Prima, thanks again for your referral," I said.

"I'm glad Face could help again. He gets such a kick working for a real private eye."

I was satisfied with the "new me."

"Create your own visual style," Pinkie said, standing with my wife behind me, looking on.

"Elegance is not about standing out, it's about being remembered," Prima Donna said, standing with them.

"Clothes make the man," Dot said.

I knew that one. "Yes, naked people have little or no influence on society," I said.

Dot handed me my omega-gun. I gave my wife a kiss on the way out.

When I hopped through the same vortex as I strolled down the street, my swagger was back. So was my trademark "uniform"—tan fedora and tan slicker. Underneath, an elegant vest over an ivory dress shirt, a wool-like fitted, stretchy dress pants, with my new aqua shoes. And last, but not least, my omega-gun in its upscale shoulder holster. This street detective was ready for some action.

Chapter Forty-Six
The Matchmaker

In the criminal world, there was the Shadow Market, the shopping center for the criminal class. You bought and took your illegal goods with you at the same time. Most were constantly moving, but others were part of legitimate businesses like the former Cat Walk. But with all of them, like the Naughty Room, you needed an intro to get in. Walk-in buyers were never welcome, as everyone was always on the lookout for the police or other criminal gangs. However, not all "matchmakers" were created equal, and many were not above leading individuals into ambushes; but the one I was meeting was a legitimate, honest criminal who was vouched for by people I knew.

I descended in my loaner hovercar and smoothly glided along the ground to what had to be a kid waiting for me on the street, leaning against the wall. I thought, shouldn't he be in school? My vehicle's phone rang and a man's face appeared on the dashboard display box when I answered.

"Cruz."

"Yeah."

"Give my man the money."

I rolled down my driver-side window. The kid cautiously walked to me as I leaned out with a small bag. I tossed it to him. He caught it and moved back to the wall. He fed the whole wad of cash into a portable counter in his clothes with one hand as he dialed his mobile with the other. Quite the multi-tasker, this kid.

"Security is tight on this one," the man on the screen said. "You want an alias?"

"Well, that would be stupid. I'm sure more than a few of the event's attendees will recognize me by sight."

"I'm sure they will, seeing you killed and got their fellow brothers and sisters in crime arrested."

"I don't think any of them are bringing flowers to graveyards or visiting anybody in prison."

"I doubt that, too. I'll leave your name at the front. Ask for 'Dancer.' That'll get you in."

"Good. What can you tell me about this Nazareth?"

"I've been in the business for almost forty years and I've never seen anything like this. Crime bosses and organizations I've only heard whispers about are crawling out from every deep, dark bottomless pit there is for this one. There's supposed to be people from Up-Top too that no one ever sees."

"What about the cops or the Feds?"

"Get this. They'll be there too as participants, not to arrest nobody."

"What? That can't be true."

"It's true. Everybody wants this item bad, even the good guys. They can't stop the event and they can't arrest nobody for walking into a legitimate place. Technically, it only becomes a crime when someone takes possession of the item. So they have to play it this way."

"Have you heard of the guy running this thing?"

"Malicious Insider is his street name. Ask one group, and no one's heard of him before. Ask another group and they say he's been a major operator in Ghost Market for ages, specializing in the most secret of secrets. Shadow megacorps. Government black ops R&D. Who can say what the real deal is? But so what? When was the last time a real Nazareth of this greatness happened before? People will fly in from all over the globe just to watch."

"Are they allowing people to carry in there?"

The man laughed. "There will be more guns in that place than Metro PD Police One. An armed society is a polite society." He laughed again.

"Nice doing business with you. I put a bit extra in there for you."

"My man told me. You're the clientele I wish I had more of. Maybe I can interest you in my other services. I do other kinds of matchmaking. Maybe the interracial variety who want to walk on the wild side."

"Interracial? You mean cats and dogs, foxes and chickens? Is their money in pet matchmaking?"

The man hit the screen on his side with his head, laughing. "I mean human matchmaking."

"Oh, Earthers and Martians."

"No."

"I'm not good at guessing."

"I got clients, criminals who like dating cops. And I know for a fact that there are cops out there, especially the female ones, who want their own gangster to practice their apprehending skills and more private, more intimate arresting activities with the handcuffs."

"Thanks for that mental picture."

"If you like, I can get you pictures and videos."

"I might go blind."

He laughed and knew that I had all the services I need. "You know plenty of cops and plenty of criminals. I pay referral bonuses, if you're ever interested."

"I'll keep that in mind."

"Do reach out again if you need another proper match to a member of the opposite criminal class. Stay alive, Mr. Cruz."

"I plan to."

"Happy V-Day in advance to you and the misses."

His face disappeared as it disconnected. The boy outside at the wall was also gone.

Chapter Forty-Seven
Tag

When I first met Tag in my Electric Sheep case, he was just a kid. He was still one of the major players in cyberpunk, the term for the mostly youth geek subculture, who lived most of their life in the VR world or, as he would constantly correct me on the right terminology, VL—virtual life.

Back then he was often jacked-in himself, but also did endless scraper jobs. He was one of the best scrapers out there, but more than a few people knew he was connected to me. The hardcore cyberpunk world was an unforgiving one. When you got to Tag's "old age" of thirty, you were retired from much of the scene. Retirees drifted into the criminal Net world, became VLer (VEE-LER) addicts—people who "lived" most of their life in virtual reality, or got a cushy anti-cybercrime job in law enforcement or the megacorps. Tag took a page from my book and went into business himself. The "kid" was now married with a new kid.

I found him in an upscale arcade bar, one of the many he owned in one of the trendier districts in the supercity. The ceilings were flashing neon electric blue; the floors flashed hot pink, and the walls were black. Here virtual lifers congregated, sitting in ultra plush recliners, but the plug-in interface wasn't helmets or goggles, it was a full-body capsule or chamber. I still called them VR coffins and found the whole thing kind of creepy. An entire ground-floor establishment filled with people in capsules from one end to another, with the sounds of hundreds of conversations via each chamber's audio. All under the watchful eye of cyborg security and two roving waitress servers in hoodies.

Tag met me at the door of his big office in the back. The room had walls lined with monitors and floor filled with computer towers. Some monitors had surveillance feeds, but most were running code of endless searches for clients. He was looking good, thin, sandy blond hair, still wore eyeliner, and tattoos covered his hands to his elbows.

"Come into my parlor, Cruz," he greeted.

We got caught up on family small talk while he pulled up a stool for me. He didn't have one desk full of monitors; he had several. And while we talked, he moved from one to another.

"You're not still mad at me for hiring Spiders."

"It hurt, Cruz. I have to admit."

"Tag, I couldn't bring that kind of heat down on you. Besides, they'd be watching you like hawks with X-ray eyes."

"Cruz, the Council of Corporations does that, anyway. They try to hire me almost monthly."

"No, Tag, believe me. If they thought you were working on my NeuroDancer business, you'd be under a level of scrutiny not even you could withstand. Couldn't do that to you."

"You think they didn't know about Spiders."

"Maybe. Spiders may not be as good of a scraper as you, but he's definitely more paranoid than you."

"Yeah, he sleeps with his wet-wear on. That's hardcore. But the ND business is a wrap?"

"Tag, I have the real job for you."

He stopped moving to another desk. "The real job?"

"Remember that picture in school of an iceberg floating in the Antarctic Ocean?"

"The tip above water is the smallest part."

"Spiders is the tip. You're the rest of the iceberg. The job is big, Tag?"

"I don't care about that. Like you, I can be picky about my work. I need interesting and challenging."

"What about impossible?"

"Impossible?"

"Outsmart the Council, the police, organized crime, and everyone else."

"Impossible?" Tag repeated. I had his full and undivided attention.

"I think there'll be enough work to keep your entire global network busy."

This was the meeting I had with the kid over a year ago. It was even before my Biopunk and Moon cases. That's how long we'd actually been working the full case. I called it my NeuroDancer case, but after her demise, it had always meant the Starlight case. As I said before, you had to get there first.

Chapter Forty-Eight
Bite-Size

With my network of safe houses over all Metropolis, finding a place to hide temporarily or for the long haul, to set up a temp HQ or new one altogether, like we did in Wharf City was easy. We'd taken up in offices for hire in a residential megatower to get ready for the big day.

The apartment opened into a sparse main living room, but we were in the adjacent larger room with twin beds which had guns, rifles, knives, ammunition laid out on top of them. One bed had weapons that PJ and one of Quix's ex-mercs were loading up. Quix and two other mercs were at the other bed, being used as a weapons table.

I popped in with a tray of beverages. "Break time," I said.

PJ was in a business suit that I'd never seen before. Very upscale sleeveless dark suit, to show off her buff bionic arms, and a silver blouse top. The men had on suits too, except they'd swapped out the expensive slacks for stretch black jean fatigues and black combat boots. They'd always be ex-military.

"Cruz, I've been meaning to ask you about today," Quix said.

"Sure," I said as I set the tray on a circular table in the corner.

"We're going to this criminal auction."

"The Nazareth."

"The most dangerous gangsters and megacorps on the planet are expected to be there."

"Among others."

"Who others?" PJ asked.

"Intelligence units of different countries, undercover police."

"All these people will be armed?" Quix asked.

"Quix, it'll probably be one of the safest places on the planet."

"How so, Cruz? Four armed people as your backup, even if we could carry in everything on these beds, means nothing in a crowd of equally or better armed hostiles."

"No one's going to shoot us. Think about it. If they said no weapons, everyone would still try to smuggle them in any way they could. Weapons that couldn't be easily detected. No one would be safe that way. This way, with everyone being able to bring in what they want, everybody is safe."

"I don't know if I agree with the logic."

"They have other safeguards, too. Besides that, all parties have to have a licensed legal representative to notarize their buy-in to the auction. You'd be surprised how many criminals don't know a legitimate attorney, and there's not enough time for them to get one of their criminal ones legal."

"Wize Gal," PJ said.

"Yes, we'll pick her up after here. After our next team member arrives."

"What else?" Quix asked. "This operation seems way too risky."

"Besides everyone being armed, the main leveler is that everyone given entry will be known by everyone else."

"How?" Quix asked. All his men stopped checking their weapons and sharpening their knives.

"Everyone's DNA will be checked, except for Bar-registered legal professionals, and all names added to the official attendance list."

Everyone looked at each other, then at me.

"They're taking my DNA?" PJ asked, with her bionic arms folded.

"Guys, grow up. Everyone knows us and they could get our DNA anytime they wanted. We're not that important. We'll be spectators, not bidders. The beauty of the DNA rule is that no one unknown will be there."

Quix grinned. "That's why the authorities are allowing this."

I nodded. "And the criminals and megacorps there don't care who knows who they are. They're bidders. That's what all this is about. Getting the inventor of the device."

"If you don't mind me saying, Cruz, you seem to be very well-informed about this Nazareth," Quix said. "My contacts tell me there's hasn't been a true Nazareth in Metropolis in like two hundred years, and this one will be ten times bigger, and a hundred times more dangerous."

"I spent a whole day and night reading their rule book," I said.

"Rule book?" they all said in unison.

"How can you expect people to follow the rules if you don't read what those rules are? They have a rule book for all attendees."

"Who are we waiting for, Cruz?" PJ asked me.

"You know him," I said. "Once he gets here, let's load up and leave."

Quix and his men looked at each other. I never saw them look at a time-piece but they always knew the time.

"We have six hours to go," Quix said. "Why would we leave now?"

"We want to make sure we have plenty of time. I'd rather be early to this thing than miss it all. We'll never see this again in our lifetime," I said.

#

I first met Bite-Size in my NeuroDancer case. He was a roly-poly of a guy with spectacles, and chain-smoked. He still ran the Netsite Movie-Town Madness and knew more about movies and their history than anybody in Metropolis. But lately, he'd stuck his toe into producing short films for first-time filmmakers.

His knock on the door came about an hour later. He was greeted at the door by PJ and two of Quix's men all pointing laser rifles at him.

"Ah!" he screamed and dropped to the ground.

"Bite-Size! Get up from there!" I yelled.

I pulled him up and dusted him off. He was wearing a dark suit under his slicker and a neck scarf. I led him inside and straight for the mini-fridge.

"Let's get this man a drink," I said.

Bite-Size still had his eyes on the others.

"They're with me, Bite-Size," I said. "Our security detail."

"Yes. I understand. Gave me quite a fright, though."

"You'll be fine."

"Can I smoke in here?"

"Aren't you too young to smoke?"

Bite-Size smiled as he fished out his cigarettes from his pockets. "My parents have been saying that to me for years." He had one of those strike-tip ones and lit it with one hard tap on his pocket. He took a puff. "When do we start, Cruz?"

"Are you ready for your close-up, Bite-Size?" I asked.

"Born ready, Cruz. Born ready."

"Then let the action begin."

Chapter Forty-Nine
The Nazeth

Quix's new vehicle was like an armored mini-bus. He drove and PJ was in the passenger seat—she'd call shotgun before I could utter a word. I was in the second seat alone. Wize Gal would sit with me. Bite-Size was in the third row seats with one of Quix's men. The rest were in the fourth row seats.

We got to Wize, the place, in no time. Wize Gal waited in a purple business suit and black slicker over it, and the hood lightly over her head. She held a briefcase in her hand. I opened my door as we descended from the sky to her, and she jumped in as the vehicle hovered.

"This is the team?" she asked.

"The team," I replied.

She introduced herself to Bite-Size. They'd never met before. The early part of the drive was them alone, talking. We learned that Wize Gal was a movie buff too, but not the movie encyclopedia of all film history like Bite-Size.

"What did I miss?" she asked out loud. "I wasn't at your final meeting, so what did I miss?"

She saw PJ and Quix glance at each other in front of us. She then turned to me. "Cruz, what's going on?"

"Nothing's going on. You know everything. We had our meeting before I had my meeting with them."

"My role is to notarize the promissory note buy-in of five million dollars."

"Five million dollars," everyone said.

PJ turned around to look at me with a frowning face.

"It's not Liquid Cool money, so you can turn back around," I said.

"Who's money then?" she asked.

"If you must know, City Hall is paying for it," I said to her.

"Not a very informative briefing you gave your team, Cruz, if they don't know those details," Wize said. "What else, Cruz? What other surprises?"

"Everybody will be armed," Quix said.

"That one, I guessed. Any type of shadow market lets the clients come in armed. Too much trouble to frisk everyone all the time, and to guarantee that the area will be weapons-free is practically impossible to achieve. What else?"

"DNA," PJ said under her breath.

"What about DNA?" Wize asked her, then looked at me.

PJ turned around again, and I fully briefed Wize Gal about the Nazareth's unusual precaution.

Wize glared at me. "Cruz, I'm a member of the Bar and under no circumstances will I be giving my DNA to a criminal organization."

"No need to worry about it, Wize."

"Why, Cruz? Because they already have it?"

"Because you're a member of the Bar and your identity is already known. No DNA needed."

"Lucky for you then, because I would have turned right around and left."

"Wize, I wouldn't compromise your legal principles. You know me."

"I'm started to. Since I missed your briefing, who runs this Nazareth?" Wize asked.

"I was told by some guy called M.I."

"M.I. As in MI-5 or MI-6, perhaps?"

"As in some guy who calls himself Malicious Insider."

"Malicious Insider?" Wize laughed.

"Criminals love their street names."

"Does M.I. wear anything in tan?"

"What do you mean?"

"What do you think I mean? I'm not the only one in this vehicle thinking it."

"I'm not involved in this," I said as Wize laughed under her breath.

"We're going to the Nazareth to observe and make sure it all ends the way it should."

"Why is Bite-Size here? What's his specialty?" Wize asked.

"He's here to confuse the bad guys."

"Someone's already confused here."

#

I'd been in bad hovertraffic before, but every lane from the slow lane to the fast one was crawling. Metropolis sky lanes were always chaotic, but it was organized chaos. Twenty stories up with large hovercraft, like trucks and tankers, in the bottommost virtual lanes, buses and RV hovercraft in the lanes above them. All personal and commercial hovercars were in the main virtual lanes above them both. The hated hoverbikers zipped around wherever they wanted but were still in a designated virtual lane structure. We were caught in a hovertraffic jam like we'd never seen before.

The only vehicles that could fly where they pleased were the police, firemen, and garbage trucks. Also, megacorp zeppelins floating where they wanted, but they paid the city massive monthly fees for the privilege.

Our destination was called The Sticks. It was an open paved over space between more than one district, one of which was Mad Heights, or more commonly called Mad City. I'd been there before, almost died there, and never wanted to go there ever again.

"Where in the Sticks are we going?" Quix asked, looking at his dashboard traffic tracker. "That seems to be the source of the slowing traffic."

"Glad we left when we did," I said. "We'll be looking for a Bond Street."

Wize shot me a look, and PJ turned around, smiling.

"What?" I asked.

"This is all you, isn't it?" Wize asked.

"I have nothing to do with this."

"Okay, James," Wize said.

#

As we got closer, we could see that multiple exits were closed, which was the main reason for the bottleneck. People wanted to get off sky lanes somehow, but more and more traffic cops were appearing because of the number of hovercars illegally breaking away.

"Quix, get off the freeway whenever you can," I said. "We'll be faster on the regular streets."

We finally got off the freeway only to hit slower traffic. It was a complete mess, and it took almost forty minutes to reach our street and see what was causing the snarl in the hovertraffic.

"Bond Street ahead," Quix announced.

"Despite what you all are thinking, Bond Street was the main jewelry and precious metal market square back in the day when we were the megacity of Old Metropolis and not today's supercity," I said. "Back then, buyers came from all over the planet too."

"Criminals?" PJ asked.

"No. All legit back then. Probably some crooked sellers somewhere, but it was all above board."

Then we saw them. Crowds of them. We'd never seen so many sidewalk johnnies in our lives. The street was infested with them. That's why hovertraffic had slowed. There was no place for anyone to land on the street. People flew over the street but had to bypass it, and circled multiple times before giving up because every inch of the street was covered with johnnies.

"Cruz, this is a complete cluster," Quix said.

"We'll have to do some walking, then. We're all healthy. Walking is good for you, as my ma would say."

"Where do you think we should park?" Wize asked with a grin.

"How would I know?" I asked. "Quix, just follow one of the vehicles not circling around and see where everyone's going."

Pop-up entrepreneurs. You had to admire them. Makeshift parking lots complete with their own security started from about a mile away from the entrance to the street. It was obvious that before this day, none of these parking lots ever existed. But most of the hovervehicles landing had their own armed security to stay with their vehicles.

What was also obvious was that the lots were filling up with very rich, very dangerous criminal gangs.

"We're walking?" Quix asked me.

"Yes, we'll be fine," I replied.

"Should I leave a couple of men with the vehicle?"

"We should stay together. I don't think your hoverbus has to worry itself about being stolen by these criminals."

"Finally, we are in complete agreement," Quix said. "Men load up," he yelled to his men.

"I'm loading up too," PJ said to him.

"And lady," Quix added with a chuckle.

Wize Gal stared out the window at hovervehicle passengers exiting. As we got out of own vehicle, I had the same feeling as when I was in the Council of Corporations boardroom. The surrounding criminals: neon-suited gangsters and crime lords—thuggish or freakish-looking men or slinky or buff-looking women wearing more gold, diamonds, precious gems than Fort Knox, cyborg soldiers, samurai soldiers, cyborg samurai soldiers. The weapons they had under their jackets. Swords, machetes, axes, medieval maces, and war hammers. The largest and fattest rifles and guns we'd ever seen. There was no way to sugarcoat it: these people were more than dangerous. Quix was a seasoned ex-military, ex-merc like his men, who'd been in actual wars. They were nervous. If professionals like them were scared, we'd better be too.

Someone could have choreographed the walk to Bond Street for some action movie, but it was real. Bite-Size stayed in the center of all of us. I led the way with PJ on one side and Wize on the other. Quix and his men had our back. The strange thing was that no one talked. It was as if we were all marching in a mile-long funeral procession, but with the tapping of the muzzles of rifles or other hand weapons on the black cobblestone pavement.

#

When we reached the crowds of sidewalk johnnies and sallies, it was utter pandemonium. Johnnies were fearless by nature. They had their turf and were more interested in chatting it up, joking, drinking, and scamming each other. They were in their own little world. However, the ultra-violent, ultra-evil criminals and we ourselves had to maneuver around them to get to where we were going.

Wize stopped for a second.

"What?" I asked.

"I thought I saw one of your men."

"One of my men? Who?"

"Phishy."

"Where?" PJ asked.

"Can't see him now. Maybe it wasn't him," Wize said. "Where is Phishy anyway?" she asked me.

"He has his own mission he's working on for me."

"A secret mission," PJ said to Wize.

Once past the living barrier of sidewalk johnnies, all arrivals were slowly funneled to the main entrance. We had reached what looked like an ancient bunker, or was it a giant hoverplane hanger made of dark gray stone? In my Classic Cyborg case, I'd seen more dangerous cyborgs than I ever wanted to see. This was that multiplied by a factor of ten. The Nazareth security guards also rated high on the deadly scale. At the entrance, they all wore the same black jumpsuits with laser shotguns in hand. All were cyborgs—arms, chests, faces of metal, and wearing dark glasses.

We finally reached the cyborg admitting guards.

"How many in your party?" one asked.

"Party of eight," I replied.

"Name?"

"Dancer," I said.

He found my name on his electronic clipboard and checked it off.

"Give me your entrance fee," he said.

I reached into my jacket and out came a card. The cyborg grabbed it with metal hands.

"Who's the attorney?" he asked. I pointed to Wize.

He handed her an electronic pad and a stylus pen to sign.

"Payment received and notarized for a Mr. Cruz, party of eight, non-bidding," the cyborg said to his fellow thugs.

Another one, with no weapons, slapped the back of my hand with his fist. I could see my picture and name appear on the tablet of another guard. He did the same to the rest of my team.

"The scan won't work with full cyborg arms," he said to an annoyed PJ.

"What do you want me to do?" PJ yelled at him.

"You got legs, don't you?"

"Be very careful about what you do next," she said with a sneer.

The man smiled, knelt down, and tapped one of her exposed calves. "There you go. In and out."

The cyborg guards waved us in.

We slowly walked in. The scene reminded me more of raving fans gathering for a concert rather than the criminal auction it was. From our vantage point, it was like standing in a hollowed-out mountain and people were everywhere, as far as the eye could see—criminal people, evil people. With the Nazareth multi-million buy-in, many in the criminal world wouldn't be able to get in. With its requirement of a legitimate attorney to notarize your payment, a DNA scan and "sharing" list would keep millions more away. But tens of thousands still surrounded us, hundreds of thousands, or more criminals, waiting. If an asteroid crashed and blew up the gathering, Metropolis might be crime-free for an entire year. But then I remembered we were looking at a sliver of a fraction of the real criminal class in the supercity and lots of the attendees were also from out-of-country and, literally, out of this world. Visual proof of job security for all law enforcement on Earth.

"Do you see what I'm seeing?" PJ said to me.

I'd noticed too. "Yeah."

"Is that real?" Wize asked.

We were all staring. The lights in the mega-auditorium were dim, but we could still see across to its furthest walls. I'd seen real giants before. They were rare, like true midgets, since neonatal science could eliminate most of the genetic abnormalities that plagued humanity in ages past. But the man we spotted in a light-colored suit was a true giant. He had to have been at least eight feet of bulging flesh, standing like a statue with dark glasses on his face. I was certain we weren't the only ones who couldn't take our eyes off him.

"Bite-Size, is this you?" I asked.

"Me?"

"Some kind of movie thing."

"Cruz, what are you talking about? I can't make giants."

"Maybe he's on stilts," Quix said.

"That's Mr. Big," someone next to us said.

The information came to us from a member of a gangster party of twelve. From his accent, I guessed from a Northern African nation. The members, though, all had that East Euro look based on their facial tattoos down the sides of their faces. As with everyone in the place, the price of their suits and jewelry combined probably equaled the buy-in fee.

"Mr. Big?" I asked.

"Crime lord here in Metropolis," the man answered.

"Never heard of him," I said.

"Never heard of anyone here, but doesn't mean we don't exist, have existed, and could wipe you away and everyone you know with the snap of a finger."

"Is your organization equal or better than Mr. Big's?" I asked.

The man stared at me for a while. He was quickly sizing me up, and one of his people whispered something in his ear. "No one's bigger than Mr. Big's organization," he said.

"Thanks. Good luck with the bidding, then."

"We're spectators."

"So are we," I said, smiling.

I don't know if it was what I said or if they didn't like my cologne, but the gangsters moved away from us.

I felt something poking me in the side. It was Wize's fingers.

"Are you crazy?" she said angrily.

"Cruz, do not engage these people in conversation," Quix said.

"With people like this, it's conversation that keeps everything cool and calm."

"Boss, I have to disagree with you here," PJ said.

"Okay, let's find a spot to keep me away from everyone."

"Yes, that's an excellent idea. Cruz, I can't help noticing how cool and calm you are."

"Wize, you all forget that this place is not just crawling with criminals. The good guys are here too."

"If anything happened, we'd be long dead and mutilated before any law enforcement could intervene," Quix said.

My team was being very negative. They man-handled me away to a spot between two less scary groups of criminals. Yes, the place was scary. As you waited, all you did was look at everyone around you, and they were doing the same. Conversation was minimal even within groups. Everyone was sizing up everyone else around them. Sweaty hands on machine-guns, swords, machetes, and knives. We were all standing in the middle of a powder keg. The slightest thing could blow up the whole thing. The Nazareth could end before it ever started.

#

The waiting was our greatest enemy. Part of having street smarts was knowing when you were the lamb in the den of wolves, a den where all the wolves wanted to kill each other.

Holographic singers at special functions were common even in an anti-robot, anti-android city like Metropolis. We all heard music begin.

The selection of holographic musical performers available was mind-boggling. Centuries to choose from, but the most popular seemed to always be from the nineteenth and twentieth. A singing holographic Aretha Franklin (an American singer and musician) descended, floating above the crowds, appearing out of thin air. Though the image was normal-sized, her voice didn't echo as if being broadcast through a giant cavernous structure, but as if she were performing right in front of you. Her band included a Prince Roger Nelson, known as Prince (another American singer-songwriter) and a James Marshall "Jimi" Hendrix (an American guitarist, singer and songwriter) on electric guitars, a Glenn Gould (Canadian) on the piano, and some male quartet UK Prime rock band called the Beatles (John, Paul, George, and Ringo) as backup singers. They floated in the center of the auditorium for everyone to see them perform. Attendees directly under them moved back to see fully see them too.

Aretha Franklin AI's singing was almost hypnotic, and would have made the later NeuroDancer proud.

O say can you see, by the dawn's early light, What so proudly we hailed at the twilight's last gleaming, Whose broad stripes and bright stars through the perilous fight, O'er the ramparts we watched, were so gallantly streaming, And the rocket's red glare, the bombs bursting in air, Gave proof through the night that our flag was still there; O say does that star-spangled banner yet wave O'er the land of the free and the home of the brave!

Every nation and even Up-Top had their own version of the "Star-Spangled Banner." But past elementary school, the only time you heard it was at special high-ticket sporting expositions or the final game of team sporting events. However, most probably had never heard the original raw source-material version performed by the Aretha Franklin AI. A performance that was every bit as human and unique as its originator—the smokiness of her voice, the slow tempo, the breathlessness, the emotion of the person and the words. The music instrumentality or backup vocals of the other AI performers diminished none of its power. They just made it better.

When the song was done, everyone was speechless. The AI rose from the ground into the air toward the top of the hollow mountain of an auditorium and faded away into nothingness. People looked at each other, not knowing what to do. So I did. I gave a rousing applause.

Like the dominoes falling, the entire place filled with crazy maniacs, psychos, sociopaths and the like applauded and cheered "Bravo!" like hover-hockey fans or middle school students with their parents.

Well, at least for now, none of us had to worry about dying horribly in a battle royale shootout.

#

When all the applause died down, a spotlight engulfed a new figure in the center of the auditorium. A white Janus mask covered his head—left half smiling, the right half sad, and dressed in a black suit and loafers.

"Welcome all, to the Nazareth!" he said in a booming voice.

I felt someone kick me. I looked at my team.

"Where's Bite-Size?" PJ asked in a whisper.

I looked, and he was gone, but I gave them a reassuring look. "He's fine. Probably went to the restroom."

"Whatever, Cruz," Wize said to me, while Quix and his men laughed to themselves.

"I am your host, known in the Ghost Market as the Malicious Insider. I walked in here like all of you did, so you all both know who I am, and you don't know who I am. But it matters not. What matters is we are all here for a unique event. When completed, this event will never happen again in our lifetimes, possibly not for centuries.

"All of us know of the item we will simply call The Device. The joke is that there are many in this room who could have easily acquired The Device many years ago on the dark Net. But they all thought it to be a hoax and let it get away. Such a mistake will never happen again, but the loss was still no less profound.

"It found its way from an undisclosed government lab to an undisclosed megacorp black ops division, then to a singer-dancer still celebrated around the world by fans, known as NeuroDancer. I had thought of having her AI sing to us to kick off the proceedings, but I didn't want to cause a bloodbath since in this room are many of her victims. The Device worked and the late NeuroDancer was systematically building her network of power to rule over all of us. Unfortunately for her, she sought and hired the very individual who would bring about her own death. Through her own hubris, she was the instigator of her own end.

"I too could have The Device. But I am a superstitious person. I believe there are things in this world and in this universe that are cursed. They destroy those who try to possess them. The Device came out of the darkness and the race to possess it began anew. Then it seemed it all ended one day in Alpha Ville. New master, or mistress, and the old device destroyed forever in fire.

"But the device always had both a possessor and creator. Even with its possessor and the device no more, the creator remains. But does the curse follow the creator too? I believe so. However, for those of you here, many who have come from many miles away, you disagree. You don't believe in curses. You believe you can tame a new device from its creator and possess it for your own ambitions and desires. So be it. I will be the seller, and one of you here will be its new possessor. The Nazareth begins! Who will start us off with the opening bid?"

"I will! Twenty billion dollars!" How the man spoke sent shivers down one's spine. Mr. Big's shouted declaration made everyone immediately turn to look at the living giant. Little did I know that in a future case, I would meet up with him again.

The damage was done. With those words, the crime lord had placed the item far out of the reach of most of the bidders at the auction. Any good will from a mesmerizing singing Aretha Franklin AI to calm the gathering had vanished, as if it had never existed. People standing anywhere near Mr. Big and his very large and scary-looking entourage moved away.

#

People had already begun leaving. Whether it was because they were cut out of the action or were genuinely concerned they might get killed in a gun battle, we didn't know. I knew if Quix had a choice, he and his men would never had been at the Nazareth. The rest of my team was only here because I asked them. The official start of the auction was both exhilarating and frightening.

Then I saw her. Madame President of the Council of Corporations was alive. She approached in a shimmering charcoal gray kimono-style dress and a blue pearl necklace around her neck. There had to have been at least fifteen big, brawny cyborg samurai soldiers around her.

"Madame President," I greeted. "It is still president?"

"Yes, Mr. Cruz. I've been re-elected for a full term."

"Unanimous?"

"Of course. I've already brought on new members to the Board to fill all vacancies. A new, exiting era is ahead for the Council."

"I enjoyed working with your AI."

"She enjoyed working with you, too."

"I'm sure you're glad to be among the living again."

"I am. Thank you for saving my life, Mr. Cruz."

"You're very welcome."

"I will not be staying to the end, as I had planned. That all changed when I saw you arrive."

"You couldn't have been surprised."

"You're right, Mr. Cruz. As impossible as I thought it was, I wasn't. I will leave you to it then. With you here to watch over things, what can go wrong? Until the next time."

"Next time."

The Council President and her suit soldiers left and were soon gone from the building.

I looked at my team. "Another satisfied client," I said with a smile.

#

The bidding was like a vicious volley back and forth among participants. Each bid increasing by ten percent, higher and higher. Then a bidder demanded to see the "item." Time itself seemed to stop.

We'd wondered about this part of the auction. But the Nazareth rules applied to the "item" too. Three Nazareth cyborg guards pushed it in—a man strapped onto a hoverthrone and the whole thing encased by a glass. His mouth was gagged and his eyes covered by clear goggles, but anyone could see the horror on the man's face. A fourth cyborg guard with a scanner had the other three lift the glass container up a bit, then tapped the scientist's exposed arm strapped to the arm of the chair.

They moved the scientist to the center of the auditorium. People moved in closer as the three cyborgs stood guard around it and the fourth walked to a waiting Mr. Big. The DNA scan would reveal the man's identity to those who knew what it was. One of the few people on the planet who did was the crime lord. The powers of the world and Up-Top were seeking to purchase a human being for his secrets.

"The bid stands at one hundred ten billion," Malicious Insider announced. "Do we have another ten?"

A hand went up. "We double the bid!"

Spectators gasped. The new bidder was dressed in a shiny white suit. We all knew a spaceman when we saw one, but was this a crime boss, megacorp agent, or undercover cop?

The giant crime lord gritted his teeth and visibly clenched his fists. More people in the auditorium left for the exits.

"Please, all, let us keep to the rules of the auction," Malicious said. "The bid will be accepted, however, only one more sky's-the-limit bid will be allowed in the Nazareth. Incremental bidding only. The bid stands at two hundred twenty billion. Do we have another ten?"

Mr. Big made the counter bid. The spaceman made the higher bid. A new female bidder in green joined in, then a new group in suits and wearing motorcycle helmets.

Shots rang out, startling everyone. The motorcycle-helmet-wearing bidders were all dead on the floor. Madame President stepped from the crowds with her cyborg samurai soldiers pointing their laser machine-guns.

"At least one of you should survive. Tell your bosses that the Council of Corporations of Metropolis will always be the most powerful of any on Earth or Utopia. I look forward to their next assassination attempt, and should expect the reverse."

The CC President looked at me, smiled, and did a slight bow before turning to leave the building encircled by her corporate soldiers. So her real reason for attending the Nazareth had been revealed.

"Everyone, can we continue with the Nazareth proceedings?" Malicious Insider said in a booming voice. "Do we have another bid?"

#

Mr. Big erupted in a rage when the bid reached a trillion. He stormed out of the auditorium building with his crew, cursing and punching at the air. We were still there, but the crowd of tens of thousands had shrunk to only a few hundred.

"Cruz," a voice said, and I turned to see Bite-Size standing there, pointing at the crowd near the main entrance. The team was surprised to see him. "What's wrong?" he asked them.

"We thought you were..." PJ began.

"Thought I was who?" he asked.

"Never mind that. Who are you pointing to?" I asked him.

"Here he comes."

Run-Time's VP, Mr. Mick, approached us with a dozen corporate samurai soldiers. He didn't look pleased.

"Mr. Cruz, I didn't know you were interested in secret criminal auctions for kidnapped scientists."

"What are you doing here?" I asked.

"We have an interest in the participants," he replied.

"You or Run-Time."

"Both, but we can talk about that later. I suggest you leave now and get as far away from here as possible."

"Why?" I asked. "Most of the people have left."

"Have they? Or are they waiting outside? Also, all the sidewalk johnnies gathered around the area, which at least kept any of the parties from landing their craft, left twenty minutes ago."

The team and I looked at each other.

"I'll check it out," Quix said, and gestured for one of his men to follow.

"You have a good afternoon, Mr. Cruz." Mr. Mick turned and left with his suit soldiers.

#

Malicious Insider raised his arms in the air. "Bidders, we must now conclude the Nazareth. I'll take the final highest bid from each of the parties, skies-the-limit. We begin."

In ten seconds, we heard numbers we didn't think could be true. How much money actually existed on Earth and Up-Top combined? We didn't know, but the numbers were unbelievable.

"We have a winner!" Malicious announced.

A hooded man dressed all in crimson stepped forward and touched the glass of the imprisoned scientist.

"Congratulations, sir. The curse belongs to you. I regret to inform you that if you can get away, you'll have to shoot your way through competitors and the police, but you would have expected this."

"We have," the crimson man said. "Our Martian spaceships are hovering above."

"Transfer the funds per the rules of the Nazareth and the container's kill-switch will be disabled."

"Simultaneously?"

"Yes."

The Martian touched his ear. "Funds transfer complete."

Malicious Insider pulled back one of his sleeves and pushed a button on a wrist device. "Kill-switch disabled."

That's when the Martian fired a plasma gun and blasted a hole through the Nazareth host's chest, and all hell broke loose.

#

One shot. My explosive round shattered the hoverthrone's glass container, impacted the poor scientist's chest, and the whole thing exploded, knocking everyone, the Martians, the few hundred people gathered around, and me off our feet.

"Run!" I yelled before I had even hopped back up.

The shootout that we feared had begun. I'd never been cursed at in Martian before, but the crimson man and his fellow off-worlders took aim. Luckily, Quix and one of his men gave us cover fire from the entrance, which surprised the Martians. The Nazareth cyborg security detail opened fire on the Martians, too. But the pesky Martians had some kind of invisible force shields to block the distant incoming fire.

PJ fired her favorite laser rifle and hit the main Martian right in his torso. I dropped two others with my gun as we bolted. Quix's men with us and Wize Gal also joined in the firefight, which now involved everyone in the auditorium.

Bite-Size was screaming as he ran past us all to get outside faster than the rest of us.

I had no choice and shot the kid in the foot. He went down hard and started crying. But he soon saw why I stopped him from stepping outside. The Martians weren't lying about having their spaceships above, which were now hovering close to the ground with cannons pointed at the entrance.

"Exit Stage Left, please," I said and pulled Bite-Size away down the pathway that ran along the wall away from the main entrance. The team followed me with Quix and his men never ceasing their firing at multiple targets shooting at us.

The last thing I remembered was a flash of light, heat, my ears feeling funny, then nothing. I faded to black.

Chapter Fifty
The Booty Shakers

The aerial blast that knocked us all unconscious had also blown up the Martian flying saucer. I didn't think we had any hovercraft capable of that. Then I saw that the attacking craft was another flying saucer. We could see everything clearly from our spot because of the gigantic hole in the Nazareth structure.

We dusted ourselves off, got our bearings, and marched outside, along with all the remaining criminals inside. The sky was filled with Metro PD, Interpol, and other agencies, which likely included X-Branch, if that was even a real agency. Then we were all arrested.

The police had arrested me before on nonsense. They even jailed me one time, along with both my future-now-current parents'-in-law. They were the ones who deserved it. I was just caught up in the dragnet. This time, we were told we'd be arrested for our own safety and to get us out of the area.

On the news, we learned multiple criminal gangs got into a grand aerial hovercraft shootout with each other and authorities, with laserfire and more hitting the Nazareth building. The battle turned the entire area to rubble, and all that remained of the building was a giant crater in the earth. There was no mention of the Nazareth, or even the simple question: why were all these gangs, cops, and spacemen, including Martians, at this one spot in Metropolis, at the same time to have such a grand battle with each other?

I wasn't the only one then, who'd used the once-in-a-lifetime gathering for their own purposes. The CC President used it to eliminate overseas and off-world rivals. Other gangs used it to eliminate their competition. Law enforcement used it to identify, capture, and kill all the organized crime street gangs and criminal corporate cabals they could get at. The world knew nothing of Starlight, and that was how it would remain.

Metropolis Police Central stood at the opposite end of the street from City Hall. It was the cubical fortress headquarters for the supercity's five-hundred-thousand plus police force—and that's where we were taken. Not to a jail cell, but to the waiting area.

The outer waiting room of Police Central was always like a massive zoo, with people all over the place waiting their turn to be helped DMV-style by counter police. Finally, we were called back into the inner quieter and nicer waiting room.

An officer came out to us and gave us the official okay to leave. We were cleared, per Chief Hub's directive, and wouldn't even need to give a statement. Also, we were sternly told, per Chief Hub, to go home. The officer didn't need to repeat himself.

"Are we allowed to ask questions?" Wize said as we all walked to the parking structure where we could call a hovercab.

"You could, but don't expect any answers."

"I see Mr. Bite-Size is no longer limping despite getting shot in the foot," Quix said.

Bite-Size pretended not to hear him.

"Where's Phishy?" Wize asked me. "Interesting how all those street people showed up at this Nazareth."

"Sidewalk johnnies and sallies aren't street people. They're sidewalk johnnies and sallies. And Phishy is out there being Phishy," I replied.

"How many other people did you have working on this caper with you?" she asked.

"Caper? Oooh. I like that word. I need to figure out ways to use it again."

"I notice you have denied nothing," Wize said with a smirk.

"My boss has been playing spooky mind games on us," PJ said, watching me.

"Guys, it's over. That's the important thing. It's over. We're in one piece, and we're going home."

We'd reached the pedestrian bridge from Police Central to one of the city's parking structures. To the side were elevators and the steps to the ground floor.

"Does everyone have transportation on its way?"

"My parents are coming for me," Bite-Size said.

"How old are you?" Quix asked him, laughing. His men chuckled.

"I need to save money," Bite-Size said, flustered. "I'm an amateur film maker too, and it's not cheap."

"Quix?" I asked.

"My guys are on the way," he said, shaking my hand. "Already got another job, so stay out of trouble, Cruz. Remember, you're supposed to be a street detective, not a secret agent."

"Don't I know it."

"My people are on their way," Wize Gal said.

"My people are on their way too," PJ said. "What about you?"

"My ride is already here," I said, pointing. Descending from the sky was a dark silver Bee hover-speedster bug. "Mrs. Cruz has arrived."

"I hope you won't be taking on any more Council of Corporations clients ever again," Wize said.

"Absolutely, hell no, never again," I responded.

#

"I'm picking up you up from police stations now?" Dot asked me when I piled into her little speedster.

The wife's look reminded me of an international female spy. Her trendy outfit included a white headscarf over her shiny hair, dark glasses, and a faux-leather navy blue slicker. Her silver bracelets and rings sparkled in the light. Too bad we couldn't fly convertible-style for the wind to whip through our hair, but that would blow off my fedora and her stylist headscarf. And I didn't want to get hit in the face by a bug. Not cool.

"Not arrested, Mrs. Cruz, simply a guest of my pal, the Chief."

"A guest, huh?"

"Oh, I have a surprise for you," I said with a wink.

"Surprise? I thought the case was done."

"Oh, yeah. That's done and gone."

"Cruz, I'm not going on any more vacations with you. No more dead bodies and stuff."

"But you enjoyed wearing that Sherlock Holmes cap on Jules Verne's Island, and so did Kat."

I heard faint giggling behind my seat.

"If your surprise is a short vacation, that's dead on arrival too."

"No, that's not it. I got two surprises."

"Two?"

"What's wrong with one? Cruz, I'm driving. I don't want any shocks to the heart while I'm driving."

"Funny you should say that."

"Funny how? What did I say?"

"Heart."

"What about hearts? Your heart or mine."

"Ours." I raised my hand, fluttered my fingers, and pulled a long rose from my hand. "Happy Valentine's Day, Mrs. Cruz."

Dot laughed. "You remembered." I gave her a quick kiss. "Cruz, I'm driving." I got back on my passenger side. "How did you do that?" she asked.

"I met this kid at a convenience store and he does all these magic tricks as a hobby. He showed me a few things. Now I got skills."

"Yes, Cruz, you got skills."

"Oh, and surprise two."

"Which is?"

"Knowing you were off, I say we head over to Booty Shakers for a date night!"

"Yes!" she shouted.

Booty Shakers wasn't just a dance club. It was one of the platinum dance clubs in Metropolis. You didn't set foot inside unless you planned to dance non-stop all night long and have obscene amounts of fun. No one ever left there unsatisfied and when you did, you were ten to twenty pounds lighter from all that sweating on the dance floor. Dot and I were dancing maniacs.

"But we need to do something about Junior and Kat."

"Well, I got two surprises too," Dot said.

"Are those surprises named Cruz-Control and Kat?"

I reached my hand around and found my targets. Two munchkins hiding. I was already tickling them when Junior and Kat popped up.

"Daddy," they yelled, giggling.

For a six- and three-year-old, they surely dressed better than I ever did at their age. Cruz Jr. had his little black fedora and Kat was like a clone of Dot with her white headscarf. Both of them were in tan outfits; I guess to match the return of their dad's trademark attire.

"Seat belts!" their mother yelled at them.

"We don't have to make any pit-stops after all, then."

"We can't take them to the dance club, Cruz."

"Why not?"

"It's V-day!" Junior yelled, helping his sister buckle her seat belt.

"Dancin'!" Kat yelled and started wiggling around.

"Aren't you going to tell us about this case you finished?" Dot asked me.

"We can talk about that later."

"Is your deadly game over, Mr. Cruz?"

"Yes, it's finally over, Mrs. Cruz," I said, smiling, but masking a sense of deep relief and reflection.

We'd come a long way from our Phobias Anonymous Support Group. Being a street detective in Metropolis was dangerous; there was no way around it. But that was okay. It was the price for being one of the good guys in this supercity.

I noticed an orange glow peek through the clouds. "Look at the sun," I said. "See the sun, kids?"

In Metropolis, it was rarely seen so clearly in all its splendor. It mesmerized the kids as we flew into the sunset, heading to our favorite dance club for a family Valentine's Day outing. At least that wasn't a vacation, so I wouldn't attract any trouble. No crazy maniacs, only plenty of dancing ones.

As for the Starlight case, I'd never speak about it ever again.

Review Request

Dear Reader,

I hope you enjoyed *You'll Never See Starlight Again.*

<u>Can You Write Me a Review?</u>

If you enjoyed *You'll Never See Starlight Again (Liquid Cool, Book 10)*, I'd greatly appreciate an honest review on one or more of the following sites:

Reviews are the best way for readers to discover good books. My writer's motto is simple: "Readers Rule!" Thanks so much.

Always writing,

Austin Dragon

Continue The Adventure

<u>**Get Your Next *Liquid Cool* Books!**</u>
These Mean Streets, Darkly (Liquid Cool Prequel Short)
Liquid Cool (Liquid Cool: The Cyberpunk Detective Series, Book 1)
Blade Gunner (Liquid Cool, Book 2)
NeuroDancer (Liquid Cool, Book 3)
The Electric Sheep Massacre (Liquid Cool, Book 4)
I, Alien Hunter (Liquid Cool, Book 5)
A.I. Confidential (Liquid Cool, Book 6)
Biopunk Blues (Liquid Cool, Book 7)
The Moon Is A Good Place to Die (Liquid Cool, Book 8)
Write Me a Murder on Jules Verne's Island: A Liquid Cool Cozy Murder Mystery (Book 9)
You'll Never See Starlight Again (Liquid Cool, Book 10)
Liquid Cool Box Set (Liquid Cool Prequel and Books 1-3)
Liquid Cool Box Set 2 (Liquid Cool: Books 4-6)
Liquid Cool Box Set 3 (Liquid Cool: Books 7-9)

<u>***Liquid Cool: From the Crazy Maniac Files* mini-series**</u>
Classic Cyborg (Book One)
Digital Samurai (Book Two)
The U.F.O. Case (Book Three)
Liquid Cool Box Set 4 (Liquid Cool: From the Crazy Maniac Files Mini-Series: Books 1-3)

Also by Austin Dragon
See all my books in science fiction, epic fantasy, and horror at:
http://www.austindragon.com/books

About The Author

Austin Dragon is the author of over 30 books in science fiction, fantasy, and classic horror. His works include the sci-fi detective *LIQUID COOL* series, the epic fantasy *FABLED QUEST CHRONICLES*, the international futuristic epic *AFTER EDEN* Series, the classic *SLEEPY HOLLOW HORRORS*, and the new *PLANET TAMERS* military sci-fi series. He is a native New Yorker but has called Los Angeles, California home for more than twenty years. Words to describe him, in no particular order: U.S. Army, English teacher, one-time resident of Paris, ex-political junkie, movie buff, Fortune 500 corporate recruiter, renaissance man, futurist, and dreamer.

He is currently working on new books and series in science fiction, fantasy, and classic horror!

http://www.austindragon.com/books

***

www.ingramcontent.com/pod-product-compliance
Lightning Source LLC
Chambersburg PA
CBHW071213210726
48293CB00002B/410